HIDDEN HEARTS/ SMUGGLED HOPE

Jolene O'Dell

The Well Publishers

ISBN-13: 978-1-954658-06-6
ISBN-13: 978-1-954658-07-3 (Digital)

Cover design by: Kathy Bruins
Printed in the United States of America

CHAPTER 1

A man stood off to the side of the concourse, towering over those surrounding him, holding a sign with a name on it. Vivian leaned around an embracing couple and squinted at the sign and the man behind it. Her name was scribbled in a wobbly hand across the piece of cardboard. The holder had a lock of black hair fell boyishly across his forehead, and he broke out into a sly grin, his eyes crinkling at the corners. His black leather jacket strained under his muscles as he beckoned me over.

Vivian swallowed and raised her hand in acknowledgment. She was pulling a rolling carry-on behind her and had a large, black leather bag slung across her shoulder. The man reached for her carry-on which she handed over to him. His bright smile continued as he directed her away from the terminal. Through his smile he whispered so softly that she wondered if he were speaking at all.

"You're being watched. Act like a tourist." Vivian choked back a panicked urge to look over her shoulder.

"My name is Li Jian Wei." Jian introduced himself loudly to her, likely for the benefit of her followers. "You may call me Jian. Let's get you checked into the hotel and then we can finish going over the itinerary and finalize what you'd like to see while here,"

"Sounds good," Vivian replied, trying not to sound shaky.

Jian and Vivian weaved their way through the crowded Shanghai airport heading for the taxis. The crowds grew thicker, and Vivian's throat constricted nervously. She peeked back just as Jian grabbed her hand and pulled her into a little shop, but she didn't see anyone watching them. "The Ministry is having you followed. Play along," he whispered again, softly.

"You must be famished after your long trip. These are popular right now." He held up a green package and waved it back and forth. "Seaweed Snacks." Vivian's nose wrinkled up involuntarily and Jian laughed, putting the package down. "Protein, that's what you need." His focus never left her face, but his eyes darted to the side, taking in the scene behind her. Jian shoved a pack of peanuts into her hand and steered her to the check out.

"Thanks, you never know how long it will take to reach the hotel," Vivian said, clumsily opening the package and shoving a peanut in her mouth.

The two moved back into the crushing crowd with Jian gripping her arm securely. Vivian tried to smile but it was a weak attempt at best. Outside, Jian walked purposefully to a waiting cab, gently guiding a stiff Vivian into the back. He chatted amiably with the driver in Mandarin as they waited; traffic clogged the main thoroughfares and dropped their progress to a crawl. When the driver swerved sharply, Vivian slid hard into Jian's side with an oomph. Suddenly quite aware of his closeness, she slid back over to her side.

She prayed, thanking God when they pulled up in front of her hotel. She wasn't sure what she was more thankful for, that the ride was over or that she wouldn't be thrown into the side of a handsome, buff young man again. Vivian gratefully stepped out of the cab and stretched while trying to nonchalantly look around. A few other cabs pulled up along the street, but no one got out of them. *Strange*, she thought. *Maybe a few hotel guests called for cabs.*

They checked into the hotel and went up to the 16th floor.

The hallway was bright and clean and enormously long.

"You're in this room," Jian tapped a dark wood door with his knuckle, "and I'm right next to you. I'll be back in a few minutes. Do not open the door for anyone else." He was still standing outside Vivian's door as she closed it.

Vivian locked the door behind her and turned around to inspect the room. It was quite posh compared to many of the other hotels she'd stayed in. She passed through a large sitting area before reaching another door. She pushed it open to see a king size bed with a bright red duvet. She cautiously placed her suitcase on the bed and scanned the rest of the space. From where she stood, she could see into an enormous bathroom.

She heard a faint knock coming from the front room and she jumped. She hurriedly made her way back to the door where she peeked through it to see Jian standing outside her door.

"I was beginning to wonder if you'd fallen asleep," Jian joked as he entered the room, closing the door and locking it behind him.

"Really got in that 30 second powernap." Vivian smirked. "Who were...?" Vivian started to say but the withering look Jian gave her silenced her.

"So, where do we start? There's Disneyland, Circus World, the Bund, Pearl Tower, Yu Gardens, The Jade Temple, shopping. What are you in the mood for? Jian smoothly recounted a list of attractions in Shanghai.

"Why don't we decide on the way?" Vivian offered.

"Great idea!" Jian agreed, a hand on the door. "Do you have everything you need?" he asked, nodding toward her black bag.

"Yes, I'm all set." Vivian stepped up to the door as Jian unlocked and opened it for her. They headed back toward the elevators. She was surprised he hit the button for floor number three. She stared at him curiously and opened her mouth to ask but Jian near-imperceptibly shook his head. He stretched animatedly and seemed to be pointing toward the corner. She saw it now. A camera. The Chinese did not play around.

The elevator dinged for floor three and they exited silently.

Jian led them to the far end of the hallway to another set of elevators marked in both Mandarin and English "EMPLOYEES ONLY". He punched the button for basement then, after they entered, the hold button. The elevator ground to a halt.

Vivian's eyes grew wide, but she said nothing. Jian shrugged a shoulder and quietly spoke, "We're okay in here. They don't tend to survey their workers on these elevators, but I am certain your room is bugged and maybe even tapped for video. We're going to deliver your load first. I want it out of your hands. We'll talk more when we're in the tunnels," he added reassuringly.

"I'm sorry if I'm doing this all wrong. It's my first delivery." Her light brown eyes darted back and forth, and she pulled on her scrunchy nervously.

"You're actually doing well for being so young and new at this," he replied, releasing the hold button. The elevator shuddered as it moved to the basement. "That bit in the hotel room about deciding on the way was brilliant," he said, admiringly.

"Thank you, I thought it would be best if we didn't give a location, they could go to. What if we weren't there?"

"Give me your phone," he ordered out of the blue. Vivian looked confused but dug it out of her enormous black bag. He fiddled with it for a few moments and handed it back. "We use an app with pre-programmed backgrounds of attractions in all the different cities we operate out of. That way you can take any selfie and give it the appropriate background to 'prove' that you were there," he explained as the door slowly screeched open.

"Handy!" Vivian quietly replied, peeking up and down the dark hallway they had stepped into. Far to the left lights were aglow and people were moving about, but they didn't go that way. They went to the right, and the dark shadow stretching out ominously. They rounded a corner and came to a sudden stop.

Jian moved a large trashcan aside and slid a panel out of the way. "You first." She stepped through into total darkness, leaving behind the shadowy hallway, which seemed bright compared to this. Jian slid the panel closed. Vivian's heart pounded in her chest, the darkness pressing in around her. Jian turned the flashlight mode on his cell nearly instantly. Without thinking she gripped Jian's arm tightly. Vivian noticed a smile play at the corner of his lips.

"These tunnels connect multiple safe-houses and sympathetic businesses. We even have a few cab drivers." Jian pulled her hand down to his and threaded his fingers through hers. Vivian was surprised at how comfortable that felt but she walked on in silence. "We will head up to the street level a few blocks away and take one of those cabs to a safe-house. Then maybe we can get something to eat, if you're hungry, and we can take a few selfies to satisfy any nosy police."

The tunnel smelled of earth and stagnant water. No light peeked into the darkness aside from Jian's phone. Their footsteps echoed in the passage, nearly obscuring the sound of tiny feet scurrying along their route. Vivian cringed inwardly, an involuntarily shiver running down her spine, either from the creepy crawlies or the mere fact that they were sneaking through a hidden tunnel smuggling bibles into a foreign country. The punishment for their activities could be very severe, especially for Jian. Another shiver shook Vivian's frame. While she was ready to make a stand for Christ the consequences were great if they failed.

They went the rest of the way in silence, turning left and right until Vivian had lost all sense of direction. She'd never be able to find her way back if Jian wasn't with her. The sound changed as they went from crunchy gravel to smoother paving stones. Vivian peeked down one side tunnel at a distant figure back lit by a pale, eerie light. Eventually, they slowed to a stop. Jian dropped her hand and held his finger up to his lips. He slowly slid a panel open, and a pale beam of light split the darkness. He peeked through and waved his hand for her to step out.

Vivian was surprised to see they were in a parking garage, another garbage can blocked part of her view. By the time she turned back to Jian, he had the panel shut and she couldn't even guess which one it was. Jian smiled ruefully at her, that stray lock of hair hanging near his right eye again. She turned quickly to hide a smile. That rouge bit of hair was awfully cute on him. *Stop it*, she chastised herself, *you need to focus on the job*.

He tugged on her arm and nodded toward a stairwell. They climbed for several levels before coming out on street level. Jian led them past several yellow cabs to an unmarked door. He knocked three times before shoving it open and pulling her in behind him.

A balding man sat behind a packed desk; he was wearing a blue jumpsuit that was covered in oil stains. He put down the papers he was holding and spoke rapidly to Jian who replied just as rapidly and jabbed his thumb in Vivian's direction. The balding man nodded his head once and with that went back to his stack of papers.

"We are using one of their taxis. Let's go." Jian grabbed a set of keys that hung along the wall and put his hand to the doorknob. Vivian followed, amazed to see how The Society worked in the field. It was completely different to see it firsthand.

Jian practically stepped over to a compact car that was yellow on top and gray on the bottom and grinned devilishly. "Your chariot awaits my lady." He bowed deeply to her. Vivian's stomach fluttered a little and she laughed lightly. He held the back door open for her and she was surprised at how disappointed she was that she had to sit in the back.

Once settled inside Jian easily navigated traffic and Vivian looked out the window. She took in the skyscrapers and the dark alleys.

"Can I ask you a few questions?" Vivian was uncertain when it was safe to talk and when it wasn't.

"Yes, we are safe. Most taxis aren't, but these are longtime supporters of our cause," Jian replied, his eyes never leaving the road.

"How long have you been doing this?"

"Many years. I grew up doing this on one level or another.

I've been so many people sometimes I forget who I am sometimes," Jian admitted, a hint of sadness hanging on his words.

"You mean identities you've taken on?"

"Yes, so many different identities." He looked back at her in the mirror. "How old are you?"

"Oh no! You first!" she laughed defensively.

"I'm twenty-two." He looked so much older than that.

"I'll be twenty this year. In July, actually." Her face lit up in a soft smile, her excitement for celebrations obvious. "So will we meet up again after this mission?"

"I'm not sure how much they've told you, but we will meet every two months in a different city to do this. I am your assigned point-man. The fewer faces you see the better. Less you can spill when you are caught. We will continue this until the authorities become suspicious and then we take a break. Oftentimes, we can get a year or more of active missions before they begin to suspect."

Vivian's heart beat a little faster. She would get to see him every two months indefinitely.

"They hadn't told me that. They gave me two rules. Don't get caught and don't get personal." Was his head hanging for a moment or did Vivian imagine it?

"We're here," he said quietly, getting back to his serious businesslike self. Jian pulled up to a tall building and drove down into a parking garage. Jian found a parking space between a White Pearl Lexus and a 1992 Jaguar. Vivian joined him as they walked to the stairwell.

"We need to camouflage you. Do you have sunglasses? A hat?"

Vivian dug into her large, black, leather bag and donned a pair of large, yellow sunglasses and a warm winter beanie. She looked to Jian for approval and his grin suggested he agreed.

"Why so many stairs? Haven't you people heard of elevators?" Vivian was only half joking. Her legs were burning by the time they'd gone a half dozen levels.

"There is one, but it has a camera." Jian said, jogging up the stairs. "We have to go up to the 18th floor. Think you can make it?" A smirk crossed his face as a look of horror overcame Vivian's.

"I'll be fine." At least, she hoped she'd make it. Jian did seem to slow down a bit, but he kept them moving. He glanced nervously behind her as they rounded each landing.

After what felt like years, they paused on another landing with a gray, steel door that had a large 18 painted on it. Cool air hit her sweaty face with a sharp sting, flooding her with relief. Silently, she followed him partway down the hallway to a plain, black door, where he knocked three times, paused, and knocked twice more.

The door was unlocked and swung open by an elderly looking man hobbling away quickly, his cane tapping along the tile floor of the entry of the apartment. Jian followed with a distinct familiarity. Vivian quickly followed the two down a hall and into the living room.

"Welcome, courier. Place your bag on the table," the old man ordered Vivian as he watched her like an ancient eagle from his perch atop a stool. She obeyed him and was a bit shocked when he dumped her belongings into a small, gray tote and set it aside. Then he began to carefully and intricately pull the stitches out of the lining.

He gingerly took a dozen books out of the bags hidden compartment. The books were thin and black with bright red lettering on the front in Mandarin. In English she read "On Protracted War", each one indicating different volume numbers. The old man opened a volume and handed it to her.

Vivian took the proffered book and squinted at the Chinese characters. She couldn't make heads or tails of it.

"It's Psalm 91," Jian said, peering over her shoulder. "Whoever dwells in the shelter of the most high will rest in the shadow of the Almighty. I will say of the Lord, 'He is my refuge and fortress, my God, in whom I trust.'" When Vivian looked up both men were smiling so broadly, she couldn't help but be at ease.

"We can print our own Bibles here in China, but it speeds up the process to have pre-printed versions ready to go. Breaking them into three volumes makes them lighter and easier to transport. And if we paste them with propaganda like this," Jian said, tapping the outside of the book, "it almost always passes the visual test of loyalty."

Vivian handed the book back carefully to the old man. He leaned back over the bag and pulled out several dozen memory sticks.

"We give these out as well for the believers. The digital copy of the Bible is well hidden within the files. Your bravery in doing this job is noted and appreciated by the millions of brothers and sisters in Christ here in China," Jian finished. Vivian felt humbled to be part of such a great cause. Growing God's Word in a nation that was so suppressed was an honor. She would happily face prison time to bring God's Word to the nations.

"Courier, you and point-man have coffee while I sew. It will take me thirty minutes," the old man said, dismissing them with a wave.

Jian led the way to a small galley kitchen. A bright red coffee maker stood on the counter with a tower of pods next to it.

"What's your flavor?" Jian asked, grinning broadly at Vivian.

"Hmm ... something chocolaty, I think." Vivian decided, smiling back at Jian. She watched him pull two mugs out and pop a pod into the coffee maker. It whirred to life and soon spit out fragrant coffee into the plain white mug. A few minutes later, the two had moved into the only bedroom. It had a sitting area on one end and storage in the back. A tiny sleeping mat was wedged against the wall behind a storage shelf.

Vivian sat down in a worn, brown chair and lifted her "cuppa joe" to take a sip. She eyed Jian as he sat next to her in a matching chair. Jian looked up and met her eyes. Vivian blushed and looked down at her mug. She cleared her throat nervously and tried to refocus.

"Why does he keep calling me 'courier?'"

"We do not share names unless absolutely necessary. To protect as many people and layers of the organization as possible." Vivian nodded at him between sips of mocha.

"So, we'll meet every other month in a different city. What do you do in between?" Vivian asked conversationally, tapping her foot on the ground nervously.

Jian sighed "I work. Just like you," he said flatly, watching her response. She visibly stiffened at his curtness and looked down at her feet. "Vivian, the less you know, the better," he said softly. "I'm sorry…" he started to say but she cut him off.

"No, it's fine. I get it." Her tone was sharper than she meant it to be, she didn't mean to sound offended.

They sat in awkward silence for several minutes. No sound came from the living area where the old man sewed the lining back in her bag. As the minutes ticked by and their coffee cups emptied, Jian shifted in his chair and cleared his throat. Vivian glanced at him and smiled meekly.

"Listen, I know this is all new to you but once you get into a routine this will go smoothly. Where do you want to go eat?" He seemed to be trying to smooth things over without saying as much.

"Well, I'm not dressed for fine dining, so not something glamorous." She was dressed nicely, but casually, in hot pink shorts and white button-down shirt, the bottom tied in a knot.

"Have you decided where we're going to pretend I took you?"

"I was thinking of the Jade Temple and maybe someplace else, but I haven't decided. Anything to eat around there?"

"Yes, the Muslim Market has really good street food. Hand me your phone." Vivian dug out her phone and handed it him, curious. He fiddled around for a minute and then stood up and waved her over. "Let's take our Jade Temple selfie now."

He held the phone at arm's length and then laughed as he looked at the screen, snapping a picture anyways. He turned the phone to show Vivian. Her head was barely in the frame. He squatted down a bit to get closer to her, putting his arm around her shoulder and pulling her close. They both smiled shyly as he snapped a few more pictures. He dropped his arm and stood up, leaning in to show her the photos. Vivian, a little bit unnerved being so close to this tall, handsome, young man, reached for her phone and stepped back.

A soft tap, tap, tapping came down the hall toward the room. Their heads snapped up at the same time to see the old man standing there with her finished black leather bag.

"You must leave now," he insisted, holding out the bag. Vivian rushed forward to grab it. The old man turned away without so much as a wave. *He has the "don't get personal" rule down*, Vivian thought.

"Let's go." Jian was right behind her as she stepped into the hall. Vivian slung the bag over her shoulder and opened the door. The two headed off to the cab waiting in the parking garage.

An elderly woman squawked at a young boy who swiped a Mandarin orange as Vivian stood in the open-air market. The elderly woman's crinkled eyes were half hidden underneath a wide-brimmed straw hat. She sat between a pile of bright red shiny fruit and an assortment of green vegetables. The smell of savory meat cooking wafted through the air. Vivian's stomach growled, reminding her why she and Jian were standing there.

"Let's get our picture in before it gets too dark," Jian suggested, his eyes darting from faces, to handbags, to clothes, trying to catch anything out of place.

Vivian pulled out her phone and took a quick picture of the elderly produce dealer. Then another of the little boy who was drooling over a cauldron of cooking meat a few stalls down munching on a bit of orange. She held the phone out to Jian. He pulled her over to stand in front of the woman's produce. He squatted down and held his arm out, pulling her in next to him. A face popped up behind them just as he took the picture. He dropped his arm and spun around quickly and yelled at the little boy in Chinese.

"I don't want anyone in the background that could be found and questioned," Jian whispered to Vivian. He deleted the picture and swiped back to see the previous pictures. "You cannot take pictures of bystanders, it's too dangerous." He deleted those, as well, and they took another one quickly before anyone else could photo bomb their effort. "Let's eat!" Jian said, excitedly and much louder, steering Vivian down a few stalls to a smoking grill.

"What is it?" Vivian asked, eyeing the meat nervously. Her bravery only went so far.

"It's lamb. This is a Muslim market, so everything here is Halal." Jian paid for several bamboo skewers of the aromatic meat. He handed one to Vivian and carefully took a bite of his own.

"Mmmmm." he moaned, his eyes closing briefly, juice dripped down his chin.

Vivian took a petite bite and was pleasantly surprised by the flavorful lamb. It was spicy but not so much that even her delicate tongue could not handle it. They ate silently and strolled by a few more vendors. They threw away their bamboo skewers in a trashcan and wandered down to a noodle cart.

Jian spoke in rapid Mandarin and snagged a bowl of steaming noodles. He handed one set of chopsticks to Vivian and took another for himself. She raised an eyebrow at him but took her chopsticks and expertly grabbed a few noodles. It was strange to be sharing food with this man, their chopstick occasionally clicking against each other. Her senses were on overload from the variety of life bursting around her and from being so near Jian.

They slurped down the noodles and moved on to pork buns farther down the aisle. Vivian stopped next to stare at a vendor with bright red piles of… something. She cocked her head and scrunched up her face.

"What are those?" she asked, extremely concerned, as people

munched on the knobby-looking items.

"Chicken feet. Want to try some?" Jian offered. Vivian slowly shook her head no and backed away, bumping into Jian, nearly tripping. He burst into loud, raucous laughter as he righted her.

"Come on, let's get some dessert. It's around the corner up here." Jian led her to a vendor with long skewers of fruit that were coated with a slick shiny layer of sugar.

Vivian glanced back at the chicken feet before eyeing the lines of fruit suspiciously. "What is this?"

The young woman minding the stand eyed him hopefully, talking animatedly. She cast Vivian an angry look and handed a few skewers of crab apples and grapes to Jian, holding onto them and saying something to Jian. He paused and spoke softly to her. Her dark eyes shot to Vivian then back to Jian. She let go of the skewers and looked somber.

"What was all that about?" Vivian asked him, glancing back at the scowling young woman.

"She thought we were a couple. She was concerned that I was tainted by a dirty, rich American devil. I told her you were dying and traveling the world was your final wish."

Vivian snorted out loud. "You told her what?"

"Yeah, she was quite mad that I had fallen prey to your womanly wiles." He waggled his eyebrows at her. They laughed together and headed back toward the cab.

"This is really good, but then again you add sugar to anything, and it tends to be pretty yummy," Vivian's mouth was sticky with sugar goo. Jian smiled at her and absently reached out to wipe a goo spot from her lip. He paused, his hand wavering in the air near her face. He came back to life and swiped the glob of sugar off her lip and smeared it on his pants. As he turned away Vivian wondered if his hand had been shaking. She shook her head; she must've had it wrong.

***

CHAPTER 2

A light breeze played with Vivian's long, silky, black hair, tossing it around her face as she stepped out of the cab that dropped her and Jian off at their hotel. She swatted the stray hair away from her eyes and followed Jian into the hotel. With the task finally off her mind, and a bit of her nerves with it. Vivian finally noticed the ornate lobby. It was filled with business types, tourists, families, and foreigners. As she entered, Vivian glanced around, taking in the color scheme of white and gold, the soaring marble pillars, the snow-white porcelain floor. The centerpiece was an art installation that consisted of long pieces of glass filled with golden lights, reminiscent of a wired Chihuly.

The pair strode purposefully to the elevators. Jian was scanning the foyer nonchalantly when he visibly stiffened. A group of three men, who had been milling aimlessly near the elevator, stopped dead in front of them. While the men did not wear uniforms, they had standard military cuts, and two stood at ease. Jian placed his hand on Vivian's arm to steady her but she was still shaking.

One man, shorter than the rest and a little portly in his business suit, waved for Jian and Vivian to follow him to a darkened sitting area. The stout little man spoke with a gravelly voice and pointed his stubby finger at Vivian. She pulled back away from his accusing glare and felt Jian's hand tightened on her arm reassuringly. Jian spoke smoothly, his voice not showing any of the quavering anxiety or fear that Vivian felt.

"Pull out your phone. He wants to see the pictures." Vivian fumbled in the bag and had just pulled out her phone when one of the men seized her bag roughly from her. Vivian squeaked a protest but didn't try to pull it back. She unlocked her phone and pulled up the pictures. The husky man peered over the phone as she swiped across the screen showing the various pictures she'd taken at the market and showing the Jade Buddha Temple. Jian smiled knowingly and nodded at the phone as the portly man spoke to him. A guard examined her plane ticket closely.

"He wants to know how long you are here." Jian told her, still showing an impressive amount of confidence in the face of their intense scrutiny.

"Tell them I plan to be on my flight without delay. Chicken feet aren't appetizing enough to keep me here," Vivian said cockily, snatching her black bag from the snooping men. One was holding up her makeup case while the other pawed through her belongings.

Jian snorted at her response but relayed her message to them. The portly man stiffened for a moment. His associates looked ready to grab the bag back. He broke into a broad grin and must have repeated her words to his guards because they were soon chuckling. A few more words were exchanged and with an apologetic smile toward Vivian, they were gone.

Vivian wanted to melt into the seat they were standing besides, but she knew she had to maintain her composure, at least until she was out of sight. She was going to be searched and questioned on a regular basis and she would need to be as calm and collected as Jian had been. Resolutely she turned and made a beeline for the elevators.

She started as she pushed her door closed only to have Jian catch it and walk into her room with her.

He pulled out a small device, reminiscent of a small phone and began walking around the room. He stopped at the hotel's wall phone and unplugged it. He peeled apart the apparatus and pulled what looked like a small silver button out. He mimed drinking a glass of water and pretended to drop the button into it. She ran off to grab a glass of water and rushed it back to him. He moved into the bedroom and the bathroom and soon had nearly a dozen of the devices sitting at the bottom of the cup.

He made one final stroll through the hotel room before turning back to Vivian's questioning gaze.

"You handled all of this like a seasoned informant. I must commend you on how well you held it together. You must have been extremely nervous."

Vivian blushed slightly at Jian's compliment and rushed to change the subject. "We can talk freely now. Are these bugs?"

"Yes, this little thing," he held out the black device he had used, "scans the area for both audio and visual bugs. It appears there are no video feeds in this room. Usually the more they suspect you, the more instruments they use. No video is good, they don't think you are a major concern."

"Won't they find out we've removed these and come back?" Vivian's eyes were wide with concern.

"No, they have cleared you, so no one is listening right now. They've moved on to other threats." Jian took the cup over to the sink and dumped the water down the drain catching the devices before they hit the sink.

"What are you going to do with them?" Vivian asked.

"I'll crush them and then flush them."

"Why don't you drop it down the heat vent?" Vivian suggested, looking around the room for vent.

"That would work in another country. Our vents are in the ceiling." He pointed to a vent where the ceiling met the wall. "May I have your phone?"

Vivian pulled her cell phone out and handed it over to Jian. He expertly swiped and pecked at the keyboard and handed it back to her as it was dialing. His own phone went off a moment later.

"I programmed my number into your phone and now I have yours. I'm going to leave you alone tonight." Jian said, his eyes on his phone as he added Vivian's number.

"Um, are you sure? Is that safe?" Vivian's face was clouded with fear.

"Yes, I would not leave you alone if I had any concerns. I will be right next door, and you have my number now if you need it."

Jian shoved his phone in his pocket and reached out her and patted her back. Vivian could feel herself shaking nervously. Jian pulled closer, then suddenly dropped his hands and walked over to the door. He gave her a confident smile and left her alone with her own thoughts.

Vivian locked and bolted the door after him, unsure what she wanted to do. A shower sounded amazing, as the long flight and even longer day were catching up with her. She dropped her bag on the sofa retreated into the bedroom. Her suitcase was still on the bed where she'd left it. She pulled out a yellow tank top covered with daisies and a pair of matching sleep shorts and headed for the shower.

The bathroom was massive, with a granite counter that stretched at least 8 feet in length. A large soaking tub stood on one side with a matching shower opposite it. Brass accents reflected the light of a stunning crystal chandelier. Vivian dropped her clothes onto the long counter and started the shower. She was lost in thought, trying to process the day's events, nearly ready to get in the shower but the steam gave her pause. She readjusted the temp before stepping in. It felt like a welcoming hug after her long travel day and her run through the city with Jian. Vivian thought of him as she washed her hair, wondering where they'd go in the morning. *Stop thinking about that man*, Vivian scolded herself, *you've got enough on your hands.*

Cleaned up, with a full belly, and exhausted, Vivian fell asleep and didn't so much as move until well into the next morning.

Vivian stretched underneath the luxuriously soft and silky sheets, woken momentarily by some noise outside, and snuggled back down into the soft feather bed. A sharp knock at the door caused her to shoot out of bed, groggy and disoriented. She rubbed her eyes and stumbled to the door. Peeking through the peephole she saw Jian looking nervously up and down the hallway. She unlocked the door and carefully pulled it open. He slipped in the small crack and locked the door behind him.

"I was worried when you hadn't come by my room yet or called me. Are you feeling alright?" Jian turned around from locking the door and took in Vivian's disheveled hair and sleep wrinkled clothes.

"Do you realize what time it is?" Vivian yawned loudly and shook her head.

"It's almost noon." Jian said emphatically. "Are you alright?"

"Yeah, I slept like the dead. Jet lag is no joke. Sorry for worrying you. I was safe and sound snoring away." She laughed lightly. "Or at least I hope I wasn't snoring." She looked awkwardly down at her tank top and shorts. Jian seemed to finally notice that she was still in her pajamas, and he averted his eyes as if she were almost naked.

"Um, I'll be right back. Give me a few minutes," Vivian stammered and ran off to the bedroom to get dressed.

Jian had the coffee maker whirring to life by the time Vivian rejoined him in the sitting area. She was dressed in a long, summery skirt with matching tank top. "You look great." He murmured as he looked down at his khakis and navy-blue polo shirt and blushed.

Vivian dropped softly onto the sofa and took a deep breath. Her long hair was brushed to a silky sheen and in a loose braid down her back. "What do you want to do today?"

"First, coffee. And I'm supposed to be asking you that question. Where do *you* want to go today?" Jian had walked over to the counter and poured two cups of black coffee for them.

Vivian thought for a few moments and decided she didn't have the energy to go gallivanting around Shanghai. "Let's stroll through a museum. Maybe dress up a bit and go to a nice dinner, since I fly out tomorrow night," she decided, looking over her cup of coffee at Jian.

He nodded his head. "That sounds like a good plan. Let's get going."

Vivian leaned against a pillar at the exit of the terminal, her fingers drumming impatiently on her thigh. Her eyes darted from one face to another looking for her ride. A young couple walked by holding hands, a woman pushed a screaming little girl in a stroller, an elderly man shuffled along with his wife, and a tall, dark man stepped out into view. A little boy practically bounced up and down by his side.

Vivian's face lit up despite her exhaustion. She grabbed her suitcase and joined the tall, dark man and the bouncy boy.

"Hi Dad! Hi, Evan!" Vivian said, her voice strained from fatigue.

"Welcome home. Did everything go all right?" Her father's Kenyan accent was crisp among the soft southern accents floating through the air around them. Her little brother's eyes were jumping from her face to their dad's face.

"Who cares! Whatcha bring me?" Evan burst out, grabbing the handle of her rolling suitcase so he could pull it behind them.

"Ha! Glad you care so much about me, you little brat!" Vivian shot back at the child messing his hair up knowing that it would bug him. Evan hit her hand away and tried to fix his hair. "Yes, Dad, it went fine. I'll tell you what I can back at the house. Has Livi gotten back yet?" Vivian watched her father's face carefully. He merely smiled and shook his head.

"No, she's due to be back tonight. I'll get her but it will be after Evan's bedtime." Her father grinned down at the grumbling 9-year-old.

"Awww, Dad, do I have to stay home?" Evan whined as they weaved through the Nashville airport.

"Yes, son, you will. This way, Vivian." Samuel Kimani wrapped his arm around Vivian's shoulders and guided her through the airport toward the car waiting in the parking garage. Vivian's feet sluggishly moved forward. "We'll talk tomorrow, Vivian. You need to rest."

Vivian slept through the car ride and most of the day only dragging herself out of bed, no light came through the curtains. She stared blearily at her trying to figure out how long she had been asleep. She threw a robe on and made her way to the living room where she peered out the window looking for her father's car. It wasn't in the driveway. Evan was sitting at the table slowly eating a bowl of ice cream when she walked into the kitchen.

"There's pizza in the fridge," Evan mumbled through a mouthful of chocolate ice cream. He swiped a dribble off his chin and tried to grin at her.

"Yuck! You are so gross?" Vivian complained. She mussed his hair and helped herself to cold pizza.

"So, what do you do there, anyway? What's the point?" Evan asked, a dollop of chocolate on the tip of his nose from licking the bowl.

"I'll tell you when you're older. Now go brush your teeth and get ready for bed." Vivian shooed her brother off to bed, leaving the kitchen in silence.

The quiet of the kitchen was broken by the sound of the garage door opening for her father's car. Vivian jumped up excitedly and ran to the door, throwing it open for her sister. Livi bounced into the room and grabbed Vivian around the neck in a rough hug.

"Wow! How do you have so much energy? I'm ready for bed again. I've got my days and nights so mixed up," Vivian laughed as her sister swung her own black, leather bag onto the table.

"I'm always up for anything, you know that!" Livi extracted herself from Vivian's arms and sat down at the table. Her face, tan like Vivian's, showed more fatigue than her voice suggested.

"Well, girls, I'm going to bed. We can talk tomorrow when your brother goes off to Aunt Rachel's."

The girls munched on cold pizza for a while in silence before curiosity got the better of Livi.

"So, what's your contact person like? I got this sweet, old grandma. In fact, she insists I call her Nai Nai, which is Grandmother in Mandarin, I think." Livi's eyes, darker than

Vivian's, danced excitedly, as she reminisced about her trip to Taiwan.

"Well, mine wasn't exactly a pensioner," Vivian said evasively. Livi's eyes went wide with wonder.

"You got a hot guy, didn't you?" she blurted out. Vivian immediately and loudly hushed her sister, but there was no getting around Livi's questions.

"Young, yes. Handsome, yes. But he's just my contact, that's it,"

"Okay, you must tell me all about him. Leave nothing out." Livi might have been eighteen, but she gossiped and gawked at boys like a fourteen-year-old.

Vivian rolled her eyes, but there would be no sleeping for her unless she gave her sister some information. Well, less information and more gossip.

"He's tall, at least six feet, if not taller and buff. He speaks English with barely a trace of an accent and obviously fluent in Mandarin. He's twenty-two and mentioned that he's been doing this on and off his whole life. I have a picture of us." Vivian pulled out her phone and showed her insistent sister their selfies.

"Oh, you are such a liar. He's way more than handsome, he's downright sexy!" Livi squealed as she snatched the phone to swipe through the pictures.

"You know Dad hates that word." Vivian sat back and yawned, watching Livi go over each photo for every detail. "Don't even think of telling Dad about him. I'll handle that."

All three siblings represented a different aspect of their parents. Vivian, the oldest, somehow had managed to look a little like her Thai mother and a little like her Kenyan father. Livi was heavy on the Asian features and Evan heavy on the Kenyan side. When their mother had died giving birth to their brother when Vivian was 10, she had to become the caretaker for both younger siblings. She had to grow up overnight. Livi somehow managed to stubbornly resist growing up despite being only 11 months younger than Vivian.

"I think this guy is cute!" Livi remarked as she handed the phone back.

"This isn't a dating service, Livi. If we get caught, we're looking at serious charges. I hope you realize what you've signed up for."

"Yes, I know how serious this biz is. But that doesn't mean I can't enjoy the scenery while I'm doing it!" She waggled her eyebrows at Vivian, who just moaned in frustration.

"I'm ready for bed." Vivian got up and turned to go but Livi's voice stopped her.

"This trip made me miss Mom a lot. Maybe it was being so close to Mom's homeland. I don't know, but I just thought about her so much." Livi suddenly turned serious.

"I miss her a lot, too. Sometimes I forget what she was like but then you come in the room, and I remember. She was bubbly and quirky just like you. Always making up things for us to do or places to visit. She was so much fun. Sometimes I get a little bit jealous of that. I wish I could be a little less serious." Vivian left her sister to contemplate her thoughts and headed back to bed.

CHAPTER 3

A pleasant aroma tickled Vivian's nose slowly pulling her from her sleep. She opened one eye and saw the light streaming in through her gauzy white curtain. She yawned and stretched out in her bed; her thoughts as scattered as the light pouring into her room. Eventually she rolled over and opened both eyes.

"When are you going to get up!" She jumped and sat up staring at Livi who was laughing from her chair in the corner.

"Livi! Get outta here!" Vivian yelled, throwing a pillow halfheartedly toward her.

"I was delivering you the nectar of heaven and you throw a pillow at me? Nice way to show your gratitude. See if I do anything nice for you again," Livi stuck out her tongue and pointed past Vivian to the nightstand where a steaming mug of coffee sat.

"Thanks," Vivian mumbled as she scrambled out of bed.

"Dad said he wants to talk to you. I'm taking Evan to Aunt Rachel's house, bye!" Livi waved dramatically, smiled, and left. It only took a few moments for Vivian to jump into the shower. She wrapped a towel around her thick hair and trudged off to her father's office.

Vivian's father, Samuel, was at the great oak desk in his office. *Probably writing his sermon for next week,* Vivian thought. She sat down on the love seat that was surrounded by bookshelves, heavy with tomes.

"I'll be right with you." Samuel said, continuing to type away at his laptop for a few more minutes. He finally shoved his chair back and stood up stiffly before joining Vivian on the love seat.

"I want you to tell me everything that happened. Not the sugar-coated-dad version. I want to hear the version the council will hear." Samuel's face was serious. Vivian swallowed hard and tucked her hair behind her ears.

Vivian explained what happened while her father nodded slowly. She was looking down at her hands by the time she finished, waiting for the lecture she was sure was to come.

"I worry about you. This is something that your mother or I would have done but I really don't like you girls being involved." Samuel paused for a moment, a look of painful concern darkening his face. "Still, I support your decision. When does the council want to debrief you?".

"This afternoon, I believe. I'll have to check my email. Anything else?" Vivian took a breath, feeling a little relieved after their talk.

"Yes, tell me about your contact."

"Ugh, did Livi say something to you?" Vivian moaned and rolled her eyes, promising herself she would be having words with Livi when she got back.

"No, actually, she didn't say anything to me about this." Samuel's eyes were narrowed suspiciously.

"He's a young Chinese national. I don't know anything about him since we're not supposed to get personal. Can we please be done? This is painful!" Vivian stood up quickly, not waiting for her dad to answer.

"Ok, I just want you to be safe," Her father gave her knowing look.

"Bye, Dad! I'm going to get something to eat and then head off to the council debriefing." Vivian waved her hand in the air and left her dad to brood on the love seat.

Jian moved through the alley as quickly as he could looking for places to hide. *In just a second, I will hear their footsteps*, he thought. Right on cue he heard feet slapping the damp ground. He squeezed behind several dumpsters shoved up to the back of an apartment complex.

Putting one foot against the brick wall and one against the metal dumpster he wedged himself up out of sight. The air was bitterly cold from the recent January freeze and smelled of moldy leftovers and cigarette butts.

Several men shouted and ran past his hiding spot. One of them slammed his fist against the dumpster, angry that they had lost him. He'd be stuck here for several hours as they waited around, hoping he would come out of hiding so they could nab him. But he would never give them that satisfaction. He was a master at waiting, even in cramped spaces. He had developed patience as a child, one that never had enough to eat and spent more time on his own than anyone he knew. Survival skills were his mainstay from an early age.

While he tried to focus on something other than his cramping muscles, his thoughts turned to his most recent contact. Vivian. He had been quite surprised at how well she had handled the stress and danger. His thoughts turned to how her hair had glinted in the sunlight. A small smile played at the corner of his lip. He jolted back to reality, aware that the agents were bustling up and down the alleyway. He couldn't afford to get distracted now.

Jian glanced at his watch. It had been an hour already and he could hear the men snooping around in the alley still. While they suspected he was connected to the underground church, they had no idea what his role was. If they brought him in it would be a standard interrogation. Despite knowing that his stamina could outlast theirs, his foot braced against the metal dumpster was starting to slip, his shoes wet from slogging through thick snow.

His foot shifted with a loud screech and his heart dropped

into his stomach. There was movement in the alley and shouting. Rough hands pulled him out into the open and shoved him hard into the ground. Fists and feet flew fast and furious. He relaxed against the pain instead of stiffening. He'd been beaten enough in his life to know how to leave his body and float outside of the pain and humiliation. After a few minutes a sharp voice called them to a stop.

"Let's move him to the precinct to interrogate him. You three stay here and wait to see if any contacts come to meet with him. Everyone who comes this way is suspect," the one in charge commanded as Jian was handcuffed.

Jian took stock of his injuries, which included thorough bruising, a bloody nose, a busted lip, and it felt like he had a rib out of place. It hurt to breathe. They patted him down and took his phone and his wallet. He wasn't worried about that, though as he deleted all info from it often, so he didn't think there would be anything they could use against him. He walked silently but upright, despite the throbbing pain, knowing they would target whatever hurt the worst when they interrogated him.

The station was a dull, worn out red and the Chinese flag hung proudly in the front. The windows were dark and dingy, and the front lobby was lined with equally dingy rust red seats. Several people congregated in a corner whispering together, likely waiting to hear news of their loved ones. An officer shoved him forward suddenly, causing him to trip over his feet. When he righted himself, they shoved him, harder still, through a door into the back.

The interrogation room was a gray room that had probably been white at some point. It looked like every interrogation room that he had ever seen, and he'd seen many of them. Always one table with a single chair on the far side, with a window or mirror the authorities could see through.

"Sit," his captor barked, smacking the back of his head. *Lord, help me to shine for you in the face of this persecution. I pray I can protect the innocent and endure what I know is to come*. He sat heavily in the wood chair and adjusted his hands, trying to get some relief from being pinched by the cuffs.

"So, you're with the Christians. As you know all unauthorized religion has been banned. Consorting with unapproved Christian groups can have some very serious charges" The interrogator was short and round with very little hair on his head. He was among the least intimidating interrogators Jian had ever had.

"Americans are infiltrating our great country. They seek to bring their extreme ideology here to brainwash us through their supposed religion. What is your part in this? Talk! I want to know!" the man screamed passionately and slammed a fist on the table.

Lord, forgive me what I must do to get out of here and to protect my brothers and sisters in Christ, Jian pulled himself up as straight and tall in the chair as he could.

"I walk the despicable Americans through our land showing them our great country. I make them show respect to our great leader, Mao, may his words live on forever. I bring them to our ancient sites to remind them of their insufficient and inferior subsistence. Why would I disrespect the Party by connecting with people who are indoctrinated by the evil foreigners?" Jian spat on the ground with a disgusted look on his face.

The interrogator was taken aback by the intensity of his tirade. He seemed pleased by Jian's impassioned speech, but Jian wasn't done. *I need to cement his belief in my patriotism.*

"We must stand together against these foreign invaders who rape our youth's minds and influence them with the ways of so-called liberty. Real, true freedom in China is to freely share, with pride, what the Party has done for the people!" Jian finished with devotion and joy written all over his face.

"My, my, you are the most patriotic suspect we've ever had sitting in here. What do you do for a living?"

"I am a tour guide. With great pride I show the greatest of our treasures, the Party!" Jian told the man, a proud smile spreading across his face.

"You don't work with the dissidents?" the man probed, his

confidence clearly collapsing.

"Why would I?" Jian looked pained at the accusation.

"Um, I'll be right back." The man sucked in his paunch as he slumped out of the room. *Most likely going to confer with his superiors, then he'll come back and apologetically release me,* Jian thought expectantly.

Jian rubbed his wrists and whistled "Amazing Grace" as he stepped out onto the street. He would have to lose the agents that were tailing him, dump his phone and wallet, and go into hiding for a few weeks, but he should be able to reappear in another city soon to help the church.

CHAPTER 4

Sitting before the council for the debriefing had Vivian's hands shaking. She knew that this was simply standard procedure, but she couldn't help but feel intimidated. The group she smuggled for was simply known as Visionary Vantage, although the underground workforce referred to it as, The Society. The organization was shrouded in secrecy to protect itself in the case of a breach. Anti-Christian attitudes were prolific around the world.

A group of twelve council members, six men and six women representing different ethnic groups, sat around a large conference table. They took turns asking questions.

"You were being followed by the time your contact met you at the airport. What did you do that had them suspicious upon your arrival?" an Asian woman asked Vivian. There was no condemnation in her voice, but Vivian still felt remorse over how things happened. She wrung her hands nervously in front of her.

"Jian told me they suspect anyone coming from North America. They have secret police on incoming flights to profile possible smugglers. I was profiled before I even arrived." Vivian hoped there was nothing she could have done to avoid their suspicions.

"When did you make your delivery?" a bespectacled man with a thick Middle Eastern accent asked her next.

"I dropped my luggage as soon as we arrived at the hotel,

then we went straight to the tunnels. We made our way to the delivery location then resumed my cover story as a tourist."

"When you were stopped by the police in the hotel lobby, did they seem convinced of your cover story?" another man asked.

"They did. I produced the pictures taken at the temple we had "visited" and they let us go on our way. The entire interaction only took a few moments." Vivian was getting concerned that she'd done something wrong. "Can I ask, please, what I should have done differently?"

"No, child, you followed proper procedures and were calm under pressure. We are quite impressed with your first trip. There is, however, another concern. We have lost contact with Jian. Which means he's either been detained, or he suspects he will be detained shortly," a grandmotherly African American woman informed her.

"Oh no! Is it because of something I did?" Vivian was sure her career of smuggling was over before it had even begun.

"There are always things to improve child, but our main concern is for Jian's safety, we can investigate how he was compromised once he returns. We are confident he will not share anything about the organization when he is interrogated. However, we do not want to lose him; he is far too valuable. Jian is one of our most effective agents. He performs more missions than the next three most prolific agents combined." The Grandmother replied, calming part of Vivian's concerns.

"Will he be alright?" Vivian asked, her throat constricting around a large lump.

"We are working hard to locate him right now. Would you like us to update you when hear anything?"

Tears threatened to well up in Vivian's eyes, but she refused to let them spill. She hadn't cried since her mom died, so why was she falling apart in front of the council about her contact going missing? She simply nodded her head to stave off the tears.

"You may go. We will call you with any updates." With that she was dismissed. Vivian moved into waiting room and retrieved her gym bag.

The Society owned a compound outside of Nashville near Franklin. It held everything one could need for training the smugglers, agents, and support staff of The Society. She wandered for a bit, looking for some way to burn off her nerves after the debriefing. The complex included a full gym, a sparring arena where they taught martial arts and self-defense, classrooms for various classes, and a computer lab for language training. During business hours there was even a cafe. But Vivian decided that a run along the many trails that wound through the hilly woods was what she needed.

She changed quickly in the women's locker room and got a language teaching app going on her phone. She was trying to learn Mandarin to help her smuggling efforts, but it was slow going. *Maybe if the narrator had a Southern accent, I would get this faster*, Vivian laughed to herself.

Out on the trail the Chinese instructor barked common phrases in her ear as she loped along. "Nǐ hǎo ma?" She repeated the phrase several times while trying to breathe. She gasped out a quick "Wǒ hěn hǎo, nǐ ne?", her feet pounding along the path. "Good, now repeat that five more times." The narrator chirped. Vivian groaned but steeled herself and choked out the phrase again. The track, covered with a light dusting of snow, wound its way between paddocks filled with thoroughbred horses. Many were retired racers and enjoyed a peaceful existence as trail horses.

Vivian's thoughts turned to her father. While he supported her and her sister's decisions, he wasn't thrilled with the danger it put them in. He understood all too well the danger of being a Bible-believing and Bible-preaching citizen. He had spent many a night in jail for his beliefs.

Her phone vibrated. "Hello?" Vivian managed between heavy breaths.

"Vivian, this is Mrs. Kaminsky, the council secretary. I wanted you to know that Jian showed up at a safe house for medical care." Vivian gasped loudly but before she could ask any questions the secretary went on. "He'll be all right. He had a busted lip, a broken nose, and a dislodged rib. His rib will heal just fine, and he'll be back on schedule to meet with you in six weeks. I'll send you the travel information when we're closer to your departure."

"Okay, thank you for the update." Vivian's voice was a little shaky as she hung up the phone. She bent over with her hands on her knees, hit with a sudden wave of anxiety. Those injuries were not life threatening but it was certainly another aspect of this job that Jian would have to face. Somehow, he had gotten them to let him go, but that didn't usually happen. Many brothers and sisters in Christ were sentenced to years in prison or the re-education camps ... labor camps with a side of brainwashing.

The anxiety and nausea passed so she stood back up. Finishing her run was the last thing she wanted to do. She tried to refocus on the language app, but the words found no purchase in her scattered thoughts. She really needed to talk to Livi to work through all the enormous feelings overwhelming her because Livi dealt with dramatic emotions all the time. She would know what to do. Livi's debriefing was scheduled for just before dinnertime. She might be able to catch her before Livi started her own work out in the gym.

***

Jian cringed a bit as he pulled his black tee shirt on. His rib ached with every movement, but he refused pain meds and muscle relaxers. He agreed to drink the herbalist's specialty tea though he wasn't sure what was in it. He was itching to get back in the field and the Society was working on replacing his passport and ID, but he had been ordered to stay put for now. He was scheduled to move on to Taiwan in a week.

The room he was staying in was a lean-to off the back of an alley level apartment building deep in the city. Most of the safe houses were in the slums, through mazes of alleyways, in dark basements, or seemingly abandoned buildings. Very few were upscale apartments and condos. The residents of the upscale buildings tended to be nosier. The low-income neighbors kept to their own business and didn't often blow the cover of an agent.

Having grown up dirt poor this felt comfortable. This felt like home. He could smell his host cooking dinner. Something about the simplicity of life here made the food taste so much better than at fancy restaurants or from high class chefs. It was peppered with the love of ancient Grandmothers, recipes that were verbally passed down from one generation to the next.

He cautiously twisted at the waist and stretched very carefully. He would join the hostess for dinner then arrange to replace his possessions. He stepped out of the lean-to into a walkway separated from the alley by a wooden fence. The neighborhood was alive with chatter, the smell of a hundred homes making dinner, and the clatter of the residents doing life. Jian pulled the door to the house open and was quickly directed to sit on a stool and drink his tea.

"You will not heal if you do not drink. It only works if it is in your stomach," the little grandma scolded him in Mandarin. "Powerful herbs and powders in there."

Jian grunted and blew on the steaming hot cup of tea. The bitter tea burned as it went down. Most traditional teas, he had found, were bitter or tasted acrid. It was not prepared with taste in mind.

"I need to replace my things. When will The Society send the money?" Jian asked the old widow.

"Patience is power; with time and patience the mulberry leaf becomes a silk gown." she tsked. She reached over to pat his shoulder gently before going back to the meal she was preparing. He knew better than to ask more questions. There was no rushing the Chinese grandmothers. They moved at their own pace, one that was outside of watches and clocks.

Jian hurriedly finished his cup of tea and stood up to put it with the dishes, but she waved him back to the stool and poured him a refill. He tried to hide the shudder that shook his body, managing a half smirk for his host. The knowing smile she sent back seemed a little too pleased at his obvious discomfort. *It's like they think that the more awful it tastes, the more it does*, Jian shook the smirk off his face.

He took his time on the second cup knowing she would refill the cup when he was done. She finally bowled up some lion's head meatballs for him with a side of pork buns. He thanked her with a grunt and ate heartily. Why did injuries seem to make him hungrier? Grandmother narrowed her eyes at him but there was a hint of a smile at the corners of her mouth.

He helped her clean up, drank another cup of tea mostly to appease her, and moved to the front living area. She snapped her fingers and pointed to the love seat. He obediently sat down and watched her pull a cell phone out of her pocket. Her fingers deftly swiped and tapped across the screen. Jian shivered, a slight breeze came through the closed window. Summers in the city could grow to sweltering temperatures and winters could be bitter cold.

"What you need will be delivered in two days. Then you can go to the market and buy new clothes. You will stay here with me until they deliver your supplies. Now, come with me. I have work for you."

Jian couldn't help but smile. Two more days of awful tea. He could survive that.

Vivian's life between smuggling runs was quite boring. She worked for a service agency that catered to rich musicians in Nashville, either running errands, walking dogs, or doing other gofer requests. Livi, somehow blessed with their father's height and mother's exotic beauty, modeled and was often an extra in music videos and commercials. The money for them both was good and the work consistent and flexible.

Vivian and Livi shared a car, so they had to coordinate pick-ups and drops offs. Usually, Vivian was behind the wheel since her job required travel and Livi's usually did not. The errand of the day seemed to be dry cleaning. She was on her fourth run of the day listening to another Mandarin lesson and trying to work on her enunciation when the phone rang. "Call from Mrs. Kaminsky", her phone announced. She quickly pulled off into the parking lot.

"Are you ready for your next assignment?" The Society's secretary, Mrs. Kaminsky, asked cheerfully. "You'll be going to Guilin. This area is known for the Karst mountains which are the famous rounded mountains as seen in many forms of Chinese art. The caves and caverns are seen as portals to another dimension of peace and balance. I am going to email you the confirmation information for both the hotel and the flight. We've been watching China closely since your last trip and your name has not come up once, nor your contact's name. Though he will have a new identity and phone number, just as an extra precaution, when you arrive. Make sure to use his new name." She rattled the information off excitedly, barely pausing to take a breath.

"Be looking for an email with the information and plan to come in to have your phone reset and updated for the trip. Lord, keep Vivian safe from the hands of the wicked. Protect her from the violent, who devise ways to trip her feet. Have a safe trip." Mrs. Kaminski ended her ramble with a prayer that sounded like it was from Psalms.

"Thank you, Mrs. Kaminski. I'll be ready." Vivian said, butterflies fluttering wildly in her stomach and anxiety pulsing in her chest. The air inside her car felt hot and suffocating. She fumbled with the buttons on her door and finally pushed the right one bringing the window down. She sucked in a deep breath of chilly but clean air, but she still felt like she couldn't breathe. She forced herself to take slow,deep breaths. *When anxiety was great within me, your consolation brought me joy, When anxiety was great within me, your consolation brought me joy.* Vivian recited on repeat until her heart rate came down and she was breathing normally again. *Okay, time to finish these errands.*

CHAPTER 5

"No, not that one. The floral blouse. Yeah, that one. Also, that cute smokey blue shirt with those trousers." Livi, who was gifted with a great sense of style, supervised Vivian's packing. Her own packing was done. The girls' trips were coinciding again, allowing them to travel partway together. However, to maintain their covers they had to pretend to be strangers once they left the safety of their house.

"There, my luggage is packed. Where are you going this time? Sorry I didn't ask you earlier. I guess I'm a little more worried this time," Vivian apologized, realizing she'd been extremely self-involved.

"Hong Kong. And I completely understand that you've been concerned. What with the hotel lobby police stop and your contact being detained and beaten? It really puts the danger of this job into perspective." Livi affirmed her sister's reason to worry, and Vivian appreciated it.

"From the little bit of research I've done, Guilin is a more laid-back city, very used to foreigners. I'm hoping that means it'll be a bit safer. Who's dropping you off at the airport?" Vivian set the wheeled suitcase on the floor and picked up the black bag loaded with Bibles, in print, audio, and e-version, within its thick leather lining.

"Sebastian. What?" Livi looked guiltily at Vivian. "Not everyone can be matched with a hot tour guide, okay?"

"You haven't told him anything, have you?" Vivian asked.

Something in her gut told her that this would not be Livi's chosen career for long, she just didn't seem very committed to the group.

"Of course not. I don't want to compromise the organization. I might not do this forever, but I won't ruin what they've spent years building up." Livi seemed hurt at the suggestion that she would sell out. "He thinks I'm doing a photo shoot."

"I know you wouldn't do it on purpose. I guess I'm just jittery." Vivian looked around her small room. The walls were bare and off-white, like a college dorm on day one of a new year. There was nothing unique about it. It was boring. Just like her. She shook the self-doubt out of her head and turned back to Livi.

Livi stood up and held her arms out to Vivian. The girls hugged each other tightly, but Livi seemed a little aloof. Vivian hoped her sister wasn't still irritated by the suggestion she could inadvertently give away the group's purpose. Livi pulled back first and turned too quickly for Vivian to read her face.

The airport was almost empty when Samuel dropped off Vivian at 11 PM. He prayed over her as usual before she made her way to her terminal. On Vivian's last trip to China, she had been profiled the moment she touched down in China and now she wondered if she had been profiled before she had even left the U.S. She stood at a map, trying to look like she was hunting for her gate, but her eyes flicked up, watching for anyone watching her.

Vivian breezed through security without trouble and waited in the private lounge The Society kept stocked at the airport. She stood in front of the mirror in the lounge's private bathroom. She studied her reflection from her long, black, silky hair, and light brown eyes to her slim blue jeans and pale pink cotton blend tee shirt. She nodded at her reflection, pleased with what she saw. Would Jian like what he saw? She glanced at her watch. She needed to get to her gate soon for pre-boarding.

Seattle's airport was dead. Only the terminals heading for Asia were even slightly busy. Vivian looked around trying to decipher who could possibly be a CCP agent. Was that old lady with the floral handbag and a service dog a Chinese agent? What about the man in a dark corner working on his laptop? He was glancing up at the terminal regularly. Was he watching for suspicious people or just anxious to get on the plane? She caught sight of Livi but ignored her sister. Sharing a flight seemed to happen on occasion.

Most travelers had luggage and were preoccupied with themselves, looking at social media or talking to the person next to them. But there were a few that appeared to be traveling extremely lightly. They had only small carry-ons and were nonchalantly watching everyone at the gate. It dawned on her why she might have presented as a smuggler. She was obviously nervous and preoccupied. Aren't most tourists giddy with excitement about what they are about to go do and see? With that quick bit of insight, she breathed a prayer of thanks and shifted her mindset.

She walked over to a group of travelers and bubbled about her excitement for the upcoming sights she was going to see. The strangers looked at her oddly and moved away but she kept the "naively excited tourist" persona going for the entire trip. Even her sister gave her a strange look.

Her charade kept the possible secret police, and everyone else, away. No one wanted to sit near the chatty single traveler. She annoyed the flight attendants, but she neatly convinced everyone that she was going to China to take in the sights. She did manage to get some sleep on the long flight after drifting off between rounds of checking the time. Her sleep was restless, though, as her mind drifted toward China and what might await her there. She arrived early in the morning on a Thursday.

***

Vivian nearly walked right by him with his black hair shaved down to nearly nothing. "Hello, you must be Vivian?"

"Oh, yes, are you my tour guide?" Her face lit up with excitement. "What's your name, again?"

"Li Chang Jie. You can call me Chang. We need to hurry to our gate for our flight." Vivian canted her head a bit but took the name change in stride.

"Nice acting job, I nearly bought it." Vivian flushed with pride. "There's no one following us. What did you do on your flight? The other travelers acted like they couldn't wait to get rid of you," Chang whispered to her as they wound their way through the large and confusing Hong Kong airport.

Chang looked around and noticed a young woman that looked very similar to Vivian, joining an aged woman. Vivian glanced their way, as well and sighed, her shoulders relaxing a fraction.

"I thought that being nervous had caught their attention last time, so I did the opposite this time. It seems like it worked. What's with your hair?" Vivian asked and playfully swiped her hand across his scalp.

"Cover, you know?" His stomach swooped from her playful touch. Chang's stomach did a few flips just being next to her. Why was she so captivating? *Head in the game*, Chang scolded himself. "We're taking a van over to Guangzhou and then an 8-hour flight to Guilin. Let's grab something to eat for the ride."

The hand-off, this time, went smoothly, and Vivian and Chang were playing tourist again. Vivian's eyes swept across the scene before her. Twin pagodas reached high above the water of a glistening lake. Greenery skirted the base of each pagoda, one gold and the other silver and red. Clouds in the sky loom low and gray, threatening to burst as tourists scurried about making the most of each moment before they did. It was surprisingly warm for March, near 70 degrees, when the average was 50 degrees.

Vivian noticed Chang watching her as she gazed up and down each pagoda, captured by their beauty. She wondered if he'd been here before with other contacts. She could thoroughly appreciate the architecture and culture. Her eyes took in everything. The mixture of tourists, the boats on the water, the threatening clouds. And him. She caught him watching her again. Heat crept up his cheeks and he looked away.

Water sprinkled on his head, drawing his attention back to the sky. Vivian laughed, her arms out to her sides and was turning in a slow circle, her head canted back, looking up at the clouds as if welcoming the coming rain.

Chang smiled and laughed. He grabbed her gently by the arm and pulled her toward the first pagoda. “Let’s take the tour while it’s raining. An underwater, glass tunnel connects the two, so we won’t have to get wet.” His hand slid down her arm and grasped her hand giving another gentle tug in the right direction.

“Hei!” a voice called through the now steady sprinkle. Chang and Vivian halted and slowly turned toward the caller.

Rapid Chinese flooded the space between the police officer and the two standing like statues. Vivian felt her heart race and her stomach began to turn. Chang, normally completely cool under pressure, seemed to be searching for the right words. He spoke haltingly then held up the hand that was holding hers. He slipped his fingers between hers and squeezed. A wave of dizziness and confusion swept over Vivian as her eyes darted from Chang to the officer and back.

The tension finally broke as the officer strode up to them and slapped Chang heartily on the shoulder a few times and nodded a broad smile in Vivian’s direction. Her eyebrows scrunched up, but she obediently turned and walk toward the pagoda with Chang.

“What was that all about?” Vivian whispered frantically, still eyeing the officer who was calling to a foreign couple as they fumbled with umbrellas.

“I had to tell him you were my girlfriend. When he saw us holding hands, he was concerned. You’re a foreigner, so he wanted to make sure I wasn’t kidnapping you.” Vivian’s stomach knotted fiercely when Chang uttered the word, “girlfriend”. She slowed to a stop and looked down at their fingers intertwined.

“The things we do to not blow our cover!” Vivian laughed,

trying to brush off the word. The nervous smile on Chang's face melted into something more real at her laugh.

"Hei!" The officer called again, leaving the foreign couple to walk from the plaza from underneath the cover of their brilliant red umbrellas. He held out his hand toward Vivian and spoke quickly to Chang.

"He wants to take our picture for us. Hand him your phone," Chang interpreted, the plastic, nervous smile plastered back across his face. Vivian dug around in her bag, now empty after handing off the volumes to another smuggler and pulled out her phone. She got the camera app ready and handed it to the officer, hoping he wouldn't see how badly her hands shook.

The two turned slightly so the pagodas were in the background and gave pained smiles. The officer barked out an order, nothing Vivian could understand, but something in the tone of his voice that made her want to obey.

Chang cleared his throat and looked down at her. "He wants us to kiss." The order came again, with more force. Vivian felt the warmth of Chang's fingers intertwined with hers, his arms pressed tightly against hers. She canted her head up and cocked it sideways a bit. Stiffly, Chang bent down and planted a rapid kiss on her lips and pulled away just as quickly.

The officer erupted and waved at them. Clearly Chang had been too quick to get a good picture. Chang sucked in a deep breath and leaned down to try again. His lips hovered over hers, hesitantly, waiting. A smile tugged at the corners of her mouth, drawing her lips up. Chang touched her lips softly; she could tell he was trying to respect the rules of their relationship. It was difficult, with the officer barking words of encouragement at them. She could feel his heart beating rapidly through his shirt.

Vivian's free hand reached up to his face and the moment her fingertips touched his cheek he pressed harder into her lips. Fire roared to life inside her, a fire she'd never felt before. Her hand caressed his cheek, and his hand cupped the back of her head, pressing her mouth into his a bit harder. The world fell away, she even forgot about the rain that was falling on them. Another few moments of passionate kissing and reality seeped back in.

Vivian was the first to drop her hand and take a small step back. Chang's hand flew up to his scalp and rubbed the nearly bald surface nervously. The officer cleared his throat and stepped up to hand back the phone. He mumbled something apologetically and averted his eyes before scurrying off to harass another tourist.

Chang tugged a silent Vivian toward the nearest pagoda. Now they needed to play the part they'd started and finish the tour as a "couple". Vivian glanced up at Chang. His eyes seemed far away. She wondered if he were battling a storm inside his head and heart as she was. What was that fire that had blazed so deeply in her core and why were her thoughts still lingering on the feel of his lips on her? These questions and more plagued her as they went about the tour. They were equally distracted and barely looking at the stunning scenery.

It wasn't until they were in the glass tunnel that Vivian realized they were still holding hands. She gently extracted her fingers from his grip and walked over to the glass. A fish swam by, unconcerned with her presence. She continued staring at the glass, distracted by a change in the lighting. Her eyes refocused on the curved glass of the tunnel and saw Chang's reflection. Was that disappointment on his face? Was it from her letting go or from before?

"When we reach the surface, we'll have to follow the relationship script, again." Chang's voice seemed to bounce off the tunnel wall and back to her ears even though he was whispering. Vivian stiffly nodded her head and turned to continue toward the next pagoda.

She felt bad giving Chang the cold shoulder, but she didn't want him thinking she was some flighty American girl that would crush on him simply because they'd shared a kiss. It was a great kiss and her insides still quivered thinking about it, but she wasn't about to fall head over heels for something as trivial as a kiss. Distracted, sure, but not blushing and batting her eye lashes.

By the time they'd reached the gold pagoda and taken the elevator to the top the rain had stopped. Mist swirled over the lake that seemed peaceful, despite being packed with boats hauling tourists about. Vivian was ready to start back down the elevator and suggest they search out some tucked away noodle shop when she ran into Chang, who had stopped directly in front of her. She was too tiny to see over his shoulder, so she had to peek her head around him. The officer from the plaza was standing there grinning broadly, likely remembering their rather convincing kiss.

Vivian slid to Chang's side and slipped her arm around his waist, leaning her head against his right bicep. The muscle tightened then relaxed as her fingers brushed his warm, taut skin, having snaked them up underneath the hem of his shirt. He reached around and pulled her into his side hard. He leaned down and planted a kiss on top of her head. Somehow, in the middle of this awkward moment smack dab in the middle of a Chinese tourist trap, this felt completely normal. Like she always held him tight, and he always kissed her in front of strangers.

The officer smiled and nodded again, seeming satisfied that their relationship was real but to seal the deal Chang leaned down and looked into her eyes, as if asking a question. Vivian caught on quickly and tilted her head up slightly, lifting onto her toes. Chang's lips brushed against hers gently then with more pressure. He was more careful this time, reserved and in charge but with meaning behind the motion that made her wonder what he was thinking, or better yet, what he was feeling, because she was an emotional mess. More so from this kiss than from the first one that had caught her by surprise. It was his reservation that she questioned. What would it be like to kiss him without regard to officers and rules of their relationship?

She shoved the thought out of her head and smiled at the officer, who thoroughly enjoyed the little show. He walked away leaving them to jump through the open elevator doors. The rain had cleared out the other tourists, so they had the lift all to themselves. They dropped their arms and stepped away from each other.

Chang sighed deeply and smiled awkwardly at Vivian. “So, hungry yet?”

“I thought you’d never ask!” Vivian laughed as the tension of the moment dissolved, as did the questions she had.

CHAPTER 6

Vivian sat at a long table in a stuffy conference room. Twelve pair of eyes stared at her, expectantly awaiting her answer. She swallowed hard and stared at the mannequin again. It wasn't so much the mannequin that scared her, it was the shape it suggested that bothered her.

"We've found that the authorities are realizing the black leather bags are being used to transport the Word. We are going back to a classic tradition of disguises. The cloth is similar to the material in the lining of the black bags and will minimize the ability of body scanners should you be required to go through one," a voice informed her. Vivian knew without looking the speaker was the head of the council, a venerable woman with a slight northern Georgian accent and warm brown skin that was accentuated by a bright canary yellow dress.

Vivian wasn't bothered by the idea of wearing a disguise. It was this particular disguise that made her nervous. Her eyes traced the womanly shape of the mannequin, following the bulge in the abdomen, suggesting this object was with child. She hadn't told anyone about the run in with the officer and their kisses. The thought of pretending to be his pregnant spouse made the heat rise to cheeks. Her heart was pounding, and she was sure the council could clearly hear it.

"Your other option, my dear, is to skip this next trip and pick up the next scheduled one," The speaker suggested, likely noticing Vivian's shaking hands.

"No, it's fine, I'll go on schedule. I just wasn't expecting to be, well, um. Expecting." She stumbled through her words but finally tore her eyes off the pregnant dummy.

"Well, then let's get you measured so they can customize your suit. See the secretary to set that up. Many blessings to you on this trip, Vivian," Mrs. Edness said dismissively. Vivian rose from her seat and slid out the door, but not before giving the dummy one more confused glance.

***

Chang's eyebrows shot up as he scrolled through the communication with his next assignment. His heart still pounded every single time he replayed the kisses with Vivian in head. Now they wanted the two of them to pretend to be married ... and her pregnant. He groaned and covered his eyes with his hand as if that could stop his thoughts. Her pregnant with his child.

He shook his head, trying to focus on the coming job. Most of his contacts were men, divorced or widowed middle-aged business types that had little to lose if they were caught. He even had a grandmotherly woman he escorted around every other month who always had her gray hair dyed a shade of carrot, a wistful attempt to reclaim her youthful red hair. But there was only one young woman.

His thoughts drifted to their last encounter. Her arms out to the side, slowly twirling as the rain misted down on her. The warmth of her lips against his. He slammed his phone down and shook his head hard. He would not replay the details of the kiss... but it was useless, the kiss crept into his dreams, and it haunted him each night. Maybe this time she'd leave him a hint as to where her parents were from.

Chang deleted the communication when his heart nearly stopped beating. The pictures of them kissing! He had completely forgotten about them. Had she remembered and deleted them? H would remember to ask her in a few weeks.

Spring was speeding along, and it would be May very soon. It seemed like now he counted time by when he would escort her again. *Oh man, I'm in way over my head on this one.*

Livi laid on Vivian's bed and tossed a pillow up in the air and caught it, repeating the action several times. "So, were you followed again, this time?"

Vivian stood in the middle of the room looking at the maternity shirt hanging on a hook on her wall. It was a light lavender color. The suit she would wear soon, to be filled with Bibles, would stay at the complex. She would get dressed at the Society's headquarters and head to the airport from there.

"Well, not at the airport, just an officer at the pagodas. We had to act like a couple. He thought I was being trafficked," Vivian said distractedly. Her hand shot up to her mouth to cover it, but it was too late – the words were out. Livi sat up quickly on the bed, it was like a sixth sense for juicy stories sounded like an alarm in her head.

"So, did you have to hold hands?" she goaded Vivian for details.

"Yes, we held hands. It seemed to satisfy him that we were a couple" Vivian said slowly, hoping her sister's hungry curiosity would be satisfied with that. Alas, she knew that would never be enough information to scratch that itch.

"Did you kiss?" Livi asked, squeezing the poor pillow till it was ready to pop stuffing out of the stretched seams.

Vivian felt her face blanch. She was so grateful she wasn't looking at her sister. Livi's sixth sense seemed to detect Vivian was leaving out details, but Livi always had to be looking at her to be sure.

"No, of course not," Vivian lied, hoping the interrogation would end soon.

"Let me see the pictures. I've never seen the Sun and Moon Pagodas," Livi requested. Vivian composed herself and whipped her phone out, handing it to her nosy sister.

Vivian was sifting through her leggings, trying to find a pair that would stretch enough to work over the body suit she would have to wear, when her sister gasped.

"You liar! You did kiss him! Wow you guys were seriously into each other. Does the council know? Oh my gosh, does Dad know?" Livi laughed as Vivian launched herself across the bed after the phone. Vivian overshot and fell onto the floor. She tucked into a roll and stopped in front of the open door. She carefully peeked out before shutting it.

She took deep breaths, trying to calm her nerves. How could she have forgotten to delete those? Livi's big mouth would have everyone this side of the Mississippi talking about it before sunset. She turned back to Livi, who was standing by the window, giving Vivian a hard stare.

"Yes, we had to kiss to convince him. He bought the act, end of story. Now give me back the phone," Vivian attempted to say calmly, hoping Livi wouldn't see her hands shaking.

"If that were the end of the story you wouldn't have lied. This was more than a simple peck. There's a ton of pics of you two lip locked. You're completely oblivious to everything around you. Did you even notice the rain?" Livi continued, goading Vivian, lightly.

"Of course, I noticed. Now give me the phone and don't you dare tell Dad. Or the council. Nothing happened. It was an act, that's it," Vivian demanded, her hand held out toward Livi.

"You are so into him it's ridiculous!" Livi laughed, handing off the phone. She moved to head toward the door and stopped, pointing at the purple shirt hanging off the hook. "What is that? You are absolutely not that big. Why is it so big?" She waved at the stomach.

"The council has me wearing a disguise and this is the shirt," Vivian replied vaguely. She closed her eyes and wished her sister out of the room. No dice, though. Livi smelled secrets like a fox on a rabbit.

"What kind of disguise would require a shirt this big,

though? Oh, no! Wait a second." She reached up to swipe the shirt off the hook and peeked at the tag. "A maternity shirt? You must pretend to be pregnant?" She laughed loudly and slid the shirt back onto the hook.

"You must pretend to be pregnant with *his* baby? Wow! So, when are you two getting married? I mean, you might as well since we're going well past kissing to having his child. I figure marriage would have to be in the mix somewhere." Livi stared at Vivian, amusement dancing across her face. .

"It is not like that at all. It's a disguise. An act. There is absolutely nothing to this. And, yes, Dad knows about the Society's plan. He's fine with it." Vivian looked down at her phone of the picture of she and Chang kissing. She didn't realize how intimate the picture was. Had they really looked like that?

"Wow! I cannot wait to hear how this trip goes!" Livi laughed, slamming the door behind her.

"Me, too," Vivian said to herself. Her fingers shook as she paused over delete button. The Society did not need to see these; however, she knew she and Chang had done nothing wrong. Why did she feel so awful hiding it from the council then?

CHAPTER 7

Chang's breath caught in his throat as he watched Vivian waddle toward him. She was convincingly pregnant but not so large as to make one think she would give birth any second. Her nervous smile wobbled a bit, reminiscent of her stride. It was extremely hot for May in Beijing and sweat was already pouring off her face. She must have been baking in the suit she wore.

He held out his hand and she gratefully took it. They said nothing as they worked their way toward the exits. She was waddling hard to keep up, her belly heavy with her load of Bibles, and he was feeling a surge of protectiveness like he'd never felt before.

They were just about to exit the terminal when a hand grabbed Chang from behind, hauling him to a sudden stop. Vivian's arm was jerked, and she flew back into his chest.

"Ouch!" she yelled, and he felt more than heard a pop from her shoulder. Amid the chaos of the airport terminal none of the officers seemed to notice.

"What is your purpose in the country? She is a foreigner. Why is she here while so expectant?" A middle-aged security officer demanded, adjusting his hat and narrowing his eyes at Vivian.

"We are here to visit my family. She is not due for several more months." Chang, still holding her hand, tugged Vivian closer, her discomfort was not lost on him.

"We need to see your itinerary." The officer stepping in front of Chang, his arms crossed. "Come to the office, now!"

Chang gritted his teeth, shook his head and looked beyond the officer to the door he'd indicated. He grunted in agreement and began to pull Vivian with him. Although he tried to tug her arm gently, she crumpled to the floor gasping. She sat cradling her arm while fat, silent tears rolled down her cheeks.

"Are you alright?" Chang was knelt by her, his hands floating in midair, afraid his touch would make her pain worse. The officers were barking orders behind him, but he ignored them. "We need to move. Can you get up?"

Vivian nodded her head. "I'm fine." She waved him off, but Chang hovered over her, not persuaded she was okay.

With the weight of her load throwing off her sense of balance, she couldn't quite get to her feet while cradling her left arm. She was about to try one more time when Chang swept her up into his arms.

"Whuh, whuh, what are you doing?" she protested loudly. Chang marched quickly after the officials, not stopping. His strong arms carried her and her bundle easily. Through the door was a small room with a desk and several chairs. Chang set her gently down in the nearest one and knelt beside her.

He ignored the officials that had come in behind him, pulling her suitcase. The pain surged again causing Vivian's face to screw up with a pained look. The four officials looked like quadruplets in their matching navy blazers. They were all talking until the first officer raised his voice.

"Is she in labor? Is that why you are here? To give birth in our country?" At that question all the officials stopped.

Chang glanced over his shoulder and nodded his head and the room exploded into activity. He leaned in as if to give her a kiss on the cheek but brushed his lips against her ear. "Can you act like it's labor?" Vivian bit her lip and gave a curt nod.

With her left arm draped over her protrusion she rubbed her stomach with her right hand and moaned. The officials all stopped for a second and looked at her then as one went back to talking loudly, shoving paperwork around the desk, and punching numbers into a phone. Chang reached down to rub the suit's belly lovingly. It wasn't hard for him to imagine his own child in her stomach. Before he could let that fantasy fly through his thoughts the door burst open. An important looking official thumbed behind him, worry creasing his brow.

"A cab will be the fastest way to the hospital. There is a sea of cabs outside that door." The man pointed back out toward the terminal exit. Chang could see a line of waiting cabs.

"There are cabs waiting out front. I'll carry you." Before Vivian could protest, he had her in his arms again and was moving back into the crowded terminal. He hoped her moans of pain needed were mostly faking, though her face suggested otherwise.

Settled quickly into the cab, Chang gently laid his hand on her knee and gave it a reassuring squeeze. "The Reproductive Medical Facility in Xuhui District." Chang barked to the cabbie.

Vivian's eyes were closed, and she moaned with every bump of the road and through every lane change. An eternity later they pulled up outside the Reproductive Medical Facility associated with Medical College of Shanghai Jiao Tong University. The Society had had the foresight to arrange their drop off here in case something like this happened. They would leave the Bibles in a bag in an exam room, and Their contact would come back by and grab it once they had left.

Chang approached the receptionist. "We have an appointment with Dr. Li." He told her Vivian's cover name in Mandarin. She nodded and checked them in.

Once in the exam room Chang carefully set her down on the long, narrow bed. He leaned down and tucked his face underneath her hair and whispered into her ear, "Can you bear it until we're somewhere else?" She bit her lip again and nodded.

He helped her to lay back and quickly exposed the suit's belly. Chang saw a hint of her belly as she fished out the zipper. He quickly unloaded her swollen false stomach and shoved the Bibles into a bag, then slid the bag underneath the physician's desk in the corner for their contact to swipe as soon as they left.

"All right, let's go." Chang stood by the door ready to escape. When Vivian didn't come, he turned and saw her face was as pale as a ghost. "What is it? What's wrong?"

"I feel sick," she murmured, covering her mouth with her hand. Chang jumped over to her side, swiping the trashcan on his way. Vivian rolled over to her good side just in time to be sick into the waste bin. She shook violently, sweat glistening on her forehead. "I think it's the pain, stress, and heat. I want to get going." She tried to sit up but floundered for a moment before throwing up into the bin again.

Chang pulled out his phone and fiddled with it for a moment. Relief washed over him moments later as it chirped. "Our ride will be here by the time we get to the front. Can you make your stomach quiet down until we get to a safe house?"

"Don't you mean hotel? I'll try but no promises." Vivian gave a brave smile, but Chang could see the hesitation.

"We're skipping the hotel and heading straight to a safe house. We need security and privacy," Chang said, setting the garbage can down and scooping her up in his arms.

Vivian was grateful the safe house was in an upscale condominium building in a beautiful, trendy neighborhood. Chang set her carefully down on the bed in the single bedroom. He cocked his head as he examined her shoulder.

"We need to get the suit off you before I can really see what's wrong," Chang tugged her purple maternity shirt up and over the paunch. Vivian's face turned a bright pink, and she hugged her left arm to her stomach, stopping him. "What's wrong?"

"I don't have anything underneath the suit, and I can't take it off myself," Vivian said quietly, her eyes downcast.

"We need to take care of you and no one else can come help. Can you please trust me?" Chang tugged her chin up so he could see her eyes. Large, silent tears rolled down her cheeks again. "I promise I'll take care of you." Vivian gave a stiff nod and carefully moved her limp arm to the side.

The shirt came off easy, but the suit had to be twisted and cajoled, causing Vivian to grunt with pain. By the time it was off, and she was lying motionless in her leggings and bra, ready to pass out.

Chang gave her shoulder a quick inspection. "I think it's dislocated. I can put it back in but it's going to be uncomfortable. Are you ready?"

Vivian squeezed her eyes shut and nodded. Chang gripped her elbow and wrist firmly and maneuvered her arm before sharply popping it up and in. She started to scream but bit down on her lip instead. She laid there panting against the burn, waiting for it to subside. When the flare of pain had passed, she slowly opened her eyes and roughly wiped away her tears with her right hand.

Chang sat silently watching her face, his own filled with sorrow. In the awkward silence she became acutely aware that she did not have a shirt on. She moved to sit up and cover herself at the same time, but pain lanced through her shoulder, and she collapsed back onto the bed.

"Don't try to sit up on your own." Chang held a handout to her, but she batted it away. "What's wrong?" Chang looked down and his face went a shade of bright pink. "Hold on, I've got a shirt you can wear." He stalked off to the front room. Vivian could hear him rummaging through luggage.

A moment later he returned with a large cotton tee shirt with the Beijing Ducks basketball team logo on it. "I think it would be best for you to wear this, rather than something of yours. It's probably easier to get on than anything you've got. Let me help you, please." Using her good arm she shoved herself up. Chang slid the tee over her head slowly. Vivian's cheek tingled where his fingers lightly touched her skin. She slid her good arm through the sleeve and clenched her jaw as she slid her other arm through. She could feel his breath on her skin as he adjusted the folds of fabric. He looked down at her, a smirk playing at the corner of his mouth, and lowered his head to ear.

"I'll be back shortly with supplies." His breath tickled her ear, causing a shiver to run down her spine.

She leaned back on the bed surrounded by fluffy pillows wearing his shirt. It smelled like him. A vague scent of leather and something woodsy, cedar maybe? The door creaked open, and Vivian awoke with a start. She must've dozed off thinking about the aroma of cedar trees.

Groggily she tried to push up into a seated position, but pain rocked through her arm. "She cried out in pain, feeling useless and silly.

"Don't be in a hurry. Ask for help," Chang chided her, his hands steadying her then pulling her up to prop with her back against the swath of pillows.

"I brought food and some medicine. Also, we've rearranged your flights so you can stay here to rest a few extra days." Chang handed her a bottled water but she struggled with getting the cap off. She grunted in irritation and handed the bottle back to him. He silently opened it and then pulled a small white tablet out of a pill bottle.

"Thank you. I really am grateful for the help." She popped the tablet in her mouth and swallowed it with a gulp of water. "I'm used to doing the helping, not being the one who needs the help."

"I can understand struggling to be dependent. I am the same way." He cleared his throat and nodded his head back toward the door. "I bought some jiaozi and roast duck. If we can't enjoy Beijing's sights, we should at least enjoy its cuisine." He smiled broadly, apparently proud of his hometown favorites. "Would you like it now or later?"

"I'm surprisingly hungry and I've never had roast duck. Let's have it now while it's fresh."

Chang soon reappeared with food in hand, and had pulled a chair next to the bed, a plate of food balanced on his lap.

Vivian gave an appreciative moan after sampling both the jiaozi and duck. "This is fantastic. I need to a take a food tour sometime."

Chang smiled knowingly. "Americans cannot get the cuisine just right. You must be here to try the real thing."

"What else do American's fail to understand?" Vivian wondered aloud.

"Well, Chinese medicine for one, is far superior, in my humble opinion to the loaded pharmacies in the West. Why not try to be as natural as possible?" Chang said, taking another bite of his roast duck. He closed his eyes for a moment.

"Another good point. We do tend to appreciate modern science over traditional medicine. Where did you learn such good English? You speak it flawlessly," Vivian asked, leaning her head back to rest on the headboard.

"Brother Qing Qing, the man who cared for me from age ten on. He hosted more missionaries than I could ever count. They all took turns teaching me. I owe him much." Chang's voice cracked on the last phrase. He turned away quickly and swept out of the room, leaving his plate, half finished, behind.

Vivian sat up and looked between the now empty chair and the door. Her stomach flopped uncomfortably, just when she thought she was starting to know him he surprised her. She felt horrible not knowing such a dull question could cause such an emotional outburst from him.

She set her plate aside and slipped off the bed, his black tee hanging down to her knees. She crept to the door and peeked out. Chang, his back to her, bustled about in the small kitchen, putting things away. Vivian moved through the apartment slowly, her stomach in knots.

"Chang, I'm sorry." He stiffened, still facing away from her. "I'm still getting to know you so I don't know what's off limits to talk about."

"You have nothing to apologize for." Chang said, turning toward her, his eyes darker than usual. Vivian stepped closer to him, hesitantly laying her hand on his arm. He sucked in his breath and moved closer to her. He slid his arms around her and pulled her into his chest. She rested her cheek against him. "I'm sorry." He all but whispered into her hair. She closed her eyes and soaked in his warmth.

CHAPTER 8

"Well, you're lucky. You'll heal quickly if you leave it immobilized and do physical therapy when you get back from your next trip." Dr. Barnard tugged the hospital gown over Vivian's skin, now mottled with deep purple bruises. "You can ice it as needed but no more than twenty minutes at a time. Ibuprofen for pain but I'd recommend limiting them.

"I'll let the council know you'll be fit enough for your next mission. I think the plan is to have you use the maternity suit every other trip, but I'll let them explain the details. Are you doing alright?" Dr. Barnard leaned down and focused on Vivian's face. Only a few wrinkles at the corners of his eyes and a sprinkle of silver along his sideburns gave away his age.

"You mean, emotionally?" Vivian asked, waving away the doctor's concern with her good arm. "I'm fine. It was an accident."

"Very well." Dr. Barnard stood and left her alone to get redressed. Vivian's shoulder was past the acutely painful part of the healing process and had settled on inflexible. She contorted her left arm to get her shirt back on before hopping off the table.

Vivian maneuvered from the Society's doctor's office through the crowded hallways to Mrs. Kaminsky's office. As The Society's head secretary, she had role in every process of the entire institution and was known for her deep loyalty to Gloria Hayes, the head of The Society, and its council.

Vivian paused before the open door and peered around a young man. He swept his lengthy brown hair away from his glasses as Mrs. Kaminsky caught Vivian's eye and waved at her.

"Thank you, Jack, I'll be sure to pass along the message. Vivian, please come in. Mrs. Hayes is expecting you." She nodded her head toward The Society's President's office door. Vivian paused to knock then opened the door.

Mrs. Hayes' office was bright and cheery. A whitewashed desk blended into the white walls, which were covered in colorful tribal paintings. A cheery crazy quilt hung on the back of a sofa, which, along with several chairs, were arranged near a window. A vase of wildflowers sat on a coffee table, completing the layout.

"Have a seat on the sofa. I'll be right with you." Mrs. Hayes' voice caught Vivian's attention. Vivian turned away from the group of paintings to wait on the sofa. She watched Mrs. Hayes walk over to join her. The woman's curly white hair contrasted beautifully against her chestnut skin.

"So, has Dr. Barnard released you then?" Mrs. Hayes asked setting a stack of folders down on the coffee table.

"Yes. I need to keep my arm immobilized until my next trip then begin physical therapy when I return. The outlook is good," Vivian said, glancing out the window. White fences stretched out across the fields, each paddock lined with blue-green grass and filled with horses.

"Have you had a chance to enjoy the trails yet?" Mrs. Hayes indicated the scenic view that had captivated Vivian.

"No, I'm not much of a rider. But maybe this autumn I'll try it again. Dr. Barnard will have to give his approval, but I'm sure it won't be a problem," Vivian replied, turning her attention back to Mrs. Hayes.

"I know a young lady like you must not have enjoyed the maternity suit, but I can assure you it has been quite the blessing this month in getting the Bibles across the border. We had success in all the countries we tried it in. We are grateful, as always, for your help in spreading God's word." Mrs. Hayes reached up and pulled her reading glasses down from their spot perched atop her head. She squinted at a file folder in her lap. "How do you feel it went?"

"It was incredibly uncomfortable, but it wasn't horrible. How often will I have to wear it?"

"We'd like to do it every other trip. Your July trip will utilize a backpack instead, then this fall we'll have you use the suit again. How are things with your contact?"

"Things are going well. He is extremely knowledgeable. I've learned a lot from him." Vivian kept a poker face; she had no intention of sharing her personal curiosity with Chang.

"He was quite upset with himself for being involved with your injury. He's connected with us several times to check on you." Mrs. Hayes peered over the glasses that had slid down to the tip of her nose. "You're not getting too personal, are you?"

Vivian's heart began to race. Chang had checked in on her, that surprised her, and she liked knowing he was concerned about her. She turned her focus back to her boss.

"I know only his fake identity. We've not exchanged personal information," Vivian carefully answered, her poker face still on.

"Alright, but you must abide by the rules. They are for your safety as well as the safety of this organization," Mrs. Hayes warned, her sharp eyes searching Vivian's face carefully.

Mrs. Kaminsky knocked on the door before opening it, a tray of refreshments in her hands.

"Now, dear, let's have a bit of a snack while we discuss the future. I'd like to hear more about your plans, now that you've settled into the program so nicely," Mrs. Hayes said, setting aside the file folder.

Vivian swallowed hard. Mrs. Hayes might look like an innocent grandmother, but Vivian felt like she was facing down a predator, Mrs. Hayes's instincts were reminiscent of a bloodhound on the trail of prey.

CHAPTER 9

Vivian pulled her hair up into a ponytail and wished for an air conditioner. Summer in China was sweltering, especially in the southern provinces. She grabbed her rolling suitcase and hurried into the thick crowd crawling toward the exit of the terminal. As she neared the group of drivers and tour guides holding signs, she finally spotted Chang.

He wore blue jeans, a light blue polo shirt, and a baseball cap with a Chinese dragon on it. He waved enthusiastically and grabbed her luggage when she neared him.

“Welcome to our beautiful country!” Chang loudly announced to Vivian, likely for the benefit of any tails she might have.

“Thank you, sir. What terminal will we be leaving from?” Vivian asked, ignoring the possibility of a tail and focusing on her interaction with Chang.

“We’re taking a private flight. Commercial flights take too long, and they don’t fly to Chengdu Let’s grab something to eat before the flight.”

“I’m starving. I’ll eat almost anything at this point, except for chicken feet, those are still out!” Vivian said, her stomach growling in agreement. Chang laughed.

Gingerly holding their noodles and hauling their luggage, they made it just in time to their private plane, which held several other passengers. Chang followed Vivian to seats in the back of business class.

"Are these others with our group?" Vivian whispered, waving ahead of them where several others sat.

Chang shrugged as he swallowed his bite of noodles. "We don't usually know many of the other contacts. Layers of security, remember?" Vivian nodded and focused on her food, a simple stir-fry, rice, a glutinous rice ball filled with red bean paste, small salad, and a chocolate chip cookie. She pulled her neck pillow and eye mask out of her carry-on bag to settle down for a quick nap.

Just under three hours later they landed in Chengdu. The city was covered with pandas. Store fronts were plastered with panda pictures, stuffed animals, and trinkets of every kind. It felt like Vivian was walking into Dollywood, but with pandas.

"We're relatively safe here, but I'd like to do the drop off as soon as we've checked into the hotel," Chang explained. It was early afternoon and Vivian had more energy than during her first trip. The overnight flight and catnap had helped with jet lag.

Once checked in, they took public transit and then walked on foot to an impoverished neighborhood. Chang led the way to a simple building bordered by dark alleyways. They walked through the entryway, the front door banging loudly behind them, and all the way to the last apartment on the first floor. Chang knocked three times, paused, then knocked twice more and waited. After several tense minutes he knocked again. They could hear children a few apartments down squealing with laughter and critters scurrying within the walls. "Be ready to run," he whispered as he put his hand on the knob and turned it. The door creaked open, but no one came to meet them. The horrific smell of decaying flesh punched them in the throat.

Chang pulled Vivian inside with him, bolting the door behind them. Vivian was pale and stood behind him, balling up the back of Chang's tee shirt in her fists. He slowly walked through the apartment, pausing every few steps. The smell seemed to get worse the farther back they went. A partially opened door stood at the end of the hall, a pale light flickering within. Chang walked slowly up to it and pushed it open. Vivian gasped.

A young man was nailed to the wall in what had been a bedroom. His arms were extended to resemble Christ crucified. His face was grotesquely bloated, and flies buzzed around him. He had likely been dead for several days. They needed to get out of there now. Was the place bugged? Had they been followed?

Chang grabbed Vivian's fist, that was still balled up in his shirt, and turned for the door. The front door bang loudly. . He spun and dash with her back toward the kitchen. He peeked out an open window. "There, in the alleyway." Two men in suits with moved quickly toward the apartment. Vivian noticed one man had mismatched eyes, they didn't have time to see what caused the unique trait.

Chang bent over and pulled open a cabinet door that was tucked underneath a small table. Still holding Vivian by the hand, he tugged her down. Vivian ducked under the table and into the dark cabinet. In the darkness she felt around and scooted into the farthest corner to give Chang room to move.

Chang had just enough time to quietly close the cabinet when the front door burst open with a loud crack. He slid over to Vivian. Her hand glide down his arm and she interlaced her fingers in his and squeezed. She could feel his heart thumping so loudly she worried that the intruders would hear it.

Vivian closed her eyes and prayed, but something was digging into her back as she pressed against the wall. She reached up with her free hand to readjust her bag, but the object still dug into her tender skin. She leaned forward off the wall and felt behind her. A nob stuck out from the wall. With a slow and careful push, the wall silently swung open. Chang let go of her hand and slid his arm behind her. He gently pushed her through the door.

They quietly climbed down from the cabinet onto a hard packed dirt floor. Chang closed the door. He pulled his phone out and activated the lock screen to barely illuminate the darkness. There was just enough of a soft glow to see the boxes lining the back wall. Vivian took Chang's phone and shined the screen to the side of the door. She slid a bar quietly across the door and sat back against the boxes. Chang took his phone back but kept her hand in his.

Heavy footsteps echoed through the hallway. The two crammed in close to each other, barely breathing. Angry shouts bounced off the cabinets in front of them. Doors opened and closed, furniture was moved, and the chaos continued.

"Where do you think they are hiding?" A muffled voice penetrated the cabinet doors.

"Patience is a bitter plant, but its fruit is sweet. We will find them." Came the reply. "Tear apart the furniture and check the floors." The menacing voice sent chills down Vivian's spine.

Splintering wood echoed through the kitchen, followed by shattering glass. Heavy feet rumbled through the apartment like a storm. The door of the cabinet they hid behind were thrown open, a thin ray of light split the gloom. Vivian tucked closer to Chang. He wrapped his arm around her and pulled her snugly into his side as if to shield her from the utter confusion beyond the thin wood barrier.

The free-for-all continued on and off for an indeterminable amount of time. As much as Vivian wanted to check the time she didn't dare so much as take a deep breath.

"Uh, Sir, we have not found anything. The, uh, Captain is requesting an update." A timid voice broke through the noisy backdrop. Someone growled, followed by another smash.

"Then let's go give the captain an update in person. We are so close to them; I can smell it. Let's go." The menacing voice growled again, footsteps retreating. The silence that followed was near deafening.

Vivian and Chang heaved a simultaneous sigh of relief and settled in to wait.

Vivian began to nod off, overcome with exhaustion. Chang wrapped his arm around her and pulled her close. She hesitantly rested her head on his chest.

Chang's soft voice in her ear woke her up with a start. Compared to the silence in the apartment it was nearly deafening. "They're gone for now. I messaged a contact of mine so they should be here soon. Hand me your bag and hold my phone," he handed her the phone. He went to work on the lining of her bag with a pocketknife he had produced, and soon had a hole big enough to take everything out. He stacked them on top of the boxes behind them.

A scraping sound echoed through the apartment. Vivian turned off the phone and held her breath. Soft footsteps padded through the kitchen and down the hallway. A moment later the footsteps were back, and it was silent. A knock came next. Then a whisper, "Shei ai ni?"

It was apparently a code because Chang whispered back, "Jesus loves you." He slid the bar back and the door swung open. A middle-aged man was squatting down looking at them with an anguished look.

"They gone. House not bugged. They come back soon. Get Bibles! Hurry!" He spoke in halting English for Vivian's benefit. Vivian grabbed the items that had been stowed in her bag and handed those out first while Chang began heaving boxes out the small door. The three of them cleared the space quickly.

"Safe houses are not safe. Where will you go?" the friend asked, nervously looking toward the front.

"I have a friend we can stay with here in the city, but we need our stuff from the hotel. Can you get our bags to this address?" Chang texted an address to the man. He nodded.

"Alley secure. Go now." They were practically shoved out the back door. Chang grabbed Vivian's hand and dashed past a waiting delivery truck, down the alley, away from the front of the building, and into the dark night.

After several blocks, Chang pulled Vivian behind a large stand of bikes and crouched down.

"Are we being followed?" Vivian was breathing hard as she whispered, not daring to look past the bikes they were hiding behind.

"I don't think so. Can you go on? We will have to go on foot. We don't have a taxi service here."

"Yes, I can make it. I've been running a lot at home. I'm up to ten kilometers right now."

Chang nodded. "Impressive. Let's go."

They ran through the darkness for over an hour, keeping to the side streets and alleyways. Eventually, Chang turned onto a road lined with towering, well-groomed trees and flower gardens. Eventually they stopped outside a modern building, the Ascott, a glowing towering silver building. They took the stairs to the sixth floor and quietly knocked on door number 73. After a few silent and tense minutes, the door opened a crack.

Harsh words flew at them through the crack. Chang softly answered and pressed a hand to the door, pushing it open. It gave way but the individual inside continued to whisper harshly. Vivian stepped in and closed the door behind her.

"Vivian, this is a friend of mine. She is a little upset that we came here, but she'll let us use her guest room," Chang said, flipping on a light. Chang's "friend" scowled at him and shook her head vigorously.

"Should we just go to a hotel? I hate to put her out like this." Vivian eyed the angry woman. She wore a silk nightie that was not modest. Her hair was a sleek, black pixie cut and even in the middle of the night she had perfectly rosy cheeks and pouty lips. Vivian wondered what kind of friend she was. Her eyes roamed over Vivian as if appraising her. She snorted and turned back toward Chang. Apparently not liking what she saw.

"No," Chang said firmly. "We are not safe anywhere else. Dandan, can we please stay here." Chang's friend, nodded her head, rolled her eyes and walked away. Chang walked through the place like he knew it well, stopping in front of a door. Vivian finally moved her worn and weary body. By the time she reached the door, he was inside with the light on.

The room was spacious. A king-sized bed stood directly across from the door. A desk and built-in wardrobe lined the left wall, while a sitting area and open door completed the area to her right.

"Why don't you take a shower, I'll get us some food. Our luggage won't be here until morning." Weariness hung on his words and his broad shoulders seemed to be tugged downward by the weight of the day.

"That's alright. A shower still sounds good." The shower felt amazing. Scrubbing off the filth of travel and the grime from sitting on that dirt floor was blissful. She took her time and hoped there would be enough hot water left for Chang. When she finally got done and began toweling off, she noticed a pile of clothes on the counter. Curious, she lifted it up and saw it was a silk nightie and robe. *At least it shows less than Chang's girlfriend's outfit.* She quickly dressed and ran the brush from her bag through her hair.

By the time she got out of the bathroom Chang had an array of food laid out across the coffee table in the sitting area. Vivian tried to smile at Chang, but it came out as a distracted, embarrassed mess.

"What's that smirk about?" Chang asked her, his head cocked to the side.

"I was just thinking about how I still think of you by the other name. And, um, feeling slightly uncomfortable in this, um, in front of you." She blushed at her honesty as she waved at her silk nightie and robe.

Chang's eyes never left her face, but he smiled knowingly and swallowed hard. He looked down at the food on the table but kept taking a few glances in her direction. She stood awkwardly in the silk, he seemed to struggle to concentrate on the food in front of him

"Please tell your girlfriend that I appreciate the loan. I'll try to repay her for her kindness." Vivian sat in an armchair and surveyed the food.

Chang snorted and looked at her incredulously. "Is that what you think she is?"

"Well, she acted like she was. Or rather, that she had been."

"I've never been involved with her. She's the bratty daughter of a wealthy friend. She's said she was interested in me and made many attempts to date me and even tried to seduce me but I'm not interested in relationships right now. Chang couldn't help but notice the look of intense hurt that passed over Vivian's face as his final words stung her.

Vivian picked up a plate and helped herself to the food, never lifting her eyes to Chang. It was silent for what felt like hours. Suddenly Chang stood walked over and knelt before her. He took her plate and put it on the table and held her hands, but she wouldn't look at him. He reached out and tipped her chin up, so they were eye to eye.

"We need to talk about what happened. About what we saw." Chang's voice was thick with emotion. Vivian finally looked at him. A single tear slid down her cheek. He reached up to wipe it away but she turned her head away from him.

"Come here," Chang said, his voice husky. He pulled her out of the chair and onto his lap and wrapped his arms around her. Her body shook with silent sobs. She thought of the man nailed to the wall. The horrific smell of his decaying body. Of their efforts to keep the Word safe from destruction. Of Chang's clear message that she was undesirable. The sobs lessened, and she locked away her desire for Chang. Heck, she didn't even know his real name. She was acting like a boy crazy teen.

"I'm sorry you had to see that. What the PRC does to their enemies is horrible. I believe the safe house was compromised before we were involved so I don't believe we are in immediate danger. Usually, it's a neighbor bribed by the secret police." Chang rubbed her back through the silk robe.

"Would you mind if I take a shower before we talk some more?" Chang asked her. "You can finish eating then we can talk some things out. About us, I mean." Chang stood up slowly, then paused, looking back at her. He hesitated, as if he wanted to add something then closed the bathroom door. Vivian felt a small spark of hope light in her chest, but she shoved it away, afraid it would get squashed again.

She sat back down and had finished off two plates of food by the time he came back. He wasn't wearing a shirt, just his jeans. As he made his way to the sitting area, he tossed his shirt on the bed and piled his plate with food. He sat down across from her and picked up his chopsticks.

Vivian launched into the words that had been brewing in her head before he had taken his first bite. “I’d like to apologize. I know the rules. Don’t get personally involved. I would be lying if I said I wasn’t fighting against my urges and better judgment. I know I’ve made things awkward, and I’ve put you in a tough spot.”

He took a few more bites in silence, probably trying to figure out how to tell her they should get different contacts. Vivian didn’t realize she was holding her breath until she started to get dizzy. She drew in a deep breath and had to remind herself to let it back out again.

“I need a minute.” She rushed into the bathroom to compose herself. She stood with her back to the door, breathing in slowly, trying to calm the sea of regret churning in her belly. She took her time, coming to the realization that this was it. They were, indeed, done as partners.

CHAPTER 10

Vivian's eyes were a bit puffy when she reentered the room. She sat down rather stiffly and turned, opening her mouth to speak. He held up his hand to stop her.

"My name is Liang Shen Wu. My father was the pastor of an underground church and was sentenced to ten years in the work camps while my mother was pregnant with me. I never met him. My mother and I lived with my grandmother. By the time I was five my mother was usually gone, working for the church for months at a time. My grandmother was nearly blind and deaf so I had to take care of her, and she could not work. We lived off what little money my mother brought home on her infrequent visits. By the age of seven, I had begun working for a farmer. It was my job to sort vegetables and feed the rotten ones to the pigs. He beat me mercilessly, so I learned how to relax into the pain. I was paid very little and would sneak pieces of rotten food into my clothes to feed us sometimes. Eventually, I realized it was easier to steal than it was to endure another beating. It was even easier when my grandmother died. I only had to care for myself." He paused and looked at Vivian. Her eyes betrayed no emotion. He swallowed hard.

"My mother returned for the last time when I was ten. I had quit working for the farmer and stole to get by. I occasionally worked, though. One day I was caught stealing. Instead of taking me to the police department he took me to his house. He fed me, clothed me, and cared for me, not just physically but emotionally. He gave me the stability and strength I needed. He eventually gave me a thorough scolding about morals, values, and my soul. I knew stealing was wrong and knew about God, but the way he put it I realized that I was wasting my time. There was so much more to life than just getting by. He pulled me into the Bible smuggling world. I never saw my mother again."

"Why are you telling me this? You could get in so much trouble." Vivian looked thoroughly confused.

"Honestly, I don't know. I've kept to myself my whole life. I've been on my own since I was five. I'm tired. I am only twenty-two and feel like an old man. I guess I want you to know what my real name is." He shrugged and smiled sheepishly.

"So, what happens. For this trip? And, um, for us?" Vivian asked nervously.

"I can answer the first part easily but the second part I really don't know. We know the rules, but I feel like we're past that now. Do you *want* to go back to the fake names? I can arrange to get you a new contact," Shen offered. He liked her knowing his real name.

"No!" Vivian said a little excitedly. "I mean, no, that's alright. I don't want to go back to that. Just one more question. Do we keep exploring this new relationship or just …?"

Shen smiled at her attempt to cover her forceful answer. Her shyness only pulled him in more. "No, I don't want to leave things the way they are. I want to know more about you."

Vivian smiled shyly and nodded. She looked exhausted. "Sorry for keeping you up so late. Why don't you take the bed and I'll sleep on the chair," he suggested, getting up to put his plate on the table.

"The bed is big enough for both of us, and you're far too much of a gentleman to do anything," Vivian gently protested.

"No, that's alright. I've slept in mud pits and sewers. This is luxury compared to most places I've been." He was finally aware that he was only wearing his jeans and she was wearing a very thin nightie and robe.

"Please? At least come talk to me while I fall asleep. If you want to go back to the chair after I'm asleep then you can." He couldn't ignore her pleading eyes.

They awkwardly walked over to the enormous bed and climbed between the cool, smooth sheets. Vivian laid on her side looking at Shen. Shen lay there watching her sleep for a while, his emotions and thoughts a storm. Eventually he fell into a light, restless sleep keeping plenty of room between them.

◆ ◆ ◆

Vivian wasn't sure what woke her up, but she was intensely aware of someone close to her. She opened her eyes slowly and turned her head to the side to see Shen holding a book, intently reading.

"Sorry if I woke you. I was reading through Proverbs."

"I didn't drool last night, right?" Her hand flew up to check her mouth for slobber and she covered her eyes with her free arm.

Shen chuckled softly and tugged on her hand, pulling it off her face. "I doubt it."

So, that conversation last night had been real. They hadn't exactly declared their love for each other, but it was a start. It still felt incredibly intimate.

"I didn't talk in my sleep, did I?" Vivian pulled the sheet up to her chin, her shyness spilling out.

"No, do you normally?" Shen laughed quietly.

"No, but I'm sure my sister Livi would tell you differently." Despite not knowing what their relationship was going to be, she liked this side of Shen best.

"What time is it?" she looked around for a clock.

"I'm not sure. I heard Dandan leave earlier. I didn't want to disturb you." Shen slid out of the bed, and Vivian's eyes follow him across the room. He swiped his phone from the table, squeezed the side so it displayed the time.

"Wow, we slept through breakfast and lunch!" She felt so much better than last night, but her stomach growled loudly enough that Shen raised an eyebrow from across the room. He laughed, grabbing a bun from the table and tossing it to her. She caught it gracefully.

She nibbled on the cold bun, watching him retrieve his shirt from the floor. He really was impressive – tall and well-built from many years of running from police and hauling loads of Bibles. His face still held a boyishness, but it was his eyes, so full of wisdom, that gave her pause. She wanted to know everything going through his mind. He looked up suddenly, catching her watching him dress, and then down again. He was almost as red in the face as she was.

"I'm going to see if our luggage has arrived. I'll be right back." With that, he promptly made his escape.

With Shen gone, Vivian quickly got out of bed, tossed the half-eaten bun onto the coffee table, and headed for the bathroom. When she got out, her luggage sat on the bed and Shen was nowhere to be seen. It felt good to be in her own clothes again.

She opened the bedroom door and saw Shen sitting on a chair. He was busy on his phone but looked up when he heard the door click closed behind her.

"Bathroom is free," she said, looking around for last night's hostile hostess.

"She's not here. Can you take care of last night's meal while I get dressed? Then we'll figure out the game plan." He stopped in front of her and reached out, gently touching her arm. Her breath caught in her throat when she looked up, her glance catching his captivating eyes. She wanted him to pull her into his arms, but instead he pulled away slowly and cleared his throat and walked into the bedroom. Vivian stood still a moment, trying to halt the swirl of butterflies in her stomach.

Vivian carried the leftover takeout to the kitchen and started peeking in cabinets to find the trashcan but was coming up empty handed. The front door opened loudly. The woman breezed into the kitchen and dropped a brown paper bag onto the counter. She was immaculate in white high-waisted pants and a hot pink sleeveless shirt.

"Trash is in there," she said in perfect English, thumbing behind her toward what appeared to be a closet. Vivian walked the tray over.

"You know he's a playboy, right? I'm sure you're a nice little girl so I just thought you'd want to know that." She stared at Vivian for a moment.

Vivian was taken aback by Dandan's comment. "Well, I don't really know about all that but I know we're both grateful that you have allowed us to stay here. So, thank you." The front door opened and Shen came in.

"Everything alright?" Concern lacing his words.

"Oh, hi, dear. We were just talking about you. Girl talk." She smirked and shrugged her shoulders.

"Uh, huh. Anyway, thank you for letting us stay here." Shen reached around Vivian to take the tray from her and dumped its contents into the trashcan hidden behind the closet door.

"Well, I don't cook, like ever, but I brought some take-out," Dandan said over her shoulder as she strutted away.

"What was all that about?" Vivian whispered, heading to the counter.

"There's an interesting history there. She was sent away for school in Europe, but once she graduated, she had no choice but to come back to China. She hates it here. She is looking for some rich husband to take her back to Europe," Shen explained, lifting a take-out box from the brown bag. He opened it up and a spicy fragrance filled the air. "What did she say to you, anyway? You looked upset." He turned to look at Vivian.

She opened her mouth to speak, but paused, unable to find the right words. Shen seemed to notice her hesitation and looked at her quizzically. Vivian shook her head and looked away briefly. "Nothing, it was nothing. She seems to think she knows you pretty well." Shen put the box down and crossed the few steps to Vivian.

"I know this is very new to both of us, but please don't shut down on me." Shen's words were incredibly soft, but their meaning was heavy.

Vivian swallowed hard. “She said you were a player.”

“Do you believe her?”

“I think there is more history there than I know about but” she started, “I don’t think you’re a player,” she finished, and relief flooded Shen’s face.

Vivian noticed Shen had gone tense. She walked up behind him and hesitantly touched his broad shoulders. He took a sharp breath. Vivian gently massaged his thick muscles as he let the breath go, then dropped her arms and wrapped them around his waist. They stood in silence with her cheek pressed against his back, listening to each other’s rapid heartbeats.

A door clicked open somewhere in the apartment and they stepped apart quickly. They guiltily went about bringing a new load of food into their room. Dandan walked into the kitchen and stared at them.

“Oh? Did I catch someone being naughty? Would you mind taking it to the bedroom, I don’t really like to watch. I do like to join though! We could use my bedroom!” She laughed and leaned over to slip on her high heels, giving both a great view of her low-cut shirt.

Shen’s face clouded and loud guttural words erupted from him. He lashed out at her in rapid Mandarin. Before she could respond the doorbell chimed. She stalked off to open the door.

Vivian looked incredulously at Shen. “What did you say to her?” She whispered.

Shen’s face fell. “That came out more harshly than I intended. I’m sorry I yelled.”

“Baba!” Dandan exclaimed. Behind them Dandan was hugging someone.

“Ming Jie.” Shen acknowledged the newcomer.

“Zi?” The man was short, with close cropped hair, and round in the middle. Surprise spread over his face as he took in Shen.

“Yes, it is me, my old friend. Your daughter was gracious enough to allow us to stay over.”

“Us?”, he said in English, taking in Vivian standing closely to

Shen.

"Yes, this is my partner, Vivian. Vivian, this is Dandan's father. Dandan, can I speak with you?"

Shen stepped to the side, waving her over.

"I heard what you told your "partner." All's well." She turned back to her father but he walked closer to Shen.

"How many years has it been?" Ming Jie asked, stepping in to hug the younger man.

"Too many years." Shen admitted, falling into step with Dandan's father. "What brings you here?"

"Well, you. Dandan mentioned you were here. You know she's still quite enamored with you." He whispered conspiratorially and laughed loudly, smacking Shen on the shoulder.

Vivian swallowed hard and turned away. Whatever was happening between her and Shen was still up in the air. He was still on the market and if he wanted a relationship with Dandan that was between them.

"Ming Jie, you know how I feel." Shen narrowed his eyes at the older man. Dandan's father merely guffawed even louder.

"She's a woman that knows what she wants and she tends to get what she wants. She's had her eyes on you for years. Its only a matter of time, my young friend." Ming Jie smiled proudly, gazing between Dandan and Shen. "Come, my friend, let us share a meal."

"Sorry, we have plans. Vivian, get your stuff." Shen ordered, snagging the bag of take-out before waiting at the door for Vivian.

CHAPTER 11

Vivian and Shen set up a picnic on a blanket and leaned back against a large tree trunk. They slowly ate the spicy Sichuan food and chatted. The shaky wall that had been erected between them on their first meeting, as per the rules, had come tumbling down.

"What's your favorite color?" Shen asked, wiping his mouth with a paper napkin.

"Green, but not just any green, emerald green. What's yours?"

"I'm rather partial to light chocolate brown. Like your eyes." There was a pause as he shifted mental gears. "This is fun, but I feel like we're forgetting something," Shen turned to look at Vivian.

"Ya, I feel like we're getting a bit ahead of ourselves. We've completely ignored God," Vivian nodded, her eyes downcast.

Shen stood up and held his hand out to Vivian. Together they bowed their heads and held hands. "Dear Father God in Heaven, we come before you humble and grateful for your intervention in our lives. We pause now from our distractions and desires to refocus on your leading in our relationship and our lives. We deeply desire to walk this path together with you leading us," Shen prayed quietly, encouraged by the gentle pressure from Vivian's hands.

"We desire to honor you above all earthly desires," Vivian jumped in, "and we ask you to take the lead on this relationship. Above all, we are committed to spreading your Word throughout the world." Then in unison they said, "In Jesus' Name, amen."

Shen dropped her hands and stepped back, looking away. "Did I say something wrong?" Vivian sounded confused.

Shen took a deep breath and turned back to her. "No!" he protested, a bit too loudly. "Just feeling a bit overwhelmed. Praying with you and ending it at the same time just...I don't know."

Vivian took a step closer but didn't move to touch him. "A bit more intimate than expected, huh?"

Shen looked into her eyes and nodded his head. "Yeah, exactly. You see me." Shen stepped toward Vivian his arms open wide. She walked into his embrace. They held each other for a long while before eventually breaking apart.

"I'd like to ask you one thing. Why me?" She asked, shyly, sitting back down on the blanket. A light breeze ruffled her hair.

Shen looked shocked. "I have never had any interest or desire in women my entire life. Not one time has someone turned my head or made me take a second look. The moment I met you that changed. You are the first woman I have met that is as interested in sharing the Gospel as I am. Despite the risks. Most of my contacts do this for a few months then fall away because of distractions or fear. But somehow, I know, even after yesterday, you won't. How would I not be interested in you?" He paused, then much more quietly and quickly "And, it doesn't hurt that you are absolutely stunning!"

Shen watched red creep up Vivian's neck and spread across her cheeks. She tucked a stray hair behind her ear and turned back to the mess on the picnic blanket.

"Let's clean up and get some sleep, we have a long trip back to HK. We're taking the train in the morning," Shen looked down at their picnic of sorts and reached down to start collecting their plates and the take-out boxes.

"I was thinking, Shen, that we shouldn't share the bed again." Shen laughed and nodded.

"I'm a gentleman but, yes, that seems wise. Okay, enough of this talk, it's not helping!" Shen laughed again and grabbed an armful of take-out boxes.

"That train ride was ridiculously long. I'm so glad to be on solid ground again." They endured the swaying of the train for nearly twelve hours, and Vivian was over it. Her legs were jelly, and she was itching to move, especially after being locked down in Chengdu. They had just enough time to get to the airport. There wasn't even enough for a proper goodbye.

"I hope to see you again soon" Shen whispered in her ear as they navigated through the train station crowd. He pulled her to a stop at the entrance to a little shop selling snacks with a questioning look, his lips dangerously close.

Vivian turned back to look at him and her stomach did a flip. She wanted to give in and enjoy getting to know what his mouth could do but her mind said they had time for that later. She steeled her resolve. "No kissing. We have appearances to keep up in public. I've got the photos of our trip thanks to the app. Are you going to contact me before my next trip?"

"I'm not going to show up at your door, but I'll be in touch. I'll take every precaution, though." He assured her quickly. "I look forward to seeing you again," he said wistfully, before his eyes brightened. "Oh, I almost forgot in all the chaos. I have something to give you." Shen rummaged around in his bag, pulling out something small and holding out his hand. Vivian reached out, palm open, and a small necklace dropped into her hand. She held it up and saw it was a koi fish.

"Happy Birthday. In the past our colleagues had a code to know who was friend and foe."

"Ichthys. I'm familiar with it."

"We can't use the original nor the usual symbol. But I thought maybe this would work. You know, I found this before anything really happened. I might've found something a little more romantic had I known." Shen seemed almost apologetic about his pick.

"It is very thoughtful, and I will wear it proudly. I'm surprised you remembered my birthday. I barely mentioned it. When's yours?" She fumbled with the latch for a minute but eventually it clicked shut.

"I don't know. I know my age, but the exact date I might have to... ask." The last word came out slowly, but he shook his head and smiled. "I'll be able to give you an answer next time I see you." He looked at the crowd rushing by and turned serious. "We've got to get you to the airport." With that they scrambled to get a cab, losing themselves in the clog of travelers.

CHAPTER 12

Slam! Stomp, stomp, slam! Livi stalked between the dishwasher and the cupboard. Evan looked up from his tablet and scowled at his bigger sister.

"What's your problem, Livi? The cupboard pinch you or something? I kinda wish it would, maybe you'd quit!" Evan ducked as a towel flew past his head. "Nice try but you couldn't hit the broad side of a Target clearance rack!" Evan grabbed his tablet and dashed out of the room, Livi's scream of frustration following him.

"Ugh, I cannot believe him. That little brat!" Livi turned her back on Vivian who had silently witnessed the scene.

"Livi, I think we need to talk," Vivian softly told her younger sister. Livi visibly stiffened and slowly turned.

"What, so you can tell me that you don't want to talk? That I can't be trusted with secrets? No, thank you! I'll skip the humiliation. Why don't you ever tell us anything about your trips?" Livi slammed another door to underscore her point.

"Lavinia, if there is something that your sister needs to say, then you had better do some listening," their father, Samuel, said from the doorway, his arms across his chest.

"But..." Livi started to say but the withering look Samuel directed her way shut her up quickly. "Fine, but not in here. I don't need Evan into any more of my business."

Vivian snorted. *Sure, you don't want him to be involved in your business, which is apparently the details of my trip.* Vivian ignored

Livi's glare and shoved back from the table. She went to her room and waited.

Livi took her time joining Vivian. She slumped down onto the chair and turned to look out the window. Vivian sighed heavily; she was struggling to be empathetic regarding her sister's constant moodiness but decided to press on with the awkward talk.

"You're mad because I haven't given you the details of my trip?" Vivian asked, crossing her arms on her chest.

"You never talk to me anymore. I miss our talks." Livi tapped her fingers on lap.

"I saw a dead body this time?" Vivian asked, her stomach queasy just remembering the scene. Livi turned her head, just barely. *At least she's listening*, Vivian thought. "It was horrific to see it, to smell it, to taste death in the air. I cannot and will not describe what happened. I would think you could respect that."

Livi sent a searing look across the room toward Vivian. "Are you okay? What happened?" Livi asked, wide-eyed.

"Yes, I'm alright. It was very traumatic, though." She shook her head to try and dislodge the horrific memories.

"But either way, you know that's not what I'm talking about. Something happened with Jian, didn't it? Why won't you tell me about that?"

"That's what this is all about? A guy? Livi, you are unbelievable! Why on earth would that be any of your business anyway?" Vivian was astonished at her sister.

"Because we're sisters and that's what sisters do! We've only got each other. It hurts when you keep secrets from me," Livi pouted quietly from the soft armchair.

Vivian's stomach rolled, remembering in vivid detail their mother's tragic death. There was life with Mom and life without Mom. Vivian had stepped up at age ten to assist with everything – the chores, helping Livi with homework, running errands for Dad, and just keeping life as normal as possible for everyone, despite their dad trying to raise a newborn by himself and grieve. Livi would never understand how much of a burden

Vivian took on while Livi continued to run through life like nothing had changed.

"You sound so selfish. If I *choose* to share anything personal with you, it is just that, a choice. I don't owe you any details. I like our girl talk, too, but some things I am allowed to keep to myself," Vivian said as gently as possible. "Livi, I'm tired. I've spent so many years being a surrogate mom and a sister and it is so exhausting."

Livi bit her lip, looking incredibly hurt. "I know you think Mom's death only affected you and Dad, but it changed me, too." She stared out the window.

"You went on like nothing happened," Vivian said, remembering Livi staring coldly at their mother's casket.

"I didn't know how to act. I was hurting, I had just lost one of my best friends. I was just a kid," Livi said defensively.

"So was I, but my childhood ended that day. Yours went on. While you were off on play dates, I was at home doing the laundry or helping dad with diaper changes," Vivian informed her outspoken sister.

"I'm not saying that I handled it right, or that I chose the best way to grieve. But it happened and there's nothing I can do to go back and change that. You're different. This job is changing you. You've always been serious but now you're downright solemn." Livi had softened a little.

"Livi, I'll try to do better at sharing with you but some things I just want to keep to myself until I'm ready to share. And, even then, there's a chance I might not ever want to share," Vivian explained to her stubborn sister.

"Yeah, yeah, I get it. You don't kiss and tell." Livi waved her hand dismissively. "Are we done here?" Livi stood up and left without waiting for an answer.

Vivian stayed on her bed, irritation at her sister threatening to bubble out of her. She closed her eyes and breathed in and out slowly. *Lord, I don't know how I could have handled that better. I confess my frustration with her. Please be near her as the grief is fresh, again,* Vivian finished her prayer less angry.

Vivian walked over to her desk to check her email. Her first week home had been filled with council meetings, the sugarcoated version for Dad, Livi badgering her for every conceivable detail, and Evan acting like, well, a nine-year-old. She was hoping Livi would thaw out after a while but that didn't look like it was going to happen anytime soon.

While she was scrolling through her weekly schedule for her normal job, her phone chirped. She absentmindedly unlocked the phone and pulled up her notifications. An unknown number had texted her.

The message said, "*Hello beautiful.*" She almost deleted it but paused.

"*Who is this?*" she replied, still hovering over the delete button.

"*Yesu ai ni.*" came the response.

Her heart pounded in her chest. Only one person would know to say that to her. "*Is it really you?*" A fish emoji showed up and she burst into a broad smile. "*Is this safe? I don't want you at risk.*"

"*Yes, it's safe. Are you alright?*"

"*Yes, I'm alright. And you?*"

"*Yes, just lonely.*" Her heart pounded with excitement. He missed her.

"*I am, too. There's a big fish shaped empty spot in my heart.*"

"*Well I will have to find you a fish! I'll message you again soon. Take care of yourself.*"

"*You do the same.*" Smiling to herself, Vivian saved his number to contacts under the phrase Wo Ai Ni.

Rain splattered against the dreary, gray building before pooling at the feet of a somber figure. His black coat dripped, adding to the pool he stood in. His matching black baseball cap was pulled low over his face, hiding his features. He puffed forlornly on a cigarette, flicking the ashes into the small lake at his feet.

Shen watched him from a darkened doorway, pondering the danger. Enter the building knowing it was being watched or disappoint Vivian?

"Screw it, I'm going," Shen growled in frustration. He moved out into the rain, tugging the hood of his raincoat over the top of his hat. He ran across the Beijing street, dodging cars and pedestrians. Without looking at the watcher he ran up the stairs a few flights and knocked on the door of an apartment. It slowly opened a crack.

"Go away!" a voice yelled through the crack. Shen wedged his foot in the door so it couldn't be slammed shut.

"Is that how you greet an old friend? A son?" Shen felt the exasperation seep into his voice.

"Who are you?"

"Let me inside and I'll tell you." Shen pushed against the door. The old man grumbled but stepped back. He ran a hand over his thinning, gray hair and shook his head.

"Qing Qing, I need your help," Shen said, looking around the familiar apartment. A small, dark front room with worn but comfortable furniture, tiny kitchen and table that had fed people in shifts, and several equally small bedrooms that had been packed with people. No matter how tiny and tight the surroundings, the atmosphere in the rental had always been sunny and supportive, though now it seemed desolate.

"Shen? Is that you? Whatever help you might need you'd better be fast about it. I'm being watched. My watcher should be here soon," the frail old man said.

"So, you *are* the one under house arrest. I thought as much." Shen was glad he had taken the time to check out the street around the building.

"Quickly, he's likely on his way," Qing Qing hurried Shen nervously.

"When was I born? I need the exact date. I know I'm twenty-two but what date?" Shen questioned, feeling a little silly that his errand was only to keep a promise to Vivian.

"That's what you ask? It was near the Mid-Autumn Festival,

but you'd have to ask the midwife that delivered your sorry self. Now leave!" He was insistent.

"I'm not worried about your babysitter." Shen turned to look at his old mentor. Once a proud man he now walked hunched, staying away from windows and watching them furtively. "I'm worried you've lost that spark that you were known for. What's happened to you?"

"People got hurt because of me. People died because of me. I will not let another light be snuffed out because of me. Please, go..." Qing Qing didn't get a chance to finish before a knock came at the door.

"Please, allow me," Shen insisted, waving away the man that had raised him away from the door. Shen strode to the door and swung it open and smiled cockily at the undercover policeman that had a pool of water forming around his feet. His mood matched his soggy clothing.

"Finish your smoke there? No worries, I'm on my way and you won't even need to report that you were slow. Wouldn't want you to get in trouble with your superiors," Shen taunted the fuming policeman.

"You are under arrest for fraternizing with a known criminal. Step out and put your hands behind your back," the patrolman ordered, pulling a zip tie out of his pocket.

"Oh, no, I wouldn't want to bother you. Run back downstairs and enjoy another smoke. Goodbye." Shen stepped around the policeman and turned to head down the hall.

"Oh, no you don't. You are under arrest." The patrolman grabbed Shen by the shoulder.

Shen laughed and swiped his foot, taking out the legs of the guard. He fell with an oomph and tried to get back up but slipped on the puddle under him. Shen grabbed the zip tie and promptly zip tied the man's hands together. He put his knee to the man's back to hold him down, but his opponent thrashed around trying to get to something in the coat's pocket. Shen knew that most policeman didn't carry guns, that was left for the military, but he wasn't taking any chances. He pressed his knee on the man's back and swiftly brought his elbow down onto his adversary's temple. The policeman yelled out, then slumped as he lost consciousness. Shen used that moment to check the man's pockets and retrieve his cellphone, as well as more zip ties. He bound the man's feet and then bound his hands and feet together.

Qing Qing stayed in the apartment, too terrified to move. He seemed a shell of the man Shen had known. Shen glanced at him as he caught his breath.

"You must get him out of here. I want nothing to do with this." Qing Qing said, visibly shaking.

"What's happened to you? You were so on fire for Yesu. Because of you His Word spread far and wide." Shen asked, disappointed in his former father figure.

"Do you see Li Mei here? You don't because they sent her to a re-education camp, and she never returned. I came back alone. They never told me what happened to her. She's probably dead." Qing Qing's face was distraught "I don't want anyone else to die because of me."

"Fine, wallow in your regret. I'll just be off with this guy. I'll be praying for you, old friend." Shen closed the door and turned back to the soggy lump on the ground. A door down the hall opened and a head peeked out.

"He passed out. I'm taking him to the hospital." The door slammed shut. Shen swung the man up onto his shoulder. He carried the man down the stairs to the back alley and dumped him into a pile of trash. If he were to track down the midwife, he had to do it now. His unconscious victim would be coming to soon, and they would lock down the area to find Shen.

Shen ran in the drizzle until he was standing in front of the building he had lived in until he was ten. It was even more rundown now than back then. Their apartment had been so tiny he had shared the postage stamp sized bedroom with his grandmother and his mother the few times she had come home. The ceiling and sink had leaked and the shared bathroom down the hall had smelled like the homeless man who often slept there.

A siren in the distance snapped Shen into action. He ran into the building and up a few flights of stairs, carefully navigating the rotten, holey stairs. He remembered a few grandmothers that could have been his mother's midwife, so he'd have to check them out one by one.

All this to figure out my birthday, sounds so silly, Shen thought. He knocked on the first door and waited for it to open. A young woman cracked opened the door and looked Shen up and down, appraising him. She must've approved because she smiled broadly, "Yes?"

"Is Nai Nai here? I have a few questions for her." Shen asked, ignoring her open stare.

"No, she passed on a few years ago." She looked disappointed "But you could come in and chat if you wanted.".

"I'm sorry to hear that. Thank you, but no." Shen trotted off to another floor and knocked on another door. A middle-aged woman appeared at the door with what looked like her husband behind her.

"Is Nai Nai here?"

"Yes, she is. Who are you?" the man asked, looking suspiciously at Shen.

"I used to live here. I just need to ask her a question. I won't be long, I promise," Shen explained. The couple moved back from the door, bidding him entrance. Inside the tiny apartment the grandmother slumped in a chair. Her round face was lined with wrinkles, her crisp, white hair fell softly around her face. Shen stood near her.

"Nai Nai, do you remember Maylin? Floor four. Lived with Nai Nai Ting and a little boy," He spoke loudly to her in the Beijing dialect.

"Yes, Ting and her little boy. How is he? He would be a strapping young man by now, wouldn't he?" she said happily.

"Well, he's standing here before you," Shen paused a moment, realizing she had not really been looking at him, but toward him. "But you cannot see me, can you?"

"No, I haven't seen in a few years. What does Ting's grandson need?" the grandmother asked, smiling up at him.

"Did you deliver that little boy?" Shen inquired.

"There was no need; the mother delivered before I got there," Nai Nai said.

"What date was that? I know it was the Mid-Autumn Festival, which started in October that year." Shen was hopeful that somehow his elder would remember. Somehow these grandmothers remembered the most minuscule information.

"Hmm, I believe it was the first day of the festival. A lucky little tiger." She smiled gently, reaching out her hands toward his face. He knelt so she could feel along his face, down to his shoulders, and down his arms to his hands. He held her wrinkled hands and smiled, remembering his own Nai Nai. How he missed her.

"Do you remember my name?" Shen asked, getting back to business.

"No, should I?" Nai Nai asked, her head cocked to the side in concern.

"No, you should not," he said simply. She nodded her head and turned toward her family members standing behind Shen and gave them a stern expression. No translation was needed, they would stay quiet or fear Nai Nai's wrath.

Shen left quietly and carefully picked his way down the old, rickety stairs. Before he got to the front door, he pulled off his rain jacket, put sunglasses on, and turned his baseball cap around. He ditched the jacket down a hole in the steps. Out on the street he heard a dozen sirens bouncing off the surrounding buildings. He went in the opposite direction without so much as another look back at his childhood home. In his head he did the calculations. October 5th.

CHAPTER 13

"I won't ask you to tell me what is going on with your sister, but I think you should fix it," Samuel told Vivian, giving her a hard look.

"Dad, I've tried. She thinks because she's my sister she's entitled to know every aspect of my private life. There's a reason it's called private. I shouldn't have to be guilted into telling her everything. Right?" Vivian held her ground, knowing she had continually offered her sister an olive branch of peace since she had been home.

Samuel sighed deeply and rubbed his temples with his hands. It clearly upset him when his children were at odds with each other, especially the girls, they'd only had each other after their mother's death.

"I understand your point, but it breaks my heart that this tension between you. I'm just asking that you keep trying," Samuel finally said. He looked haggard.

"I have, Dad, but I'll keep trying. I think she's got some unresolved stuff to deal with from Mom's death. I think our prayers are what she needs most right now," Vivian said, waving at the kitchen chair nearest her. "Let's do that right now."

Samuel nodded and sat down. They held hands and prayed over Livi's broken heart, the process she needed to go through to continue grieving, and her relationship with her most ardent supporters, her family.

The kitchen's screen door slammed shut as Evan breezed in.

Vivian and Samuel's heads snapped up in unison. Evan skidded to a stop like he'd been caught doing something naughty. A sheepish smiled warmed his face.

"Snack time. Is that still allowed?" Evan asked, a hand already in the cookie jar and the other reaching for a glass to pour milk into.

"Yes, your sister and I were just praying. Something you could probably do more of, son," Samuel said. Vivian knew he couldn't help worrying about the state of his children's souls.

"Yeah, I do, Dad. I talk to God all day." Evan said, shoving a cookie into his mouth and grabbing the milk from the fridge.

Vivian's phone buzzed across the table. She swiped it up quickly, grateful that Evan was busy stuffing his face. He often tried to snatch her phone, convinced it held her biggest secrets. He had no idea that she had her phone wiped and reset every other month. She looked down at the notifications, and her heart started beating wildly when she saw it was a text from Shen.

"*Can I call you?*" She felt like her heart was pounding so loudly her dad could hear it.

"*Yeah, give me a minute to get to my room,*"

"Where are you off to, Vivian?" Samuel asked curiously.

"Checking email, figuring out my schedule for the week, there's a Bible study I want to dig into, and there's a few friends I've not talked to for a while, so I thought I'd give them a call. I think I'll get the calls done first. Maybe I can meet up with them before I go off on my next trip?" Vivian prattled on, her nerves making her mouth run.

She quietly went off to her room, leaving her dad to chide Evan over his manners, likely a mouthful of cookie and splashing his milk on the counter. Just as she got the door closed and locked her phone jingled. Her hands were shaking as she answered it.

"Hello?" she asked, nervous and excited.

"Oh, it is so good to hear your voice," Shen said, sounding relieved.

"I only said one word!" Vivian laughed as she sat down on her bed, surrounded by a few fluffy pillows.

"I know, but it's the only word I've heard from you in weeks. I'm lonely over here!" Shen admitted.

"Well, what did you do before me? Can't you go back to that to pass the time?" She was sincerely curious about Shen's life.

"Oh, no, I realize now I wasn't living. I was just existing. There's a big difference."

"How are you? Are you safe?" It felt like she was worried for his safety almost continuously.

"I'm fine, just lonely. I found out my birthday, by the way, but for safety purposes I shouldn't share it on the phone. I can tell you next time I see you. Your birthday is soon, isn't it?"

"Yes, Dad is making a strawberry cake. But things are a little complicated at home right now." Her enthusiasm diminished as she remembered how she was bending the truth to fit around her relationship with Shen. Her stomach was in knots.

"What's wrong? Nothing to do with the trips, right?" Shen said, sounding concerned.

"My sister knows that something happened on the trip and she's positive it involves you, but I won't tell her anything. She is struggling with the boundaries I'm trying to set up. She shares all sorts of gossip with her girlfriends and is mad I won't do that with her. She thinks I don't trust her and that I am obligated to tell her everything in my life." Inwardly, she was telling herself to come clean with her father before she took it any farther.

"Are you? In China we keep our private life pretty tight."

"I think some sisters lay around gossiping about their crushes but it's not a requirement," Vivian replied, a little exasperated.

"So, I'm just a crush then?" Shen teased.

"No! Of course not!" Vivian yelled, then clapped her hand over her mouth.

"I was just teasing! I hope you know that you are way more to me than a passing fad." His voice became a little more emotional.

"Sh-" She broke off abruptly, alarmed at her close misstep.

"What was that? I didn't catch it." He sounded confused.

"I almost said your name, but I caught myself. See, you have me all sorts of distracted! I have had a lot of time to think about this, about us. I am all in."

"Thank you for watching what you say. I've spent my entire life relying on myself and God. I didn't know I was lonely until I connected with you. It's like I didn't know I had been empty until I was filled," Shen admitted.

"I miss you. I can't wait to see you again. What will we do until then?" Vivian asked, wishing that time would speed up a little.

"I miss you, too. I think we should set up regular times to talk. And keep praying for each other. I'll be adding your sister to my list. Can I ask you to pray for someone for me?" he asked. "I can't give you his name, but it was the man that raised me after my mother left. He's completely broken right now, spiritually and emotionally. He could use God's intervention." Shen took another breath as if to say more, but his voice cracked, and he went quiet.

"Of course. When do you want to speak again?" Vivian asked, calculating dates and checking her schedule.

"What about once a week? We can text in between. Next week about this time?" Shen offered; "I'm a bit sad that our time is almost over."

"Yes, that sounds like a good plan. I didn't think we should talk every day, as much as we'd enjoy it. Be expecting texts from me often." Vivian asked, putting the call on her to-do list.

"I have a few more questions I'd like answered." Vivian let her voice drip with mock seriousness. "What's your favorite holiday? Favorite movie you can quote by heart? Do you like tattoos?" Vivian rattled off several more superficial but fun questions.

"Easter and Christmas equally. *The Princess Bride*. And, yes, I find small, meaningful tattoos quite attractive." He laughed lightly.

"What? You like *The Princess Bride*? Ugh, worst movie ever."

Vivian huffed with irritation.

"You don't like the greatest movie of all time? And you call yourself an American!" His laugh echoed gently in her ear. "Same questions for you."

"I love Independence Day. The movie *Only You*. And I like tribal tattoos." She stifled a yawn but not before he heard it.

"You're tired. Why don't we pick this back up at another time?" he said gently.

"Sleep well. I know it's quite late there right now,"

"It is, but I don't mind, especially if I get to hear your voice," Shen said as they ended in prayer before promising to talk again in one week.

"Well, this plan is the most concerning yet," Samuel said, rubbing his eyes and leaning back in his lawn chair. Night had fallen, fireflies flickered as they flew around, and a fire danced in the darkness. A loud explosion shattered the momentary stillness and lit up the sky with a dazzling array of colors.

"Ohhhh, did you see that one, Dad!" Evan called out, pointing upward.

"Wow, that's spectacular," Samuel replied, not even bothering to look up. Instead, he focused on Vivian, who was defiantly crossing her arms over her chest.

"Dad, we all know the risk and I'm willing to do my part. They can't keep relying on the same tactics for each trip, it's more dangerous keeping doing the same thing. They're looking for the large black bags so we're changing to not only backpacks but regular luggage. That's considered so old school they barely even look there nowadays."

"Can't you guys just enjoy the fireworks? Why is it always business first?" Livi said, shaking her head at Vivian and their father. She'd begun to thaw out toward Vivian, at least a little bit. She wasn't back to her normal jovial self, but she wasn't being outright hostile, so Vivian would take it.

"Dad, if we believe God's hand is in this, then we'll be fine. We must do what we can to spread the Word, even if we get hurt," Vivian insisted, uncoiling her arms from her chest and reaching out to pat her father's arm. "You raised us to not fear. So don't get all worry-wort on me now!"

"I meant fearing thunderstorms and bad grades. Not hostile countries!" Samuel huffed and looked up at the sky alight with patriotic celebration.

"Oh Dad, we all know full well that is absolutely what you meant. Stop lying!" Vivian laughed, swatting at him.

"What other reckless missions have they thought up?" he asked, only half joking.

"Well, there's been mentions of smuggling Bibles in through Hong Kong in a transport van. And there's been word of using the maternity suit, again. I think I'd rather drive the van!" Vivian told him, shuddering a bit as she remembered the horrid maternity suit. She rolled her left shoulder a bit, grateful it had healed so quickly.

"When do you leave?" Samuel asked, turning serious again.

"Early, actually. The boat is set to arrive in Hong Kong in August, so I'll be leaving in a few weeks. I'll be using the new backpack, luggage, and transport truck."

"And here I thought they were just throwing around the idea. As always, be careful. Let's get back to the fireworks before your sister sends us to bed early."

Vivian smiled at her father, although he couldn't see it in the dark.

CHAPTER 14

Shen drummed his fingers on the table, his impatience flooding the room. "Flight 206 will be disembarking shortly" A voice rung from the loudspeaker. He stood, grabbed his handmade sign with Vivian's name, and made his way to customs. He was nearly a head taller than everyone else in the horde of people waiting with signs, so it was easy to look over their heads and notice Vivian stopped in the customs line.

She would be loaded down with Bibles. If she were stopped and caught she would be detained, and he would not be able to get to her. He watched carefully as the customs agents pulled people out of line one-by-one to search their bags. He prayed silently, *Lord God, blind the eyes of these guards. Allow her to pass by unseen.*

The young, athletically built man in front of her knelt and began opening his bag. An agent rushed up to him, grabbed him by the shoulder and shoved him back.

"Get your bag open!" The agent yelled. "Let's go! We need to keep this line moving!"

The young man knelt to finish unzipping his bag when the agent shoved him aside and began turning the bag out on his own. His clothing fell out, scattered across the floor then with one more firm shake leaflets went flying.

"Aha! What is this? Propaganda?" The agent screamed, the young man cowering, his eyes wide.

"I, uh, don't know how those got in there. I don't know what those are!" He scrambled over to the items and began picking them up.

"You! Pick these up!" The agent snapped at an assistant. He turned to the young man next. "You are coming with me."

Vivian swayed from side to side, almost as if dancing. She fidgeted with her earbuds for a moment, and he wondered what she was listening to, for her face was serene. The man in front of her was dragged away, the assistant stuffing his belongs back into the young man's bag and the agents moved farther along the line. Vivian was next.

Jesus, please give her grace and blind the eyes of those that see, Shen pleaded. He looked on in astonishment as an agent clapped his hands together and animatedly threw his arms in the air.

"Let's pick it up people, gotta get through this line!" The ardent agent bellowed. The line began to move, and Vivian walked straight through the group of customs agents without any of them looking her way.

A slow smile crossed Shen's face. He was positive he just witnessed a miracle. He moved to the customs exit to catch up with Vivian. By the time he got through the crowd she was waiting on him.

"This way, Ma'am." He quietly reached for her rolling suitcase and was stunned by how incredibly heavy it was. He held his hand out toward her. She cocked her head at him questioningly. "I'll take your backpack, too." As she pulled it off her back, he watched for an indication of her old shoulder injury, but she did not so much as flinch. He grabbed the strap and hauled it over his own shoulder. The backpack was so heavy it nearly knocked him over as he swung it around.

"I've already got our ride. We have time for a meal. How was your flight?"

"Very mundane and for that I am grateful. Where should we eat?" Vivian held her head high, her face still calm and relaxed. As they pushed their way through the crowd Shen occasionally caught a soft humming.

"Our ride is waiting in the commercial lot," Shen whispered, guiding Vivian away from the sea of taxis, hotel vans, and buses. When they finally reached the large, white commercial van, Shen opened the passenger door for her and slid her belongings into the back of the van.

"Can you believe what happened in the customs line? That was an absolute miracle, they checked everyone ahead of and after you. What were you listening to?" His words came out in a rush of excitement as he shut the driver's side door and started the car.

Vivian laughed melodiously, her face wide with a smile. "I was listening to old hymns. 'There is Power in the Blood,' 'Be Thou My Vision,' you know. It kept me in the Spirit instead of worrying." Vivian yawned and covered her mouth quickly. "Sorry, these overnight flights are better, but they still wear me out."

"You looked so peaceful in that line," Shen said, navigating the flood of traffic entering Hong Kong. "I am stunned at how heavy that load is. I'll be speaking with The Society. It is dangerous to be loaded down so heavily. You could be targeted because of the bulk, you could get hurt by the weight, and it's just a bad idea."

"I requested to take more. China needs as many Bibles as it can get. If I can safely bring ten, why not bring twenty? If I can bring a dozen MP3 players, why not two dozen or even three?" Vivian gave Shen a stern look, a stubborn tilt to her chin.

He shook his head and tsked. "That was very reckless of you. Honestly, you should know better than to do something that could bring attention to yourself and the group. I'll have to bring this up to the council. I'm sorry but you cannot do something like this again."

Vivian ignored the comment and took in their surroundings. "Where are we going? Oh, and when is your birthday?"

"After we get some dinner, we'll head to Hong Kong Island. There is a boat, loaded with Mandarin Bibles, waiting at one of the marinas for us. We'll drive them to a street market in Guangzhou and from there they will be distributed. It's not terribly far, only about 2 hours from here, but there are many points of concern. As for dinner, let's get some sweet and sour pork. Hong Kong is known for it." He paused, "October 5th."

"Sounds good, wake me when we're there." With that Vivian reclined her seat and curled up in a ball with her earbuds still in. Shen could faintly hear worship music. He smiled as he wove through the congested streets.

"Where were these Bibles printed? I didn't know they brought in huge shipments," Vivian stifled another yawn as Shen stopped the large van in a parking lot near the water. She sucked the last of her milk tea up through a bright pink straw.

"They were printed in Vietnam. They don't do this often, but the need has become so great they decided to take the risk to bring in a large haul. Here, put this baseball cap on, tuck your hair up inside, and use these sunglasses. The facial detection cameras are getting more difficult to confuse." With that he hopped out of the van.

Vivian put on her new disguise and crawled out of the seat. Vivian rubbed her eyes slowly as Shen dashed around the car looking in every direction. Night had fallen over the busy city but the quiet was disturbed by a mechanical crackle and then suddenly the night lit up through the sunglasses.

"Wow, these are amazing! When did we get such cool gear?" Vivian asked.

"I heard we have a new tech guru. He is all about these new toys." Shen said, moving to the back of the van.

The gentle lap of the water should have been soothing, but she could only think about how risky this operation was. She met Shen at the back of the van and the two headed down the bank to a wood and metal dock that ran to a marina filled with expensive watercraft.

Shen, with his own cap pulled low over his face, glanced up

and down the many docks that jutted out into the marina. He grabbed Vivian's hand and pulled her to his side. She yipped softly but didn't resist. He dipped down to press his cheek to hers and whispered in her ear.

"I've missed you." His breath tickled her ear, sending shivers shooting down her spine. She jumped away and smacked him on the arm.

"Don't do that! You just got after me for a potential safety violation. We need to be serious right now." She chided him, her skin still tingling where his cheek had touched hers.

Vivian's heart was pounding still when they stopped at the bow of a luxury yacht. Its name, *Redemption,* was written in bold, red lettering along the bow. Vivian's heart swelled at the sight.

"Welcome, brother and sister. There is a loading dock just over there. If you can back your vehicle down, I can navigate the boat over there. We must hurry. The Maritime Police have been searching for us. We must leave soon." The smuggler wore black clothing and a balaclava that obscured his outline against the night sky.

"Sister, why don't you join me? We'll meet our brother at the loading dock. Untie these ropes, then meet me on the bridge when you're done. Hurry!" The man ran up the gangplank and disappeared. She looked nervously at Shen, but he merely nodded and spun on his heel, running back to move the van. Vivian snapped into motion, untying the many ropes, before darting up the gangplank. Another smuggler hauled the gangplank into place behind her. The boat's engines were already thrumming. They pulled away from the dock as the second smuggler rushed to secure the ramp. She jerked as the waves shook the boat, but she righted herself and headed for the ladder that led to the navigation room.

Vivian had to duck her head to enter the small room at the top of the boat. The smuggler with balaclava on his face shoved something at her. "Here, scan the bay for moving boats. It's a night-vision device. If you see anything moving alert me immediately. If we do encounter any Maritime Police and you're on board, you might be leaving with us."

Vivian took the device and scanned past the rows of boats into the bay beyond. The night was lit up with an eerie green haze. She panned the gadget back and forth until they bumped into the loading dock.

"Stay here and keep looking. Press this button if you see any boats moving, especially in this direction." With that he jumped down the ladder and ran to the loading bay.

Out on the dock Shen had backed the van up to the edge. He'd turned the headlights off, but the van was on and running, ready for a quick getaway. He joined the two smugglers in hauling boxes of Bibles into the van. The men worked steadily in the quiet night and were nearly done when a resounding wail rent the air. Shen jerked upright and tossed his box onto the stack in the van and grabbed the next one, working double time.

One smuggler worked alongside Shen while the other untied the moorings. Vivian came running over. "They're coming!" she said breathlessly. The smuggler helping Shen ran up the ramp and grabbed Vivian around the waist as the boat began to pull away from the dock. Vivian felt terror flood her body as the smuggler heaved throwing her over the open water. Her brain told her to look up, to try to land, but her eyes were locked on the dark waters below. Then she felt Shen catch her, his strong, gentle arms guiding her to the ground. Then her full weight hit him, and he gave a quiet *oomph*. Maybe it hadn't been so gentle.

Shen set Vivian down and gently shoved her toward of the van. As they pulled away, the marina lit up with flashing strobes from a Maritime Police boat. The *Redemption* was maneuvering to try and slip past the boat and head out to sea, but Vivian lost sight of them as they slipped between two yachts.

"Where are we going?" she asked Shen, who was gripping the steering wheel tightly.

"We're heading for the bridge so we can get off this island before they alert the local police. We need to leave the city as quickly as possible," he shot at her.

Vivian decided that asking questions wasn't helpful. So, she started praying. For the *Redemption* and her small crew, for herself and Shen and their cargo, for the brothers and sisters in Christ in China. Her list went on and on. They crossed the bridge without incident and found the downtown area quiet – which slowed them down a lot, as driving through quickly would've drawn attention.

They breathed a sigh of relief as they neared the border. The border crossing had only a few commuter buses ahead of them. Border agents waved them to the side.

"Get your passport and ID ready" He parked the van and pulled out his information. An agent tapped on the window and beckoned them out. Vivian unbuckled and slowly stepped out.

An officer barked an order at Vivian. She handed him her credentials and stayed silent. The officer shone his light at her passport picture, then at her face. He tipped her hat up a bit to get a better look, and Vivian squinted at the blindingly bright light before her hand shot up to block the glare. The officer handed her items to another agent and walked around the van to Shen, who leaned against the van with his arms across his chest. A few more threats or orders were shouted at Shen. He reached for his ID and looked over to Vivian, his face poised. A group of agents moved to the back of the van.

Vivian's heart began to pound. They were about to open the doors and see box after box of Mandarin Bibles. She held out her hand for her credentials. The agent shook his head, but Vivian wasn't taking no for an answer. She tapped her open palm with her other hand before a shout came from the back of the van. The officer handed her items back, a swift look of triumph brightening his face, then moved to join his colleagues

Shen walked around and joined her. He opened the door and tossed his items inside, then grabbed Vivian's hand and pulled her into his chest. She squeaked and looked nervously at the horde of officers a few feet away.

"What are you doing?" Vivian whispered harshly. Her breath came quickly, her heart pounding in her ears.

"If I'm going to jail, I want one kiss." He smiled cockily at her, amusement tugging at the corners of his mouth. He slid his hand to her jawline, running his thumb along her cheek. He tugged gently, inviting her closer. She smiled through her anxiety and leaned in. Their lips met for a moment before a border agent interrupted them.

Vivan nearly choked when she saw him holding two Bibles. He smiled mockingly at the two of them. She tried to step back, but Shen held her close to his side.

"Where you go with these?" The man spoke in halting English. "We are simply the drivers." Shen answered in Mandarin, Vivian caught a few words she knew.

"We are delivering these to the churches in China. We've had a big order for them. Would you like to keep those?" Vivian jumped in, speaking in broken Mandarin and mixed with English. The officer's eyes lit up.

The agent paused, examining the books closely. He flipped a volume open and squinted at the pages. Vivian's heart was racing faster than the Redemption had left port. "Shen, can we go?" She whispered.

Shen's eye's grew wide at her blunder. She clamped her hand over her mouth. The agent's head whipped up and looked between them. He narrowed his eyes at Vivian.

"What did you say?" The agent asked. Vivian understood that clearly.

"Shaun, can we go?" She repeated, sweat beading up on her forehead, she swallowed hard. The agent snapped his fingers at her and poked Shen in the chest.

"Go in peace, brother. Go now." He turned and called the others with him, leaving Shen and Vivian in absolute shock. They jumped in the van and left the border crossing.

Back on the road they were both so shocked they could only take deep breaths.

"Can you believe that just happened? I was so scared. I cannot believe I said your real name." exclaimed Vivian. Shen looked disappointed but stayed silent until they they made their way through Shenzhen to their contact at a market in Guangzhou.

By the time they had made their delivery, exhaustion had caught up with Vivian and she was beginning to shake. They dropped off the van and acquired a car owned by The Society, that Shen would hand off at the airport.

Shen looked over at Vivian, taking in her bedraggled condition. He pulled off into an alley and parked the car. He gingerly tucked a loose piece of hair behind her ear. She mumbled something and groggily opened her eyes.

"We should get you something to eat. Maybe it'll help." He looked helpless.

"I think that might help. A little food, a little nap, and I'll be alright." She smiled lopsidedly hoping to convince Shen, but he didn't look persuaded.

"Come on, let's go." Shen walked around the car and opened the door. Vivian slumped out and hung onto Shen for dear life.

"Why would they plan a trip like this? Fifteen-hour back-to-back flights with only a few hours in between? Don't they realize how hard that is?" The sun was beginning to peek over the horizon as Vivian complained, dragging her feet behind as she clung to Shen.

"I'm not sure. It must be an oversight," Shen wrapped his arm around her waist and tried to carry some of her weight. She leaned heavily against him.

"Where are we going?" Vivian yawned loudly.

"A food cart near a busy temple. They set up early to catch the early morning worshipers. They have long, deep fried dough sticks and salted duck eggs."

"I don't care what it is right now. I just want to go to bed." Vivian whined.

A few minutes later Shen had Vivian sitting on a small stool tucked against a grubby retaining wall outside the temple. He made sure she ate most of her dough stick and several duck eggs. On the way back to the car she shuffled more than walked.

"I don't think you'll be able to get yourself home, at least not safely. You'll be targeted by pickpockets or worse," Shen said, when he'd finally settled her into the car.

"What are you saying?"

"I'm buying a ticket and taking you home myself," his fingers already flying over his phone's screen, booking a ticket.

"What? That's crazy. Can you do that?" Vivian asked, barely lifting her head off the seat.

"Of course, I can. Already done! Let's get to the airport, our flight leaves in an hour."

Eighteen hours later a nearly comatose Vivian disembarked the plane in Shen's arms. "What's your father look like?" Shen asked, shrugging his shoulder to rouse her. She mumbled a quiet answer. "I need to know what he looks like. You've got to wake up." He dropped her feet to the ground keeping a steady hand on her waist.

"He's Kenyan. Black." She wiped a small drip of drool off the corner of her mouth. Shen gazed around at the crowd, his eyes darting from one face to another. Finally, he noticed a tall, thin fatherly figure marching toward them. "There he is! Oh, he looks mad…" Vivian yawned.

"Vivian, what's wrong?" Samuel asked in a rush. He

"Dad, I'm alright. Just jetlagged." Vivian straightened up, pushed disheveled hair out of her face and tried to smile reassuringly at her father.

"Who is this man and why were his hands on you?" Samuel reached for her. Shen deposited Vivian next to her father and took a step back.

"I made sure she got here safely, sir, but I'm not sure she can make it your car. Do you want to carry her or should I?" Shen asked, nodding at Vivian who was wobbling as she stood between them.

"No but thank you." Samuel stepped forward to pick up Vivian, but she took a step back, bumping into Shen. Her step faltered and she careened to the side. Shen swept her up into his arms in one swift move.

"She needs to get some sleep. Either let me carry her or could you get a wheelchair." Samuel looked thoughtfully between

Shen and Vivian. A moment later he nodded to Shen and went for a wheelchair.

CHAPTER 15

Light streamed in through the curtains as Vivian stretched luxuriously in her bed, feeling much better. Had Shen really delivered her into her father's arms? She couldn't remember.

She reached to her bedside table and fumbled around to find her phone. The clock read 12:28 and she had several unread texts. One was from Wo Ai Ni. "*Text me when you wake up.*" Sent at 8 am.

Vivian smiled and replied. "*I'm up.*"

Her phone began to ring. She squeezed the side to shut off the ringer.

"You're supposed to warn me before you call." Vivian whispered. She held her breath, listening for footsteps.

"I missed you. This was the quickest mission yet, and we had no time for us," came the reply. Vivian smiled and pulled her pillow over her head to try to muffle the sounds of conversation.

"I know. I think this was the hardest one yet. I'll debrief today and find out my next travel date. I'm really hoping for more travel time. This was way too hard."

"Are you alright? Have you gotten enough rest?" Shen's words were laced with concern.

"Yeah, I'm alright. I could probably use some more sleep, though."

"Do you want children?" Shen asked, jumping right into the personal questions.

“Whoa! Um, yeah. I’d like to adopt too. Why this line of questioning?”

“I’m expecting you to be expecting.” Shen hinted. Ahhh, that’s right, she would be wearing the maternity suit on the next mission.

“Ugh, I can’t stand that suit.” She groaned aloud. “Is there another reason you’re asking me about this?”

“Well, maybe someday I might want children, but really, I just want to know what you want out of life. I want to make sure we’re going in the same direction,” Shen explained.

“Well, what about you? Do you want a protégé?”

“Yes. I would adopt, but I really want a biological son. Okay, last one, where do you want to live?” Shen requested.

“I honestly don’t know. I love mountains but not hot weather. So, maybe somewhere mountainous that’s cool? I’m not sure where that would be, though. You?”

“Anywhere you are.”

“That’s so cheesy! I want to know exactly what you like.” Vivian’s heart swelled at Shen’s words, but she was after something more definite.

“I love nature. Mountains, forests, oceans, any of it. I’ve been without a home for so many years that I can go anywhere, it just matters with who. I must go but I’ll see you soon. Take care.”

Before Vivian could reply, the phone clicked, and the conversation was over. What did he mean he’d see her soon? She had no clue, but right now, she needed to get up and start the day. Her stomach was growling, and she seriously had to use the restroom.

“Brother, welcome to our meeting. We apologize that this is so late for you, but please know we deeply appreciate your service,” Mrs. Hayes, the head of the council, spoke to Shen via a video feed. He set his phone against a greasy take-out container.

“Thank you, Ma’am,” he replied, searching the screen for a

familiar face. He knew instantly when Vivian saw him on the large screen in the conference room. She paled noticeably, her eyes growing wide. She recovered quickly though, wiping the surprise off her face while the council members focus on the display.

"We are here to debrief both of you at the same time. Your report shows an intrusion at the hand-off and at the border. Is that correct, Sister?"

"Yes, there was an incident at the hand-off. When we last saw our counterparts, they were trying to outmaneuver the officers. Have you heard the outcome of that?" Shen took note of Vivian in business mode.

"Yes, we heard that sadly they were caught before they could leave Chinese waters. We will do what we can to help them but at this point it is out of our hands. Brother, tell us about the transition point."

Shen cleared his throat. "We were honest with them and offered them several of our items. They accepted and we left." The air in the small apartment was hot and dry. He desperately wanted to open a window but didn't dare while on the call, even though it was the middle of the night. Shen sneaked another peek at Vivian, she looked uncomfortable but kept an emotionless expression plastered on her face.

"We'd like to alter your normal schedule. Are you both still alright with continuing the partnership?" came the next question.

"Yes," "Of course," came two answers at once.

A soft chuckle echoed through the council room. "We will continue this alliance. The next mission will be different. Brother, you will be escorting your sister from our home-base. Your itinerary will be forwarded to you soon. We have heard your arguments for longer missions, and we agree. We did not realize the extent to which this timeline comprised your safety or health. This is the fastest we have ever asked a team to do a full mission. This change will be reflected in the timeline for your next trip. If there's nothing else?" There was a pause and

Vivian cleared her throat.

"Will there be any, um, expectations for this next trip?" She asked, with heavy emphasis on the word "expectations."

"There are always expectations. Your objective will be highlighted as it always is."

"I think she means will we need to anticipate any gestating in the family way?" Shen whispered into the phone, trying to hide the laughter ready to bubble up. The board members looked at each other, very confused. "Will she need to wear the pregnancy suite?" He finally laughed aloud.

"Oh, yes, that. Yes, that is the plan." Mrs. Hayes turned her attention to Vivian. "We believe it will be safer to have our brother escort you from the home-base. It will be far more convincing. Anything else before we let these two get back to their lives? No? Okay, thank you, again, Brother, for joining us. Please rest well."

"What are you doing, you lazy egg? Don't be a bum." A skeletal finger pointed through the thick, humid air at Shen. "An-Chen said you arranged this. Is that true?"

"Yes, Nai Nai, I did. The old building was to be torn down. Did you want to be demolished with it? Now, you can spend time outside now. Are you complaining?" Shen grinned at the old woman. She sat in the sunshine surrounded by the green bushes and flowers of a small garden. The street-level flat with a garden had been extremely difficult to find, but when he saw the pictures, he bought it site unseen. He realized that all the money he was earning, he would never be able to use. So, why not bless someone else with it?

"You don't owe me anything, young man. Why do you take care of me?" she asked, tilting her blind eyes toward the sun, enjoying the warmth of the rays. The last apartment had been so dangerous and rickety that she hadn't been outside in years.

"I miss my grandmother greatly. You're the best one I know.

Let me spoil you... unless you want me to take you back to that hole?" Shen offered, smiling at her reaction to the simply being outside.

"Oh no you don't! I won't miss the bugs or the noise or the smell. Have you heard from my other son, An-Chen's brother? He left years ago for the countryside. I miss him so much." Her voice was soft.

"No, I haven't but I will keep looking for him."

"How mad is An-Chen?" Her soft white hair was wispy in the breeze.

"Furious, but he is grateful. Next time I come, I hope to have someone with me," Shen said, moving to kneel before her.

"You're leaving again, then? What's her name?" Nai Nai asked, reaching out to cup his face, as if she were trying to memorize his face with her fingers.

Shen chuckled softly. "I never said it was a woman. But you see so much, don't you? Her name means Alive."

"I will make sure I am still here for that meeting." Nai Nai said, dropping her hands back to her lap. Shen quietly left the garden.

"Nothing?" Livi practically shouted above the din of the mall food court. "None?"

"Nada!" Vivian arched an eyebrow at Livi's incredulous look.

"What happened?" Livi asked, leaning forward as if Vivian were about to share something top secret.

"The moment I arrived we met our counterparts, accepted delivery, and then transferred it to the next in line. We turned around and immediately dropped me off for my return flight." Vivian was still weary after that awful trip.

"That's it?" Livi was still looking at her waiting for the punch line.

"Yes, that's it. This whirlwind trip was so horrible on me that they changed policy. In fact, they will automatically add in extra time for each trip from now on." Vivian shuddered, remembering how her body had revolted at the trip.

"But he brought you here himself. That has to say something!" Livi was still looking for something that would prove that Vivian and Shen were an item.

"We're just colleagues, Livi." Vivian swallowed hard against the lump in her throat. "Get over it. Who are you dating now?" Vivian asked, trying to steer the subject off her secrets and back onto Livi. She had lightened up since their fights earlier in the summer, but she still pouted as if she suspected Vivian was keeping information from her.

"Oh no you don't! I want to know more. You're hiding something, I can smell it." Livi paused to look around the food court just in time to see Evan and their dad winding their way through the tables.

Vivian celebrated the interruption quietly but didn't dare let Livi know. She picked up her bubble tea to take a sip. Evan ran over and wrinkled his nose at the sight of the drink.

"Yuck! How can you drink that? It's full of snot balls. Yuck! You're eating boogers!" He covered his mouth and snorted. Vivian just shook her head at her little brother's antics.

Samuel joined them and sat down. He looked tired.

"Dad, are you alright? I know you've been worried about me, but I hope you know that I was okay. My contact made sure I was safe the whole time. That's why he wanted to deliver me himself."

Samuel's eyebrows rose. He turned to face Vivian his demeanor serious... which wasn't unusual for him.

"Vivian, who is he really?" Samuel gave her a stern look.

"Dad now is not the time to go into this. I told you who he is." Vivian looked away, unable to look her father in the eye.

"Was it her boyfriend, Dad?" Evan piped up. Vivian shot him an annoyed look. Was she and Shen that obvious?

CHAPTER 16

"Bwahaahaa!" Vivan clamped her hand over her mouth, but she couldn't stop the laughter from coming through. Shen gave her a derisive look and shook his head before looking down at himself. He wore a dark blue cotton shirt, which wouldn't have been hilarious – except it covered a paunch, compliments of his own fat suit. He twisted and bent backward. The belly, which was filled with Bibles, was obtrusive but not horrible. He was sure it would be hot and uncomfortable, though, when having to sit for fifteen hours.

"I concede. You were right, this is not fun. Maybe men should wear one of these when they complain about assisting a pregnant woman. It would change a lot of minds." Still, he smiled humbly and did a spin before trying to bow, but the bulge got in his way.

Vivian continued to snicker, but she was also uncomfortable, having already put her maternity suit on. They were filled to the brim with Bibles on their bodies and media in the suitcases.

"Now, remember to act the part of a couple traveling on a babymoon. I know it must be troublesome but it's a necessary evil," Mrs. Kaminsky smiled coyly, straightening Vivian's collar. "Alright, you two, time to go!"

They were already at the airport, utilizing a private lounge reserved by The Society. Saying their goodbyes to Mrs. Kaminsky, they gathered their luggage and moved to their terminal. In a few hours they were squeezed into their seats, nonchalantly holding hands while watching a cheesy Kung Fu movie.

"I never thought I'd be on an airplane, with you as my pregnant wife." Shen looked at his gut, "I have clearly let myself go and need to get my health back." Shen seemed like he was feeling wistful.

"Is that what you want?" Vivian patted her belly and smiled charmingly.

He rolled his eyes. "Yes. God willing, I would want to be married with children living somewhere quiet. No more concrete jungle. No more drifting from place to place," he said dreamily.

"Do you not like your work? I'm sure they would let you find another job." Vivian suggested, wondering how deep the vein of loneliness went in his heart.

"I am in no hurry for that life. I am content with my situation and plan to continue for many more years but someday, I would like to take a step back and have the life I was never given the chance to live. I think I'll always have some sort of role in this organization, but I don't know if I will always want to be going on trips. One can become weary of doing good, and I don't want to burn out," a wistful look passed over his face for a moment.

"I can understand that. My father has taken sabbaticals before, which are longer than vacations. He would get weighed down by duties and responsibilities and the concerns of his congregation. Add in being a single father of three and he was running on fumes for more years than I can remember. I'm anxious that he's nearly back there." Vivian squeezed Shen's hand and looked down.

"Why?" Shen asked, leaning forward to and looking around.

"He's scared he's going to lose me. Either through the business or through marriage. I know he wants happiness for my siblings and I, but we've always done life together. From the moment my mom passed away we've been a team.

He's struggling with our transitions to independence. We were dependent on each other for so long it's hard to let go" Vivian paused and turned back to Shen, but he was distracted. He had a worried crease to his forehead.

He tucked his head down to whisper in Vivian's ear. "We have a listener. Next door one row up, aisle seat." More loudly he answered her question. "Yeah, I'm sure it's hard on him to parent adult's. I'm tired, I'm going to sleep for a while." With that he closed his eyes and put his sunglasses on.

Vivian stretched dramatically and turned just enough to see a Chinese national snap his eyes off her and Shen and look straight ahead. His left eye was white, like it had been injured long ago, but it swept over the crowd with cold calculation. Dread rolled through her stomach. She was suddenly nauseous and turned away from the listener to burrow into Shen's arm. She had the feeling she'd seen that man before.

"Let's get some dim sum after we see the Great Wall. After that, there's someone I want you to meet," Shen said, leaning against a wall in Vivian's hotel room. They'd delivered their load and shed their suits. "You've got your things, right?" He pulled his hat and sunglasses on. "Time to gear up."

Vivian slipped a curly wig on, donned a wide brimmed sun hat, and her sunglasses. She double checked her bag and nodded to Shen who opened the door. She didn't so much as a glance back at her maternity suit which, now empty, lay on the bed.

"Oh wait! I forgot I have something for you!" She dug around and pulled out a small box. "Close your eyes and hold out your hand," she commanded, a smile playing at the corners of her mouth. He obediently closed his eyes and held out his hands, into which she placed a small, black box. "You can look."

Shen held the box aloft and slowly opened the lid. A small iridescent koi fish sat nestled on a bed of satin. A long chain snaked out as he lifted the necklace out. "I hope it's not too feminine. I wanted to get you something for your birthday that matched the Ichthys. It can be our little code." She shrugged shyly.

"I love it. Thank you, it's very thoughtful." He hooked the necklace onto his neck and smiled. "Ready to go?" he asked, thumbing behind him at the door.

"So, who is this friend of yours?" Vivian asked, as they walked. The hotel lobby was busy, and they had to weave their way through large groups. She gripped Shen's hand tightly and looked around absentmindedly, her gaze traveling over the sea of faces. Her gaze snagged on a milky white eye staring off into space. The man it was attached to moved away too quickly for her to get a good look. Her stomach dropped. Was it the same man from the plane? She turned to ask Shen, but with the press of the crowd realized would have to wait to say anything.

"It's someone who means a lot to me. But first, we should just be tourists for once." Shen answered, jarring her from her thoughts. When she looked back the man was gone.

They walked several blocks to the subway to get to the bus station for their trip up to the Great Wall. Normally they would use The Society's app, but now that they had the time, they had decided to see the Great Wall in person.

Shen held her hand as the bus bumped along the well-worn road. His hand was warm and had the callouses of someone who worked with his hands. Vivian wondered if it was from working out.

"What do you do on your down time?" Vivian asked. It seemed like such a mundane question but one she'd never thought to ask before.

"I don't get a lot of down time. I travel between missions and if I have a chance, I try to help the Nai Nais that work with us. I've never done things that twenty-somethings do. I don't go to the movies or hang out at the bar. I don't go shopping or read many books. What about you?" Shen spoke matter-of-factly, without any apparent regret.

"I like to read, play with my brother, and hang out with my

sister. I used to paint and draw when I had time, but it's been a while since I did that. We sound boring, don't we?" Vivian laughed.

They arrived at the base of the stairs of the Great Wall to see that the steps were tall, and a little difficult to navigate, but the couple was in no hurry and enjoyed the climb together. It was cool and overcast, easing the climb. At the top, the world stretched out before them. Mountains, forests, and intense stretches of green met their eyes. As she began to turn away the sun burst through the clouds, and brilliant rays of sunlight kissed the distant peaks. They lingered, not wanting to walk away from the stunning view. They finally took their obligatory picture and began the climb back down.

"So, was that worth it? Or should we have used the app?" Shen asked on the bus ride back to Beijing.

"Absolutely worth it. I should thank our bosses for the extra time they've built into these trips. Do we go meet your friend, yet?" She batted her eyelashes at Shen.

"Yes, we'll go meet my friend," Shen laughed

As the two drew near the condominium building, Vivian seemed to grow nervous. Shen had avoided every question about them. His reticence only seemed to increase her anxiety. Shen led her to a street level unit and knocked on the door.

A middle-aged man opened the door and grunted at Shen before walking away. There didn't seem to be any lost love between the two.

She and Shen removed their shoes at the door, then Shen led her through the small abode confidently. They exited into a small garden in the back that had a sitting area set up to the side. An elderly woman with a queenly air about her sat in a worn chair in the middle of the small garden, the sun warming her old bones.

"I know those footsteps. See, I told you I would be here for this meeting, you can't be rid of me easily," she said to Shen in the Beijing dialect. Vivian wrinkled her forehead in confusion.

"Take off your hat, wig and sunglasses," Shen directed Vivian, and she freed her head of the accessories.

Shen stepped over to the woman and knelt. He held Vivian's hand and grasped Nai Nai's with his other, then joined their hands. Nai Nai's face lit up and she rapidly spun of a string of words, tugging on Vivian's hand to bring her down to her level.

Vivian slowly knelt. The sweet old lady had fluffy white hair and her eyes were nearly hidden in a squint from the large smile that lit up her face. She explored Vivian's face and long hair with her hands, all the while exclaiming excitedly. When she was satisfied that she'd memorized Vivian's face she gripped Vivian and Shen's hands, putting them together.

A slow smile spread over Vivian's face. Even this woman seemed to know that they were together.

"What's so amusing?" Shen asked.

"Just realizing that we are way more obvious than I thought we were. Even she knows we're together. My little brother is suspicious, too. We're terrible at secrets," Vivian said, then turned her attention back to Nai Nai. "What did she say?"

"She said you have a beautiful face, and she loves that your hair is so long. Most girls in the cities have short styles, including her own great-grandchildren, and she hates it. She thinks ladies should have long hair. She was also giving me marriage advice and chastising me for not bringing you here sooner. And she promises to stay around long enough to meet our children."

"Wow, she's certain about us, huh? Who is she, by the way?"

"She was a friend of my own Nai Nai, the local midwife, and the building grandmother. She is completely blind but enjoys sitting outside every day. She sits out here even in the rain. Although she really shouldn't be out in the rain." Shen turned and said something to Nai Nai, who just laughed.

"Thank you for the kind words and for being so good to Shen." Vivian said in Mandarin, squeezing Nai Nai's hand. Shen spoke rapidly and laughed as Nai Nai let go of her hands and raised her hands to the sky and sang loudly.

The middle-aged man poked his head outside and called over to them. Shen waved him off, still laughing at Nai Nai. Vivian looked curiously at him.

“You going to translate that?” Vivian asked, a little irritated at being unable to understand Nai Nai’s dialect.

“She was singing a song of thanks to the ancestors for the favor of a good woman for me” There seemed to be a slight droop to his shoulders after he spoke.

“She doesn’t share our belief,” Vivian noticed, sharing a look of sadness.

“No, she’s been a stubborn one. But I won’t give up. An Chen!” Shen called the middle-aged man, and they exchanged a few words before turning back to Vivian. “Will you please go with her son, An Chen? I’ll be right there.” Vivian agreed, but before she could walk away Nai Nai grabbed her hands pulled her close. She patted Vivian’s cheeks and smiled even more widely.

Shen waited for Vivian to walk away then turned back to Nai Nai. “Nai Nai, I know you have said you do not need Jesus, but it would bless me greatly if you could listen to the Bible. I have a little device that plays it through headphones. I will show An Chen how to use it. Would you please do this for me? I am who I am because of God. It is a gift I would love for you to receive.”

“My sweet boy, always worried about my soul. I will do this for you, but I will not make any promises. I will listen. Now go, I am tired.” Shen dropped a kiss on top of her fluffy hair and went to join Vivian.

“What was that all about?” Vivian asked as they left the little condo.

“I recorded the entire bible on audio in the old Beijing dialect for her on an MP3 player,” Shen said, guiding Vivian toward the subway.

“How long did that take you? You didn’t mention that when we talked about our free time,” Vivian looked curiously at him.

“It took a very long time. She understands Mandarin, but the old dialect is her heart language. I never considered that a hobby, so I didn't mention it. What should we do now?"

"Let's catch a movie. It'll help with my language training," Vivian suggested.

"Sure." Shen threw his head back and laughed. "You just want me to yourself."

Vivian swatted his arm. "No! I just wanted to do something ordinary."

CHAPTER 17

Vivian and Shen held hands as they crossed the hotel lobby. The elevator dinged and the doors opened. A man stood in the center of the lift, moving aside to make room for them. Shen hit a button, but the man's hand snapped out and grabbed the door, stopping it from closing.

The man with the milky white eye looked from Shen to Vivian. "You will come with me. We have some questions to ask you," the man said in perfect English.

"We?" Shen asked, moving over to Vivian and placing a protective arm around her.

"Yes, we," the man said as a half dozen officers joined him outside the elevator.

The walk across the lobby was silent, and instead of going out the main door, they turned and went out a back exit. Several police cars waited outside. Shen was directed toward one and Vivian another. Until that moment she had maintained her composure but being separated from Shen felt like being left along in the dark.

Vivian's mind raced as the squad car made its way to the station, realizing why they were targeted. Obviously, they'd wonder why she was no longer "pregnant." They should have taken more care to hide their disguises.

The station was a low blue and white building built into a long row of old buildings. The officers led Vivian silently into the lobby. She had just barely caught sight of Shen entering as they pushed her to an interrogation room. It contained only a simple metal table with one chair on each side. Several mirrors, probably one-way windows, were set into the wall, but other than that it was bare.

One guard grabbed at Vivian's bag, but she held onto it tightly. "I'm not letting you take my passport and ID," she exclaimed in English—forgetting her Mandarin entirely. The guard began yelling and wrenched the bag from her hands. She bit her lip and sat down at the table.

She waited alone in the room for several hours before the man with the white eye came in.

"So, why are you here?" he asked, setting down her bag and sliding it across the table to her.

Vivian snatched it, rooting around in it desperately. Her essential documents were not in there, nor was her phone.

"Here in China or here in this station?" Vivian asked, anger ready to burst out.

"Both," he said calmly.

"Well, I travel here often and have never seen the Great Wall. It was beautiful. I'm glad I experienced it, I was having a lovely day – that is, I was until you and your officers dragged me here. Why, again, did you bring me here?" Vivian replied.

"You are here because you have been dishonest with us. Why would you need to do that? What are you hiding?" he held her gaze.

Vivian looked the man in the face. His milky white eye met hers with cold intensity. A shiver ran down her spine. "I don't know what you are talking about."

The man snapped his fingers and the door banged open. A woman came in holding a cardboard box. She tipped it over onto the table and the maternity suit fell out.

"Why would you come here pretending to be pregnant? Why would he have his own fat suit? Let me be frank. What were you smuggling?" The man's voice was calm, and he continued to stare at her, his elbows resting on the table and his eye seeming to track her every move

"I have nothing to say to you. I want a representative from the US. I will not speak with you." The Society had taught them to not deny anything, but to refuse to cooperate. Foreigners weren't usually imprisoned if caught smuggling Bibles, but they can be barred from reentering the country. Identities could be easily faked, so that was unlikely to keep associates from The Society out of the smuggling scheme for long.

Vivian crossed her arms on her chest and leaned back in her chair. She smiled confidently at him. He stood up slowly and walked around the table. He leaned in next to her ear. Chills ran down her spine as he laughed.

"You cocky American's think you can get away with everything." He whipped his hand across her face. "You, young one, have some powerful enemies. I'm going to lose my job for this, and you know what? It doesn't even matter."

Stars exploded before her eyes and the world spun. Her ears rung and pain exploded along her arm. It took a moment to realize her chair had tipped over and she had fallen onto her arm. Rough hands pulled her to her feet. Her vision was blurry as she stumbled through hallways to a holding cell. She was thrown into a cell where she finally regained her bearings as the pain in her face finally caught up with her senses.

She had a splitting headache, and she knew a huge hand shaped bruise would soon be blooming on her face. She stood and looked around the cell. A simple cot sat on one side with a toilet-sink combo on the other. She strode over to the cot and sat down. The room was cool enough that she doubted it was heated.

She started to sing quietly, trying to keep the terror in heart at bay. A guard stood in front of the cell and yelled at her. Softly at first, then louder and louder. Amazing Grace erupted out of her. The guard continued to yell but she continued to sing her soul out, her hands shaking the entire time.

Shen smiled to himself; he could hear a sweet melody floating along the hallway. He knew that voice praising God. His own voice rose, singing the Chinese version. The hallway exploded with activity. and shouting could be heard from one end to the other. Shen was proud of Vivian, even though she had no idea how badly this would shake the investigator.

"You're coming with us," a voice shouted at Shen as the door was unlocked and opened. He stood respectfully and held out his hands for the handcuffs. The officer slammed them on his wrists and tightened them until they pinched his skin.

There was no way around Vivian's cell as they dragged him to the interrogation room. An officer grabbed the back of his neck and gripped it tightly. Shen heard her sweet voice as they neared the cell. Desperate for a glimpse of her, he craned his neck just enough to see her sitting on the cot. A large welt marred her cheek.

Fury bubbled up inside him, and he exploded. "What did you do to her?" He yelled. "Who hit her?" He whipped his head around trying to get one more glance at her.

Shen had no plans. he was simply overwhelmed with rage. His rage was beaten out of him as a dozen officers and guards took him out using batons and fists. His arms came up to protect his face, but it did nothing to stop the beating. Things grew fuzzy near the edge of Shen's vision. He turned inside himself trying to float through the pain. Eventually, he awoke in a room with both his hands and feet secured to a chain on the wall. This room had no bars, only a simple reinforced door. The plain cinder block walls were gray and dreary, matching his mood. His eyes were nearly swollen shut and his head ached terrifically.

The door slammed open, and the lead investigator walked in. He shook his head at the sight of Shen on the ground in a heap covered in blood.

"You will be locked up for a very long time, my friend. And you'll be on house arrest for even longer. Anything to say?" He walked over to Shen and tapped him on the head.

"After it gets out that someone hit an American citizen, and a woman at that, you will be demoted to scrubbing toilets and you know it," Shen spat back.

The detective growled, "I know." He went to kick Shen in the head, but Shen swung both his feet into the man's side sending him sprawling. "Stop!" another voiced yelled from the door. A woman in a black pencil skirt and cherry red button-down shirt stood at the door. Her sleek hair was pulled up in a tight bun, giving her a severe look.

"Detective Long, in my office," her voice was steel. "Li Chang Jie. We've been tracking you for months. You travel a lot. Your clients are usually Americans, and those Americans travel throughout the PRC. Why?"

Shen shifted and used his elbows to sit up and scoot back to lean against the wall. "I am a tour guide. I show off our country's most treasured places to the foreigners. This particular client is married in America. She is my lover. Because her husband is well connected, the only way we can continue our affair is to pretend to be other people. What better disguise is there?" he said, trying to sit more comfortably.

"Your lover isn't talking. She's waiting on the US Representative. Anything else you feel like declaring?" She tapped her fingers on her arm impatiently. Shen shook his head, which nearly made him pass out due to the pain. He turned away from the woman as she closed the door.

CHAPTER 18

Vivian held an ice pack to her cheek as she sat on the sofa of a hotel room owned by an American. The US Government used his hotels throughout China's large cities because of the guaranteed security and privacy. She had showered and changed, thankful that the embassy had been able to retrieve her luggage.

The American liaison looked up from her pad of paper where she was taking notes. "We don't get many international incidents like this where the father is against the relationship. How's your face?" the woman asked, walking over to peek at the magnificent bruise that had formed under the welt. "Wow! Well, he's been canned."

"Good, he has no people skills. This bruise will take weeks to fade. Please tell me you have an update on Chang?" Vivian was grateful she remembered his current identity.

"I don't. We're working on it, but with him being a Chinese national, they have jurisdiction. I'm sorry. In the morning we'll send a car to take you to the airport and have you escorted directly to your gate. Rest well."

When she left Vivian curled up on the bed and cried.

"You must have friends in high places. We are to set you free, but we will be watching you." The woman had turned out to be the precinct captain.

"I'm sure you will be," Shen said, as an officer took off his restraints. He carefully stood, ignoring the wave of dizziness, and followed the captain out. They paused at a desk to retrieve his items and paperwork with his court date before he was released into the lobby.

"My boy, let's go home." Ming Jie called, shaking his head at Shen.

"What are you doing here?" Shen asked, shaking off the man's assistance as they stepped out of the station.

"It came to my attention that you needed assistance. Dandan has been worried about you." Ming Jie said, looking both ways before guiding Shen across the road.

"You're having me followed?" Shen asked incredulously.

"She sees it as protecting an asset. She's quite taken with you, young man."

"Thank you for posting bail but I have no interest in your daughter." Shen said, stopping at the nearest corner to peek at the plain-clothed officers tailing him.

"You can't outrun her." Ming Jie called after Shen.

He walked with his head low and picked his way through the city, trying to figure out where to go. He didn't want to compromise any of his contacts, but perhaps an old mentor who was already being watched. He headed toward his old neighborhood. It wouldn't be difficult to lose his tails and sneak up to Qing Qing's apartment.

He started walking faster. He needed to find out how Vivian was doing. It would be several more hours before he could get a new phone to call The Society. He pulled out his wallet and saw that the station had helped themselves to his banknotes. He walked for an hour and circled the area several times to get a good look at his shadows. Both men did nothing to blend in. They wanted him to know they were there.

It was getting late, the sun had nearly set, and the street he was currently on was not busy. He would need the crowds of the next intersection. As he neared the busy crossing, he forced himself into a run and darted through the crowd. He crossed the street, barely missing a car which blared the horn, and ducked into an alleyway. He grabbed the first door and yanked on it. Locked. He ran down the alley a little farther, footsteps echoing behind him. The next door came open and he stumbled into the back room of a tea shop. He ran through, not bothering to apologize, and out onto the sidewalk. Then he darted into the next shop and shoved his way to the back, leaving dazed and confused patrons behind him. He pushed the back door open and sprinted back into the alley. He took off running, hoping his tails hadn't figured out his shake up.

He disappeared down another alley and hid underneath a rickety set of stairs for another hour, before heading for Qing Qing's home.

Qing Qing's apartment building had a stairwell that faced the back alleyway, in addition to the front entrance. The back entrance was unlocked and didn't seem to be watched. He climbed the inside stairs slowly and carefully. The adrenaline was waning, and he was ready to pass out.

He padded down the hallway to Qing Qing's apartment and quietly tapped on the door. The door cracked ajar, and then flew open the rest of the way and arms pulled him in. He heard the door shut behind him and the locks engage. He was led to a bedroom, laid in bed, his shoes tugged off. Warm compresses were pressed to his face as he drifted off.

"I think it's time for you to be done. This job is too unsafe for you." Samuel said firmly to Vivian. She'd attempted to cover the bruise with makeup, but the handprint was so dark it was impossible. She'd decided to stay in until it had faded enough to hide. She'd been home for two days. The Society had sent members over to debrief her, and she'd spoken to Mrs. Hayes remotely several times, but there was no update on Shen. He hadn't checked in anywhere, although they did have confirmation that he had been released on bail but they weren't sure who posted it. He was laying low for now, wherever he was. For now, she was left to deal with her overprotective father by herself. Even Livi had suggested now might be the best time to quit.

"I am an adult and can decide what is best for me. When I signed up with The Society, I knew the risks, and I knew this was a possibility. I still do not regret that. In fact, I am grateful for this job and what I have learned. I am so proud to be part of God's story. I will not walk away because it got hard. We can discuss this later," Vivian firmly told her father. She stood up to leave his office, but he held his hand up.

"Wait, please. I just overreacted. Please stay." Samuel dropped his hand back onto his desk and laid his head down on his arms.

"Oh, Dad, I know you're worried, but this is part of the job. My contact and I will lay low for a few months, we'll be given new identities and start fresh. They'll rearrange some of the safe houses and drop spots, and we'll nix the maternity suit. I'm not scarred for life, this will fade," she said, pointing to her face. Samuel lifted his head to look at her.

"What is it that is keeping you involved? Is it that young man?" Samuel asked, his voice was shaking.

"Because God called me to this. Just like He called you to preach. Did you quit when Mom died?" Vivian shot back, arching her eyebrows at her father.

"Point taken. Are you sure it doesn't have anything to do with this young man?"

Vivian shot her father a withering look and left the room without a word. She headed to her room to call Mrs. Kaminsky again to see if they had an update on Shen.

"Was Dad yelling at you?" Livi popped out of the bathroom and pulled Vivian into her room. Livi and Vivian's tastes were vastly different, and nowhere was it more apparent than in their rooms. While Vivian's was plain Jane, dorm style, Livi's was expressive and bright. Sparkles and pink everywhere, feathers and pom-poms, fluffy, fuzzy pillows, and posters of singers, bands, and models. Vivian hated it. It was too much, although her own room could use better décor.

“No, he wasn’t. He was stating his opinions but I won’t be leaving the job. I will return to China in a few months.” Vivian said firmly, irritation creeping into her tone.

“What if The Society decides to give you a new contact?” Livi said casually, as if she hadn’t just verbalized Vivian’s most dreaded nightmare.

“Then I’ll resist it. We work together flawlessly, and they would never back away from the perfect team. Why would they do that?”

As if on cue her phone rang. She just stared at the screen as The Society’s number blinked across it. She was terrified to answer it.

Livi walked over and swiped the phone and quietly answered it. Vivian stood there numbly as she finished a short conversation and ended the call. “Mrs. Hayes will be over in an hour. I’ll get Dad and Evan out of the house. Will you be okay by yourself?” Livi generously offered.

Vivian simply nodded her head and returned to her room. She was terrified that the news would be horrible. Was Shen dead?

CHAPTER 19

Shen heard Qing Qing moving through the small apartment. They had not spoken in the several days that Shen had been there. He had cared for Shen's wounds, provided herbal remedies, fed him, and read his Bible silently from a chair next to the bed.

Shen turned his head testing his body. The dizziness was gone and but a dull throb remained in the back of his head. He pushed himself up slowly and swung his legs over the edge of the bed. Carefully, he stood up, but he didn't so much as wobble. It felt worse than it was.

Qing Qing was puttering around the small front room, a small pot was bubbling on a hot plate, and children laughed out on the street. Shen's heart ached hearing those kids. How many times he had wished he could have been one of those children running through the street kicking a ball around or playing catch-me-if-you-can. No child would decide to live through such hardships.

"You must whisper. The sitters come once a day. I cannot hide you for long, nor can I feed you much. I have groceries brought here, and if I suddenly request more it will appear suspicious. I am sorry, but you will have to leave soon." Qing Qing shuffled back to the hot plate to stir his small pot. He slumped over the pot and stirred it slowly. As if he barely had the strength to resist the water against his spoon.

"I will try not to get you into further trouble, but I will not leave you like this. As a child of the King, you should be walking with your head held high, not bowed in submission."

"I told you before. I won't let others be hurt on my account." Qing Qing ladled two small bowls of congee. "This is my ration for tomorrow. I will run out of food if you stay."

"I will bring food and supplies. I can hire workers to make repairs. I can even relocate you, if you want. I will not burden you, but I will not leave things like this. If I get hurt serving the Lord, then that is between me and him." Shen ran a hand through is disheveled hair and turned away. "I'm leaving at dusk to get supplies, make me a list," Shen ordered his former foster father. With that, he turned and disappeared in the small bathroom to clean up.

After a silent meal of plain congee, he put his hooded jacket back on and wrapped an old piece of cloth around his face. He waited for dark to leave and headed for a nearby safe house. He scrambled through the dark streets as quickly as he could, keeping to alleyways and crowded locations. At the safe house he walked down the hallway to a small locker. The locker contained clothing that likely didn't fit him anymore, three-thousand yuan, a few identities he hadn't used yet, and a Bible. He stuffed the money, clothes, and Bible into the bag and looked through his identities. He pulled one out and left the others in the locker. With that done, he headed off toward the nearest market for supplies.

The market was bustling even at this late hour. Shen looked at the short list Qing Qing had reluctantly given him. Bare bones basics. The man would likely starve to death before requesting anything of substance. Shen eyed a thick cut of beef before settling on a pork loin. After loading up at the vegetable stall, he grabbed a black backpack at an accessory stall.

Within an hour Shen hefted loaded bags of basic supplies, including the food and more clothing, and hiked to Qing Qing's home. He knocked lightly on the door, and the old man opened it with surprised eyes. Shen passed the food to his friend and stashed his own items in the bedroom, before joining Qing Qing in the main room.

"What is all this?" the old man asked, sounding irritated.

"You've lost weight, you need to eat more. The danger has already passed so eat. You are here for a reason. Live up to that. Cook the meat." Shen insisted.

"But they know I don't have meat."

"If someone comes to the door, tell them you killed a rat," Shen said, hefting a bag of rice and putting it away in the cupboard.

Mrs. Hayes smoothed the fabric of her bright purple gomesi dress as Vivian poured tea for the two of them. Livi had successfully gotten both Evan and their father out of the house to give Mrs. Hayes and Vivian some privacy. She convinced them she wanted to go bowling, so the house would be empty for at least a few hours. Livi was a terrible bowler.

"Thank you, dear." She said, accepting a cup of tea. "I'm sorry for what you went through. How are you doing?" Mrs. Hayes asked.

"I'm alright. Mostly worried about my partner." Vivian paused and looked absently out the window. "I don't want to leave The Society. I realize a break is required, but I am not quitting. My contact and I have a strong rapport, and I don't wish to throw that away and start fresh with someone new. Which, speaking of…do you have an update for me?"

Mrs. Hayes raised an eyebrow. "Well, my dear, we are floating the idea of connecting you with a new handler, but I see you have a strong opinion regarding that. Why?" Mrs. Hayes, always one to cut to the chase, sipped her tea and waited for Vivian to answer without answering Vivian's question.

"After all we've been through, we trust each other and work well together Starting over means risking more missions." Vivian said, looking down at her teacup.

"Our concern, my dear, isn't with protocol, it is whether you two have become too dependent upon one another. Is there anything you would like to share?"

Vivian swallowed hard. "I do care deeply for him, as a brother in Christ and as a person. We have been through a lot together and have come out stronger because we worked together. You cannot replace good chemistry."

"Alright, my dear, I will bring your answer back to the council. We will meet in two weeks to discuss it. We would like you to be there.? Mrs. Hayes finished her cup of tea and stood, poised to leave.

Vivian stood, also, and faced Mrs. Hayes. "So, no update then? Please tell me when you hear something." It wasn't a question.

Qing Qing shuffled through the flat toward the door. He paused as a knock came again. He cracked the door open and stepped back quickly. An arm thrust through the door, shoving it open with a bang. Two middle-aged men, with slight paunches and wearing navy jackets and khaki pants, strode in grimly..

"Here's the food, old man." The bald one shoved the bag into Qing Qing's hands and sniffed loudly

"What's that smell?"

"I caught a rat." He grunted under the weight of the bag of supplies.

"Hope it was good because that's all the meat you're getting for a while. They've cut your supplies again." He laughed coldly and looked around the dingy room. "Ready to give up the names of your conspirators? Who supplies you with books?"

"I'm sure I can catch you one if you'd like to stick around a few more minutes," Qing Qing offered, a wry smile on his face.

A glare replaced the man's smirk. Without another word they backed out the door. Qing Qing quietly chuckled and, entering the tiny kitchen, began putting away the meager groceries.

"Where would you take me?"

"Inner Mongolia. I know a place close to the border, so if you must leave the country, we can get you across." Shen cocked his head at the old man from the bedroom where he had hidden. "What's changed?"

"I don't want to eat rats!" Qing Qing laughed and clapped his hands together. His eyes sparkled with amusement. It felt good to laugh. When was the last time he had laughed?

"Well, then," Shen said, "I'll make the arrangements. You will need to pack light. Until then, eat. I need you strong for the journey. And pray! We will need the Lord's favor on this." He smiled at his former mentor. "It's good to see you smile, old friend."

CHAPTER 20

A breeze teased Vivian's hair. She swiped at the stray piece, but it danced on the breeze a moment before she could tuck it securely behind her ear. She looked at the horizon where the sky was lit up in brilliant pinks and oranges.

"Well, Mom, I suppose I should say something. I'm just sitting here, feeling useless. I want to jump on a plane and head over there right now, but I haven't heard from him. We haven't gone more than a week without texting or and its been almost two months. What do I do?" Vivian sighed and leaned back against the maple tree near her mother's headstone.

"What I wouldn't give to have you give me some advice. I've been praying and praying and not getting anywhere. I've been lying to Dad and Livi and The Society. I am in so deep I don't know how to get myself out." Vivian dropped her head down into her hands and shook with sobs. "This is one of the only places I feel comfortable unloading everything." She looked up and swiped at her face. She curled up to her mother's headstone listening to the sound of the wind in the nearby maple tree.

◆ ◆ ◆

"Shen!" a crisp voice called above the din of the mall. "Shen!" The call came again.

Shen looked around absently from where he stood at the cellphone kiosk, watching his burner phone getting a quick repair job. He nearly fell over when Dandan marched right up to him and swatted his shoulder.

"Don't ignore me, it's rude. Where's your girlfriend? Or are we on another one now? You've always liked exotic girls, haven't you?" She smoothed her chic pixie cut and adjusted the sunglasses propped on top of her head.

"Dandan. I wasn't ignoring you I didn't see you. They've let you out of your crib. What sort of trouble are you causing now?" Shen looked at the vendor, mentally urging the man to hurry up, but his hopes were dashed when the man glanced up at Dandan. She wore a short black dress that showed off her long, thin legs. Her tiny red leather jacket matched her red, spiky heels and showcased her curves.

"No, seriously, where is she? I've got a date, but we can always have fun together. You know, the four of us!" She raised an eyebrow and winked, completely ignoring the repairman practically drooling on Shen's phone.

Shen snapped his fingers in front of the vendor's face in a rush of irritation, then turned back to Dandan.

"She's out of the country right now."

"Woo! A little protective, aren't we? Is she *the one*? Will there be little Shen's running around soon?" She snorted and turned a blinding smile on the small crowd gathered around the kiosk. She turned back to Shen and tugged the necklace out of its hiding spot. "Oh, a fish. Did your lover give you this?"

Shen's fists clenched at his sides. He shifted and looked around. It wasn't as crowded as usual, but he still wanted to get out of there. He despised being exposed.

Arms slipped around Shen's waist unexpectedly. He veered away, uncomfortable in her arms, but Dandan tightened her grip. Shen easily broke her hold and stepped back.

"Jealousy doesn't look good on you." Shen held his hand up toward her away, but Dandan walked into it, rubbing her chest against it. Shen dropped his hand and stepped back.

"Jealous? Of her? Why would I be jealous of her?" Dandan laughed haughtily.

“Because it’s me you want. Dandan, I am not interested.” Shen knew he’d hit home. Dandan’s smile cracked for a moment, shock spread across her face and was gone in an instant, replaced by the smugness she always wore.

“I can have anyone I want, even this moron over here.” She indicated the vendor, who was holding Shen’s phone up to him. Shen grabbed the phone, threw down a few bills and walked away.

Out of the corner of his eye he saw that someone was following him. He spun around, irritation rising.

“Why are you following me, Dandan?” He pulled up short, jerking to a halt before colliding with Dandan’s father.

“I’m losing patience with you, young man.” Ming Jie growled, his business coat a little snug around the middle, arms crossed over his chest. “She’s done waiting on you. You have had enough time to come around.”

“You know I consider you a friend, but you should stay out of this.” Shen said, his body tense.

“I would do anything for my daughter or for her happiness. Anything!” Ming Jie stepped closer, poking his finger into Shen’s chest for emphasis.

“Leave me alone,” Shen whispered before walking away without looking back.

“Go deep, Vivian!” Evan yelled, stepping back and letting the football fly. Vivian ran backward, gauging where the ball was headed. She jumped into the air, scrambling to grab the ball, but it bounced off her fingertips before falling to the ground.

“*Ooof!*” The breath whooshed out of Vivian as she pitched over backward and tumbled down a shallow incline, to the bottom of the short hill they’d been playing on. Evan’s laughter rang out, following her. She rolled to a stop and threw her arm over her eyes. Crunching steps ran up to her. A toe nudged her.

“Are ya alright?” He asked, nudging her again. Vivian

theatrically rolled over; her arms splayed out awkwardly. Vivian rocked up onto her bottom and threw a handful of leaves at Evan. She smiled, enjoying an everyday moment with her little brother.

"Let's go, little stinker! It's about time for dinner. Livi said she had something special planned." Vivian shook her head at Evan. Leaves and branches were stuck in his afro. "You look so silly!" She snickered and pulled a few leaves out of his hair, then took off toward the house with Evan in tow.

"Hey!" Evan yelled as they rounded the patio furniture on the back patio. "If Livi's cooking doesn't kill me, your bad throwing sure will!"

"Hey! My cooking isn't that bad!" They both stopped short. Livi stood in the open doorway, her arms folded across her chest defiantly. She narrowed her eyes at the wayward siblings in front of her. "At least have the decency to look guilty!" Evan laughed and dashed around Livi and into the house.

"Your phone has been going off for an hour. Who is texting you so much? Your Chinese lover?" Livi laughed, holding Vivian's phone just out of her reach and teasing her with it.

"Give me that, Livi!" Vivian swiped her phone out of Livi's hand and pointed through the door. "What's burning?"

"Nothing's burning. Nice try." Livi sniffed the air, her eyes grew wide, and she turned around slowly. A faint acrid scent wafted through the air. Vivian's phone lit up, emitting a repetitive chime. Her heart raced as she looked down and saw a number she didn't recognize. Livi raced into the house, throwing a suspicious glimpse at Vivian.

"Hello?" she answered the phone as she stood in the back of the garage out of the way of her family.

"Hi, yourself, friend," a familiar voice replied. Vivian arched her brow at his choice of words.

"Friend? Never mind...Are you alright? I've been so worried."

"Yes, I'm alright. It has been hard to lay low but I was safe the whole time. Have you been alright?" Shen said, the familiar rumble of his voice filling her with comfort.

"Yes, I'm alright." There was a pause. "It has been hard to sit out and not travel but I've been fine."

"My girlfriend," Shen quietly said.

"Sorry, come again?" Vivian asked in confusion, before her eyes went wide with the realization that he was, in fact, answering the question she had tried to cover up.

"You're my girlfriend. And I don't want to wait to see you again. Do you think you could meet me somewhere in a few weeks?"

Vivian's mind was rushing. He wanted to meet with her outside of the Society business. Where could they meet?

"Hello? Are you still there?" Shen asked, worry tinging his words.

"Yes, sorry, you took me by surprise. I wasn't expecting that."

"No, it's not alright. I've had a lot of time to think about us and did kind of throw that at you." Shen drifted off into a string of Mandarin.

"I miss you, too. Where can we meet?"

Shen grumbled under his breath a moment longer but did settle down. "I'm calm. I think we'll meet in Hawaii. I'll email you the arrangements."

"I miss you. A lot. I was about ready to get on an airplane and try to find you myself." Actually, Vivian had a ticket she needed to cancel.

"I miss you, too. I didn't think this would be so hard."

"I know exactly what you mean." Vivian tried to swallow down the stubborn lump, but it wouldn't move.

"Vivian! We're going out to dinner. Get your rear in gear!" Evan called from the mud room.

"Be right there!" she called back, then turned her attention back to Shen. "I must go. I really don't want to, I want to stay, but if I don't go, they'll come looking for me."

"And that will cause uncomfortable questions. I understand. Look for my email. I miss you. Nǐ jìu shì wǒ yào zhǎo de rén ," Shen said softly.

"Awww, you're the one for me, too."

"You've been keeping up on your language lessons. Good! Now off with you," Shen said, a kissing sound coming through the phone as the connection died.

The door opened and Evan jumped off the step. He had picked all the leaves and rubble out of his hair and combed it out. He grinned mischievously at Vivian and loudly whispered to her. "Livi burned dinner so we're going out! She should cook more often!"

"I heard that you brat! Get in the car!" Livi's voice echoed through the garage. Evan's eyes grew wide, and he whipped open the back door to the car. He slammed the door shut just as Livi stepped out

Vivian turned on her heel to join Evan in the car, but Livi grabbed her arm.

"Where do you think you're going? You know you're telling me what that was all about." Livi had her hand on her hips and head cocked to the side.

"Livi, don't start. There's nothing to tell you. A friend got a new phone and wanted to talk. In fact, we might go on a trip in a few weeks. I haven't done anything fun in months, and I think I could use a trip." Vivian couldn't even look Livi in the eye, she was talking to Livi's shoes. Guilt swirled in the pit of her stomach.

Livi looked unconvinced and huffed over to the car, throwing open the passenger door. Samuel stepped into the garage and looked from the car to Vivian and back again. He shook his head but said nothing as Vivian joined Evan in the back.

CHAPTER 21

A low rumble punctuated the deep night and Shen gripped Qing Qing's arm tightly as the bus hit a bump. He despised the idea of using public transportation to escape from Beijing, but there was no choice. He couldn't get a vehicle to take as far north as they needed to go.

Qing Qing had begun eating more, putting aside his frugal nature. His entire demeanor had changed the moment he had decided that rat meat was not on the menu. He had even begun exercising. While he hadn't put on a significant amount of weight, he had certainly gotten much stronger.

Qing Qing bounced in the seat next to Shen like an excited toddler, peering out the window and enjoying the limited view. The cumbersome vehicle began to slow as they entered a small village. The driver maneuvered to the side of the road where a group of people were gathered, waiting for the bus to take them to the border city of Erenhot.

Shen absently scanned the crowd, then stiffened when he noticed a uniformed officer among the small press of people. His hand dropped to the bag near his feet, that was filled to the brim with Bibles for his contacts in Erenhot. He looked around, noting with dismay that most of the empty seats were in the middle of the bus where he and Qing Qing sat.

Qing Qing had enough wherewithal to settle down as the new additions made their way down the center aisle. An elderly granny passed by with a large cloth sack with produce sticking out, a scrawny teenager followed behind her, then a few middle-aged business types, and then the officer.

Lord, please close his eyes to these Bibles. Allow me to take Qing Qing safely to Erenhot, Shen silently beseeched God. The officer sat down directly across from Shen, and he had to suppress a groan. A few more passengers boarded, then the bus jerked back into motion.

The officer removed his hat, smoothed his hair and looked around. He caught Shen's eye and nodded, then reached out toward the bag. Shen's heart raced wildly. The officer smiled sheepishly and laid his hat on top of the bag of Bibles, then leaned back and closed his eyes. Qing Qing elbowed Shen and gave him a knowing smile.

They settled in for the long ride. It would be eight hours if everything went well, but it was an old and battered bus, so the Lord only knew how long it would truly take. The bus rumbled its way along the roads and highways, passing by checkpoints and tollbooths.

As they neared Erenhot and the final tollbooth, a sea of vehicles clogged up the road. Uniformed officers randomly waved some through and others to the side. Shen slumped resignedly against his seat. He knew exactly what was about to happen: their bus would be waved aside and boarded. As if life were a movie and he was the one writing the script, the bus was waved apart from the rest, and chugged over to the side to await the boarding party.

The snoozing officer woke up with a grunt, rubbing his eyes. "Are we there yet?"

"We're at the checkpoint." Shen absently replied, keeping an eye on the group of officers about to board. When the officer saw his military comrades, he straightened up and smoothed his shirt. Shen looked at Qing Qing, who was fast asleep. It wasn't hard to see that he was truly worn out from so much activity after years of house arrest.

The officers made their way down the aisle, looking through bags and checking identifications. An officer slid by him to rummage through the granny's vegetable pack. Shen's heart nearly pounded out of his chest as a man stopped between he and the officer seated across from him. They chatted for a moment before the Corporal turned and glanced down at Shen's bag. He expected to be hauled off the bus and arrested, guaranteeing Qing Qing's demise in a reeducation camp or prison. But the Corporal looked at the bag and saw the officer's hat laying on top. With a smile, he swiped the hat off Shen's bag and handed it to the officer before he moved to the front of the bus and exited, waving them on.

Shen's heartbeat slowed, and it took everything in him to not jump up and praise God right then and there.

Eventually, the bus lurched to a stop in Erenhot, and they disembarked just as the sun was coming up. Resting was never easy on public transportation, and Shen hadn't even tried, knowing Qing Qing's safety rested upon those Bibles remaining undiscovered. Shen walked the flagging old man to a cab near the bus station, giving the driver an address. The cab arrived at a small, white apartment building on the outskirt of the city. Shen guided the elderly man up the stairs and to a door at the end of the hallway.

Before he could even knock the door was opened and a group of curious faces greeted them. "Here, please find a place for my friend to rest, and get him fed," Shen ordered, passing Qing Qing off to the several helpful hands. Others gathered around Shen as he unpacked the Bibles and placed them on the dining table.

"I am Pastor Ling," a young Mongolian man said. "Thank you for bringing these here. Many of our disciples have never seen a Bible in their language. Here, take one." Pastor Ling handed a Bible to another young man. He lifted it reverently and caressed the binding before opening it up. He began reading aloud in a Mongolian dialect.

Shen's heart grew in his chest at the sound of God's word, even if he could not understand it.

"It'll be alright, dear, you'll see," Mrs. Kaminsky, The Society's secretary, said, patting Vivian's hand from across the desk.

"You know why I'm here?" Vivian asked, wondering what today's outcome would be.

"Oh, yes, dear, I know more than they do. When your hands are in so many pots, and you keep everything from boiling over, people share a lot of things with you." Mrs. Kaminsky winked at her and stood.

"They're waiting on you. And, dear?" Mrs. Kaminsky paused briefly before leading Vivian to the double doors leading to the council room.

"Yes?" Vivian asked, hoping for some sage advice.

"I don't think you have anything to worry about." With that she quietly opened one of the doors and ushered Vivian in.

The large conference table was surrounded by council members. Not a seat was empty. *Great*, thought Vivian, *no one thought to take a vacation?* She crept to the empty chair at the table and sat down, wishing the floor would eat her up. The conversation continued around the table uninterrupted.

"I agree that great teamwork cannot be replaced, but safety of this organization is top priority and many different people can work well together," an Indian woman said emphatically to a dark-skinned man.

"The real solution to our concerns about safety is to focus on rural communities. We should discuss the needs of the rural communities and move more contacts out of the cities and into the countryside. The city surveillance system is hindering our efforts; we are barely staying ahead of this ever developing technology. Let us concentrate our efforts in the countryside," the man suggested.

"Here! Here!" A man with a British accent said in support. "We need to figure out why more and more of our agents are being discovered through video surveillance. Something is bringing attention to them. Are there agents that are distracted or compromising our security measures?"

"Vivian, thank you for joining us." Gloria Hayes turned to Vivian, shooting a welcoming smile in her direction. "Please tell the council your thoughts on the matter. Do you wish to continue working with your contact? Would you agree to being paired with a new partner?"

Vivian swallowed but her throat was tight. She straightened and cleared her throat, "I do wish to continue to work with my contact. However, if the council believes it to be in everyone's best interest then I will work with someone else. Strong chemistry and teamwork are important. We have built a solid bond. We have proven ourselves capable and able to handle difficult situations," she began but was interrupted by the Indian woman.

"Your capabilities are not what we are questioning. You have proven yourself to be a formidable pair. Whether or not your pairing has become too recognizable is the concern. Chinese technology will easily notice you two in the metro areas. Who your preferred partner is, is not our priority."

"Thank you, Dayita," Mrs. Hayes said, and turned to the dark-skinned man. "Faisal, can we get them in and out of the countryside without passing through the larger cities?"

"Well, we have been setting up safe houses along the borders where there are few patrols, so we could fly our contacts into a neighboring country before entering China. Entry and exit would be safer, in theory. Also, since we have been floating the idea of acquiring mining rights along the border and digging a series of tunnels between the two countries, now might be a good time to implement that."

Mrs. Hayes nodded in agreement. "All in favor of tunneling and concentrating on the countryside say 'aye'," Mrs. Hayes called for a quick vote. Her hand, Faisal's, the British gentleman, and several more shot up. Only Dayita and one other kept their hands down. "We will continue to find a work around with the technology so we can again safely enter the larger cities, but for now we will concentrate our efforts on the borders and the countryside. Now, Vivian, back to your circumstances." Mrs.

Hayes looked sadly at Vivian, and the younger woman felt her heart skip a beat.

"There is still the concern that the two of you might be growing too close, or too reliant upon one another. We will allow your partnership to continue for now, but this discussion, while tabled for now, will come back up again if need be. You will meet again next month." It was a warning to her. Vivian swallowed down her guilt. If only they knew just how deep she was in, the itinerary for her trip to Hawaii had come through just last night.

"Yes, ma'am." Vivian nodded her head at Mrs. Hayes and stood from the table. She gave a slight bow to the council before turning and leaving the room. As Vivian passed through the waiting area, she noticed a slightly portly man of Asian heritage. He seemed familiar but she couldn't place him.

She turned back as Mrs. Kaminsky called the man into the conference room next. "Ming Jie, you may go in now."

CHAPTER 22

Waves crashed over Vivian's feet, warm and inviting, but not nearly as much as Shen's arm around her shoulder. They walked along the beach, watching the sunset turning the sky a brilliant array of orange, yellow and red. colors. Guilt knotted in her stomach. She was fresh out of the council meeting where she'd been warned not to do this, where she had all but said she would not. But here she was.

"What's wrong, Ai Ren?" He pulled her in closer to his side and stopped walking, turning to face her.

"I'm struggling with something. The council made it clear we are to be business only. And, well, here we are." She looked down at their intertwined hands. It was easy to say that they weren't doing anything wrong because they were staying pure, committing their relationship to God, and praying together often, but their entire relationship was built on deceit.

"I wondered if something like that had happened. You've been a little stiff around me. Why does The Society have these rules?" Shen asked, reaching out and tugging her chin up with one finger. Vivian met his warm, brown gaze.

"To protect the organization. So that if one link is broken it doesn't bring down the entire operation."

"Exactly. What did you do in the police station after that coward hit you? Did you give them details or beg for mercy?" Shen asked.

"No, of course not. I followed procedure."

"I don't think that they desire to step in between young love or keep apart couples. They are merely looking to protect themselves. When we choose to officially announce our relationship we will have to step down and find new roles in which to serve." Shen sounded so sure of himself and the outcome

Vivian wished she could be as confident.

"Let's head back for dinner," Shen suggested, slipping his hand back into hers and giving it a squeeze.

They strolled back up the beach to their rental car, where Shen held the door open for her. Before she could slip into the seat, he pulled her back with gentle pressure. Vivian looked up, confused, and was met with an amused smile. She reached a hand up and mussed up his hair. He'd grown it long again and dyed it blond, but he was still her Shen.

Dinner that night was a quiet affair. They'd spent the week sightseeing, swimming, boating, and relaxing to their hearts' content, but now their imminent separation was looming over them like a heavy cloud.

"Does it make our relationship easier or harder, for us to meet up like this?" Vivian asked, taking a bite of poke.

Shen chewed his lomi lomi salmon thoughtfully before answering. "Honestly, in the long run I think it's to our benefit. Taking time away from the constant state of fear and adrenaline and relax while getting to know each other can only benefit us. But, in the short term, yes, it's hard to hold you close then let you go."

At what point does it become love? Vivian wondered. She was certain she was nearly there, but she was not ready to tell Shen that, not yet.

"You alright? You disappeared for a moment," Shen asked, pulling her back to the present.

"Yes, just thinking about what you said. I'll see you in a few weeks, again, anyway. What color will your hair be the next time I see you? Blue? Pink?" Vivian laughed at the mental image.

"You should try it with me! We can pick a wild color together.

I'm sure your father would love that! What did you tell him, anyway?"

"Livi is the one you should be worried about, not our father. I told him I was meeting up with a friend for a relaxing vacation. Livi's on another trip to Taiwan so I didn't have to say anything to her. I'm glad we made this trip; I feel like I left fifty pounds of stress on the sand, I'll be refreshed for the next trip."

"Well, at some point you're going to need to tell her." He absentmindedly rubbed her hand. "I think we need to make these trips a reality more often. Shall we meet again in six months?" Shen suggested, looking hopeful and fluttering his lashes at her. Vivian burst out laughing and threw her cloth napkin at him. Her heart and soul were deeper into this relationship with Shen but still burdened with shame.

Where was greenery, the trees, the grass? Vivian understood it was a desert, but growing up in Tennessee, a virtual sea of greenery, seeing a desert for the first time was deeply shocking. The Gobi Desert stretched out before their Russian utility vehicle. Brown with hints of red washed out all other colors. Even the sky seemed to be a washed-out tan.

"Is that a dust storm?" she asked the driver, pointing ahead. He merely grunted and focused on the road. She'd flown into Ulaanbaatar, then had boarded a smaller biplane that landed on a private airstrip in the south. They were making their way through the desert, avoiding the main roads. When they'd broken away from the sea of mining trucks heading south into China, they'd been standing still in traffic for hours.

The utility truck bumped along the sandy surface for another hour before a group of buildings came into view. A flood of trucks was leaving the fenced-in cluster of construction. Her driver seemed particularly happy to jump out of the vehicle, and he disappeared within moments. Vivian looked around, taking it all in. The barren landscape stretched for miles disappearing into the horizon. A half dozen weather worn buildings were haphazardly erected in the sparse space. It wasn't clear exactly what was going on here. She pulled her coat tighter against her neck as the chilly air nipped at her exposed skin. Unsure where the driver had gone, she rummaged through the luggage she'd hauled into the country looking for her personal items.

"I've been waiting for hours. Don't you know its impolite to keep someone waiting?" Shen's voice called from behind her. She dropped her luggage and almost flung herself into his arms, but she restrained herself at the last moment.

"Traffic was crazy. Be a gentleman and help me with these bags." She indicated the mess of luggage in the back of the truck, filled with Bibles and other teaching materials.

"We'll unload after dark in one of the garages. Here's our driver." Shen took Vivian's bag and pointed toward the driver. The man puffed on a cigarette as he threw open the door to the truck and climbed in, taking off just as Shen slammed the door shut.

He led the way to a nearby garage and held the door for her to pass through. They made their way to an elevator in the back and, when it stopped, came out into a dark cavern with lights running off into opposite directions. A group of men were waiting for them.

"I am Batu. Thank you for making this trip. I trust you had a safe journey?" Batu had strong cheekbones set in a sturdy, round face.

"Yes, thank you. I had an uneventful trip. Would I be able to clean up a bit before we talk?" Vivian asked, absently scratching at her neck.

"Yes, of course. The sand seems to get into every crevice. Brother, can you show her the way?" Batu asked Shen. He grunted an acknowledgment, turned to the right, and took a few steps before pausing for Vivian to catch up.

"You'll find that even if you clean up, you merely exchange the sand from up top with dirt from down here. This room," Shen opened a door and flipped on a light, "is mine. You can use the shower and change. When you're done, just open the door. Someone will come for you. It's good to see you." Shen added, giving her arm a little squeeze before leaving her alone.

Clean and refreshed, Vivian walked along with one of Batu's colleagues to a large room filled with boxes, crates, and wooden benches, the last of which were currently occupied by Shen, Batu, and several other men.

"Welcome, Sister. The driver has offloaded the delivery. Would you like to see the operation?" Batu stood, followed by Shen.

"Yes. How do you get the materials south of the border?" They made their way back to the corridor and down to a service elevator. The doors clanged shut and they jerked deeper into the earth.

"You have seen how we accept the deliveries. From there, we repack them into crates and wooden boxes." Batu explained, leaning against the side of the elevator to balance against the shaking of the lift.

"Like the ones I saw in the room where we met?"

"Exactly. From there we run them through the tunnel system to the south where the Chinese team distributes them accordingly." The elevator jerked to a stop, flinging Vivian into Shen. She quickly straightened and turned back to Batu who merely raised an eyebrow and opened the lift gate. From there they climbed onto a golf cart. Batu drove them far into the caverns of the mine, where the air was cool and moist.

"What is mined here?"

"It's sand. We collect sand from the desert and dye it and export it for crafts."

"Well, that's creative. There's plenty of sand out here."

"Indeed, there is. Ah, this is our stop." Batu jumped out of the golf cart and led them to a maintenance locker. He opened the door, flicked on a flashlight, and stepped inside. Shen slid his hand down Vivian's arm to take her hand as they followed Batu into a dark tunnel beyond. They stopped a few minutes later, and Shen reluctantly dropped her hand.

"Tomorrow, you two will go through the tunnel from here with the Bibles, using a mining cart. At the other end you will meet with the next contact. You will have two days to get back here before the next driver heads back to Ulaanbaatar

Shen, who had been oddly quiet, replied, "That won't be a problem. I am stationed there often, now, so I am familiar with it. Vivian, are you ready to eat?"

"And, a shower, the sand is literally everywhere."

The mining cart Batu had mentioned was a prehistoric beast; an engine cart in front with two small seats, followed by wagons attached behind it, all filled with crates and boxes. The cart rumbled through the dark tunnel, the only illumination coming from its headlights. They held hands, enjoying the private moment. The engine was too loud to allow any talking, so the occasional squeeze of the hand would have to say everything.

The tunnel was long and straight, with only the occasional curve. It was narrow, just wide enough for the cart and a few inches of clearance on each side. Had she wanted to, Vivian could have reached out and touched the rock and dirt walls.

At the end of the tunnel, an open gate met them. Shen stopped when all the wagons were through before cutting the engine. The silence was nearly deafening after hearing the roar echoing off the close walls. The headlights of their mining cart illuminated a large cavern. Vivian couldn't make out much more of their surroundings in the deep darkness until a pinprick of light flashed off to the side.

"Welcome. Please follow me." A tiny woman, with long black hair beckoned with her flashlight for the two of them to follow. Shen took Vivian's bag and his own, and waved Vivian ahead of him. They made their way through a network of tunnels to a small room with a mini-fridge, coffee machine, and microwave.

"The men will load the materials onto a truck and you can be on your way. You may wait here." The woman disappeared back the way they'd come.

"I have a friend I want you to meet while we're in China," Shen said, getting coffee for them.

"Which friend is this?" Vivian asked, taking a careful sip of the scalding liquid. She scrunched her nose at the acidic, bitter taste of cheap instant coffee, but she was grateful for the caffeine.

"My foster father," Shen said cryptically. Vivian recalled the story he had told her of his childhood, and vaguely remembered mention of a father figure who took him in.

"When did he move up this way? I thought he was in the capital?"

"I moved him up here myself. He needed a taste of freedom after so many years of confinement. From what I hear, he's living it up." Shen drained his cup and cringed as the bitter elixir slid down his throat. Vivian laughed, but then nearly gagged on her own mouthful. She walked it over to the sink and dumped it unceremoniously.

"We're ready." Vivian jumped as the woman popped in. They followed her out to the service lift and jostled their way to the surface. A truck was loaded and waiting for them.

"You will leave with a caravan of other trucks. You know the way, correct?" Shen nodded and threw their bags into the cab of the truck. The woman turned back to Vivian. "You may want to disguise yourself. The border is heavily watched."

Vivian put her sunglasses on and pulled the hood of her coat up, tucking her loose hair in. They loaded up into the cab of the Russian made dump truck and joined the parade of trucks flowing out of the mine.

"It will only take us an hour to get to the drop off zone. After that we'll take a detour to visit my friend," Shen informed her.

"What did he do that got him confined to his home?" Vivian asked.

"Many people are arrested, sent to prison or reeducation camps and then when they are released, they aren't free. They are followed for weeks, months and sometimes years. People the Chinese Communist Party consider a major threat are not allowed to leave their homes. People who visit them are harassed or hauled in for questioning. He was one the CCP considered too much of a threat to have freedom in society. He proselytized too often, too loudly, and too enthusiastically." Shen answered.

"It's so sad. They don't even know what it's like to truly be free. Freedom of speech, of thought, of religion." Vivian slid over to sit next to Shen and tucked herself into his side. The heat in the cab didn't work and it was cold this far north, desert or not.

"It is sad, isn't it? What's your father's church like?"

"A member of The Society has a mansion that used to belong to a country music star, he bought it cheap when it was foreclosed. We use the private theater for services. He's allowed us to customize it so we can have a worship band and pulpit."

"Was the church supportive after your mom passed away?" Shen asked, putting his arm around her and pulling her in close.

"Yes. They paid our bills, bought our groceries, and took my sister and I to school. They made sure we had clothes and supplies. But my father never allowed other people to babysit us. He would often preach with my brother in a carrier he wore. Evan's put in more time behind a pulpit than most graduates!"

"Why do you think he wouldn't let others help?" Shen asked, squeezing her hand and moving their truck away from the long train of trucks in front of them.

"We'd already lost so much when my mom died, he didn't want us to lose him, too. He made it clear that his priority would always be his children. We lost a few people that year who disagreed, they felt his priority should be the church. The rest rallied around and jumped in to help. I'm so grateful for his sacrifices."

"I am, as well," Shen said quietly.

"Why?" Vivian asked, curious.

"Because his choices helped to shape who you have become. One day I will thank him personally," Shen said soberly.

"We're here." Shen backed the truck up to a large, dark building. "Stay close to the truck and don't speak to anyone," he ordered. Vivian slid back over to the passenger seat and cautiously got out, dropping to the ground.

Shen disappeared to the back and barked orders to a group of men. They worked quickly to unload the crates and boxes, never even glancing in Vivian's direction. It wasn't long before Shen rejoined her.

"We're going to come back for the truck. We're borrowing a car, let's go!" Shen took off at a good clip. Vivian had to run to catch up. "He's only a few minutes from here. Don't tell him your name, where you're from, your nationality, nothing. If the authorities find him, I don't think it would take much to break him."

"Do you think it's safe for me to meet him?" Vivian asked nervously as she buckled up, while Shen drove through the city. The city was bland and whitewashed, as if all the color had been leached out of the surroundings.

"Yes, it's safe for a visit but we won't make it a habit." He squeezed her hand reassuringly. "There is word coming down from the council that we are going to be smuggling materials into the mountain villages. We might need to set up a base of operations to work out of, I'll work on that next. These missions won't be one or two nights and head back, the travel time will be extensive. So, you might be here for a week or more at a time."

"Really? So, we'll be spending more time together?" Vivian asked, excitement blooming in her heart.

"Yes. For all the council's warnings about getting too personal, they certainly set us up."

CHAPTER 23

Qing Qing had gained weight and color in his cheeks. Shen heard his soft voice dancing through the apartment, singing a joyful tune. "Freedom agrees with you, my old friend." Shen said, clapping his foster father on the back. "This is a good friend of mine. I wanted her to meet you."

Qing Qing turned to Vivian and took her hand, smiling and nodding his head.

"It is pleasant to meet you, sir," Vivian said in halting Mandarin. Qing Qing's eyes grew wide.

"She speaks Chinese? What is this? Where have you been hiding her, young man?" Qing Qing asked, standing to embrace Vivian animatedly.

"Yes, sir, I speak some. Not very well, though." Vivian stepped back and sat on a small footstool.

"Qing Qing, Shen has told me much about you."

Qing Qing's eyes squinched tightly as he burst into a proud grin. "God got a hold of Shen from birth. He has a blessed path. Now, tell me, what kind of friend are you, my dear?" He continued to grin knowingly at the two of them.

"No more of that, Qing Qing. She is just that, a friend," Shen chastised him, but his own heart stung from his lie. "Tell me what you are doing with your time, now that you can leave your house."

"I walk a lot. I go to the market. I do tai chi. I am cooking more, and I lead a small Bible study here. I go to the church services." Qing Qing stood and strutted across the room like a proud peacock. He assumed a tai chi position and guided his hands and feet through a series of movements fluidly. "Also, I know you two will make a wonderful couple. You are terrible liars, and your lies will hurt others one day. So stop lying to the old man." He spun on his heel and disappeared into another room.

Vivian's jaw dropped and she looked at Shen. He just shrugged and laughed. "What can I say, he's a character," he said in English. "Let's get you back. I am needed elsewhere soon."

An annoying buzz shook Shen from a light sleep. He blinked at the number before deciding to answer it.

"Yes?"

"You are exceptionally difficult to find. How are you doing?" A familiar voice echoed in Shen's ear.

"Ming Jie! I am well. How can I help you?" Shen asked, happy to hear from his old friend.

"My daughter has been asking for you, she says it's very important. I will send her number." Ming Jie replied. "Don't be a stranger, okay?" Click.

"What on earth could she want now?" Shen wondered aloud. A moment later his phone vibrated again. He took a deep breath and rolled over onto his back and staring at the thatched roof ceiling. Despite its rugged appearance, he rather liked this little hut in the middle of nowhere. Being a city kid, he couldn't get enough of nature.

With a sigh of resignation, he sent off a text and rolled off the bed to start his day. He gasped as the chilled air hit his skin, and he rubbed his arms vigorously to generate a little bit of warmth. He dressed quickly in the pale light coming through the dingy windows. Zipping up his heavy coat, he peered out to see fresh snow, and in the dim haze there wasn't a soul about.

His phone vibrated on the bed. "Must see you. Tomorrow

at 3pm." An address followed shortly after. It was the Beijing railway station. Why would she want to meet there and what was so important? His gut squirmed a bit. Something was off, but he had no idea what. His curiosity was far too great to simply not show up.

"Father, I have no idea what she's up to, but I have a bad feeling about this. Guide my footsteps until my work here is done." Shen breathed out a quick prayer. He sensed the Holy Spirit stirring inside him and felt certain that, whatever lay ahead, he was in good hands.

Shortly before 3:00 p.m. the following day, Shen peered out from behind a sales rack in the Beijing railway station. Dandan had arrived twenty minutes earlier and was pacing, looking around every few minutes. She was becoming more frantic with each minute that slid by with no sign of Shen. To the side a pair of men were tucked into the shadows. He could disappear into the crowd right now and leave her behind, but he'd have to change his burner phone again right away.

He slipped out from behind the rack to fall in behind a large businessman. He slid in behind Dandan silently and stood there until she turned around and face planted directly into his chest.

"Stop it!" Her shock melted the moment she realized she was speaking out loud. An exaggerated look spread across her heavily made-up face.

"Hello, handsome! I'm so glad you showed up! Why don't we go somewhere a little more private?" she purred, slipping her arm around his and attempting to guide him toward the shadows. He pulled free and stepped back

"I have only a few minutes before I catch my train. What is the emergency? How can I help?" He wondered if there was no emergency, yet here he was giving her the benefit of the doubt. He stepped back cautiously, every one of his senses screaming for him to run, to get out of there. A strong hand gripped his throat from behind as something sharp poked his neck.

"Don't you know that no one gets away from me," Dandan whispered harshly as darkness clouded Shen's vision.

"What about this one?" Livi asked, twirling in front of a large mirror. The turquoise dress flared out at the bottom dramatically. "I look like a British royal!"

"Wow! That dress is stunning! It does make you look a bit aristocratic. Seriously, that dress would be perfect for a beach wedding in the Bahamas but maybe not a winter wedding in Tennessee. You're a guest at the wedding, not the bride. Maybe you should wear something a little more toned down," Vivian remarked, noting the glare Livi threw her way.

Livi looked down, shrugged her shoulders, and slid the straps off her shoulders while holding onto to the cloth over her chest. "Yeah, you're right. I need something sparkly and vivid that doesn't take away from the bride."

Vivian stood from the chair provided for those waiting for the shopaholics and waited outside the dressing room.

"Will you pass me that burgundy velvet one?" Livi asked from behind the door.

While her sister changed outfits for the twentieth time Vivian browsed the racks. Her mind wandered to her own future. Would she have a wedding some day? Would it be with Shen? She shook her head to clear those random thoughts and bumped smack into what she thought was a rack. Then as she turned an *oomph* escaped the object.

"Oh, I'm so sorry." Vivian stepped back, sheepishly straightening the messy rack she'd bumped the stranger into.

"Hai xing! No harm done." The woman, who barely topped 5', swiped at her flawless black pantsuit. Her thick, black hair was pulled into a harsh bun high on her head, accentuating her angular features.

"You're Chinese," Vivian said, feeling silly for even saying her observation aloud.

"Yes, I am. Do you speak Mandarin?" The woman eyed her suspiciously and picked up a stray garment that had fallen from the rack.

"A little. Again, I apologize. My mind was somewhere else." Vivian turned back toward the dressing rooms to see her sister had still not emerged.

"Thinking, maybe, of a special young man? Shopping for a special occasion?" the woman asked nonchalantly.

"No, nothing like that, I was just browsing. My sister is doing the shopping." Something about the woman felt off. Vivian wasn't sure what, though.

"Would you like to have coffee when your sister is done? I haven't spoken to anyone in Mandarin in weeks, it would be nice to have a conversation."

Just then Livi burst through the door of her dressing room and did a dramatic spin. "Praise God! I think this is the one!" She gave another spin and stopped before the mirror to fluff and primp the dress. "Right? It's perfect, isn't it?"

"Oh, you are Christians. That is why you shouted a praise to a god? Right?" the woman asked, moving closer to Vivian.

Vivian fidgeted. What an odd thing for this stranger to say.

"Of course, we are. This is the Bible Belt, after all," Livi replied, giving the woman an incredulous look.

"I would like to hear more about this 'Bible belt', as you call it. Coffee on me?" the woman insisted.

Vivian grabbed a random dress from a rack and marched over to Livi, who raised an eyebrow in surprise. "Oh, you're trying one on. That's great, but I don't think chartreuse is the best color for you. It makes you look a little sickly."

Vivian looked down at the dress and just shook her head. "Well, you never know unless you try it on, right?" She grabbed Livi by the arm and hauled her into the dressing room.

"We'd love to have coffee with you. We'll be right out," Livi shouted as the door shut behind them.

"What are you doing? You don't know her," Vivian whispered harshly. "There's something strange about her, I don't like it. Why would she ask us about being Christian?" She helped Livi out of the velvet gown and tossed Livi's shirt onto the floor near her feet.

"Maybe they need Bibles?" Livi whispered back, shimmying into her jeans.

"Don't say anything about The Society. I can't put my finger on it, but something isn't right," Vivian warned.

"Obviously I won't say anything. Here, put the dress back on the hanger. Are you going to try that on or not?" Livi pointed to the rather ugly dress Vivian was still holding.

"No, it was my cover." Vivian said. Livi laughed and rolled her eyes, shoving her feet into her sneakers without bothering to tie them.

"Let's go have coffee with our new friend!" Livi announced as she bounced out of the dressing room, leaving Vivian to play pack mule and carry the goods.

CHAPTER 24

"Don't hurt my boyfriend!" The shrill words bounced around in Shen's throbbing head. "Please, I need him unharmed. I can't make out with him if he's beaten and bruised."

"You better not be calling *me* your boyfriend," Shen mumbled, trying to sit up, but his arms were pinned behind his back and something taut dug into his wrists.

"Oh good, you're awake!" Dandan squealed. The sound made his head pound even worse. "I'll order them to untie you if you promise to behave."

"I would never harm you and you know it," Shen growled, taking in his surroundings. They were in a hotel room, and he was sprawled across the king-sized bed. Dandan was sitting next to him, stroking one of his biceps. Several muscular men were spread throughout the room, leaning against the walls or perched on chairs.

"I kind of wish you would get a little more physical with me. I like it rough!" she chirped, giving his arm a little squeeze. "Will you promise to not run off right away?"

"How would I do that? You've got me tied up, drugged, and surrounded by goons." Shen noted that other than his pounding head and the pain in his wrists he seemed unharmed.

"Okay, untie him," Dandan ordered as she stood. A nearby goon whipped out a blade and menacingly smirked as he jerked on Shen's wrists. A moment later he pushed himself up to sit on the bed. He rubbed his chaffed wrists and hoped the pounding behind his eyes would abate quickly.

"Okay," Dandan started, pacing back and forth, her hands clasped behind her back, "I want in. Whatever it is you're into, I want in. I've been intrigued for years, and whatever it is seems to have stolen your heart. I alone get your heart. What has you so captivated? Is it drugs, smuggling, human trafficking? I couldn't pry a thing out of my father. I've even had him followed and I've come up with nothing. He just lives a boring, bland life. What is it? I can take it."

Shen laughed; he couldn't help himself. To think she thought she could have what she wanted by kidnapping him. He laughed even harder thinking about her involved with Bible smuggling. He felt a pang of guilt over that last image, realizing that God could use anyone. Even a rather spoiled rich girl.

Dandan looked hurt and his pang of guilt welled up to complete discomfort. "Oh, I'm sorry. I just can't believe you would have me kidnapped because you thought you that would work. What I do is not for me, but it is for the good of China and the world. It is bigger than one individual. I gave away my autonomy a long time ago, and simply live to serve. I smuggle Bibles." Shen stood up to stretch and the hired hands jumped up, ready to move in, but Dandan waved them back.

"You're joking? You expect me to believe that?" She sounded hurt.

"I know you might not believe me, but I am serious. I bring Bibles in from other countries. They are distributed to the underground churches" Shen rubbed his head, a faint pounding still bothering him.

"Do I have to be a Christian to be involved?" she whispered, her face scrunched up, deep in thought.

"We can go over the plan of salvation and I can set you up with a good mentor. Change who you serve, and you will find true peace and freedom."

"What if I don't want to change?" Anger, with a tinge of humiliation, spread across her face. "What if I want to work with and marry you without becoming a Christian?"

Shen eyed the door. The chain was hooked across the frame, and he'd lose precious seconds fumbling with it.

"I have made a commitment to not marry anyone who is not a Christian. I can take you to a fellow Christian. Right now." Shen offered, holding out his hand to her.

"Right now?" she asked, looking hopeful, as she took his hand.

"Alright, but don't try anything. The men have been told to keep you with me, and I don't want you to have broken legs." She snapped her fingers at the four men, and, as a group, they moved to leave the room.

The elevator ride was silent and Dandan used the time to feel up and down Shen's arms and pat his chest. His skin was crawling by the time they emerged in the lobby.

"Get the car," she ordered one of the men, and he strode out the door. Shen knew he needed to get outside while there were only three thugs left.

"Let's wait outside for him. My boss will not be pleased I've been delayed, so the quicker we can get in the car the better," he suggested, but Dandan hesitated. "I'll keep you warm," Shen pushed.

She brightened up at that and led the way out the front door. The moment they emerged Shen knew that they were only a few blocks from the train station. Traffic was heavy, and her hired car would have a hard time getting close. "Which way are you parked?" he asked. Dandan pointed to the left and they all started walking that direction.

Shen quickly slid his hand out from Dandan's, giving her an MP3 player with the Bible on it. "You want to know what captured my heart? Listen to this."

He took off in the opposite direction, running as fast as he could. He heard one person give chase, followed by several others in the distance.

He ran into the street, deciding that dodging cars would be easier than pedestrians. He jumped out of the way as a messenger bike swerved in front of him. Horns beeped, brakes squealed and the pounding feet behind him did not fall away. He aimed for a side alleyway and turned around to land a swift kick into his pursuer's gut. Shen's foot connected and the man doubled over, gasping for air. The thug's comrades were coming up quickly behind him. Shen jumped over the downed man and threw a punch into thug number two's throat. He dropped instantly, unable to suck enough air in. Goon number three landed a punch into Shen's left temple, momentarily blinding him. Shen dropped and did a leg sweep, bringing his opponent down just as the first guy pulled himself off the ground, still looking a little blue in the face. Shen sprang up and headbutted the man right in the nose. He heard a satisfying crunch. Shen took off into the shadows of the alleyway, intent on leaving the city for good.

"So, like, you're a diplomat?" Livi asked, tapping the side of her mocha absently with her long fingernails.

"No, I am a speaker. American churches invited me here to speak on the Three-Self Patriotic Movement in China and give updates on how the churches in China are doing. Where do you go to church, maybe they would want me to speak?" The woman had introduced herself as Ting when they'd finally sat down with their hot beverages, and now was telling the sisters her story.

Livi glanced in Vivian's direction. Vivian subtly shook her head. "Oh, Capital Revival, here in Nashville," Livi lied, taking a small sip from her cup. "So, what is going on with the churches in China?"

"Oh, they are doing wonderful. They are overloaded with ...What is the English word for the book?" Ting said vaguely, pausing to search for the right word.

"Bibles, you mean?" Livi prompted.

"Yes, those. We have more than we can use. We have so many

we are sending them back, in fact." Vivian's stomach lurched. Everything this woman was saying was wrong.

"I'll be right back; I want a muffin. Want anything?" Vivian pushed up from the table and paused.

"A yogurt would be great. Thanks, sis!" Livi turned back to their strange acquaintance.

"Do you have any siblings?"

Vivian slipped over to the line and whipped out her phone, dialing The Society. "This is Mrs. Kaminsky; how may I direct your call?"

"I need to speak with Mrs. Hayes, it's important. This is Vivian, by the way." She inched closer to the counter.

"She's on the other line right now, can I ... oh, she just hung up. Let me transfer you." Before Vivian could thank her, the line was ringing.

"Gloria Hayes, how may I serve you?"

"Mrs. Hayes, it's Vivian. Livi and I met a suspicious woman from China. She's claiming she was sent here to bring an update on the churches there," Vivian whispered.

"What do you mean 'claiming'?" Mrs. Hayes sounded quite concerned.

"She says she was invited by American churches to represent the Three-Self Church and that they don't need more Bibles, that they have so many they're sending them back."

"Is Livi with her now? See if you can get her card or contact information, and I'll have it investigated. But more importantly, get Livi and get out of there. Do you want me to send a driver?" Mrs. Hayes's concern had bloomed into full-fledged mama bear mode.

"No, I'll get her right away. And thank you, Mrs. Hayes."

"No, thank you, Vivian, for calling me." Vivian left the line that had backed up behind her and popped up next to Livi.

"Where's the food?" Livi looked ready to eat her paper coffee cup.

"Oh, I'm sorry, but I just talked to Dad. He needs us to pick Evan up from practice." Vivian said, using their private sister code they used to get out of awkward conversations with creepy guys. As Livi stood Vivian turned to Ting, “Do you have a business card I can pass on to our Pastor? Maybe the church would like you to come speak.”

Ting handed her a card with a smile. She didn’t seem suspicious of their hasty exit, but just to be safe, Vivian took them on a long and winding path to the car.

“What was that all about?” Livi finally asked, breathlessly flopping into the passenger seat.

“There was something very off about that woman. Did you notice she said ‘a praise to a god.’ rather than ‘praise to God’ as in the God, not just any ol’ god? We need to get this card over to The Society.” With that, the girls abandoned their afternoon mani/pedi plans.

***

“We’re running her info now, girls. We’ve come to realize that it’s possible that hostile governments might try to infiltrate us. She’s digging for information. Of all places in America to look, why Nashville? There are much bigger cities to operate out of. That’s one reason we chose Nashville as our home base, it seemed less conspicuous. Something must’ve tipped them off.” Mrs. Hayes was pacing about in her office.

“They have my real identity and can easily search for my departure city. I always depart from Nashville. Don’t we all depart from here?” Vivian surmised, nervously tugging on her long braid.

“Yes, you’re right. All our operatives leave from here. That could be it but I am wondering if something keeps happening on the other side of the pond that has them looking here. We’ll keep looking.” Mrs. Hayes looked concerned.

“Going forward, we will be flying out from other cities,” Mrs. Hayes decided. A knock interrupted them, and the door pushed open. A short, lean man with dark brown hair entered holding a laptop. As he came in, competing musical jingles rang through the room. He tapped his watch to silence one noise then pulled out a phone to quiet another.

"I found it! She's a Chinese plant. She is, indeed, connected with the Three-Self Church, but not in the capacity she claims." He stood up and crossed his arms proudly, beaming at his handiwork. He looked at each of them in turn and waved towards the laptop.

"Let me see," Livi said, nudging Vivian aside. "Wow, she is part of the MSS."

Vivian looked confused, her glance darting between Livi and the young man.

"They're the Chinese FBI, more or less." The young man said.

"She's been everywhere. How long as she been here, though?" Livi looked at the man. Color rushed up his cheeks as he moved in next to her and tapped away on the keyboard for a moment.

"Six weeks. At least, that's when she flew into Nashville," he said, looking up into Livi's eyes. He blushed again and cleared his throat before taking a small step back. Vivian tried not to smile, but the man's discomfort around her beautiful sister was rather cute.

"Well, let's have her tailed. I want to know what churches she's been snooping around in and where she's going next. I need to know how close they," Mrs. Hayes ordered. "Thanks, Jack, Good work." She turned to the sisters. "Alright, ladies, lay low and we'll keep you updated." Mrs. Hayes's phone rang, and she answered it while Jack gathered his laptop, his phone and watch jingling in unison, again.

"You have impeccable timing, sir," Mrs. Hayes was saying. Vivian turned to grab her purse and go when Mrs. Hayes snapped her fingers. Three heads turned to look back at her. She was pointing at Vivian. "You, come here. Give him an update. Keep it succinct." She held out the phone to Vivian.

Vivian nervously took the phone, figuring it was her father checking in. "Hello?"

"Well, hello yourself." Shen's voice filled her ear and her heart jumped.

"Update, okay, there is a Chinese official snooping around here. We're not sure how close they are to us, but they are in the ballpark. We'll know more soon." Vivian hoped that was succinct enough for Mrs. Hayes, who was chatting with Jack and Livi near the door. Jack was ogling Livi like a lovesick puppy.

"I have an update, too. Do you remember Chengdu? Where we stayed with my friend's daughter? Well, our hostess is trying to cause some trouble. She had me kidnapped, drugged, and tied up." Vivian gasped but he plowed on. "I'm fine. I've changed numbers again and will call you soon."

"How can you say that and act like it was no big deal. That's a big deal!" Vivian practically shouted at the phone. Mrs. Hayes patted Jack on the back and made her way back to her desk. "Be careful. Here's Mrs. Hayes." Vivian handed the phone off and turned away before Mrs. Hayes could see the tears threatening to spill over.

"Let's go, Livi." She snagged her sister on the way out, leaving poor Jack looking longingly after them.

"What was that all about?" Livi asked, jogging to keep up.

"Um, just an unexpected reappearance of a very annoying... never mind. Let's just go home. We need to get your dress hung up before it starts to wrinkle."

"He was cute, wasn't he?" Livi said, dreamily.

"Who?" Vivian looked behind them.

"Jack, silly! Do you think he'd go to the wedding as my plus one? Maybe Mrs. Kaminsky could give me his number or point me to his office. I haven't had a good date since what's-his-name stood me up." Livi droned on, distracted by her fantasy wedding date.

"You're hopeless!" Vivian laughed, running to the car and leaving Livi behind to dream walk the rest of the way.

CHAPTER 25

"Twenty-four bags, one thousand Bibles. That is one heavy load," Shen remarked as he slammed the back hatch of the car.

Vivian smiled at him, butterflies in her stomach at the opportunity to spend two weeks together. "Let's hit the road, Jack!"

"Jack the tech guy?" Shen looked quizzically at her.

"No!" Vivian laughed.

"You Americans." Shen chuckled to himself and jumped in the driver's seat.

Their priority for this trip was to avoid detection and deliver the Bibles, tracks, flannel graphs, and other teaching materials to a church in rural China. Shen sped away from the border as if someone were chasing them.

"Are you alright? You seem anxious." Vivian was concerned about him since he admitted he'd been kidnapped.

"Yes, I'm alright, I just want to get these Bibles out of our hands. It's safer that way."

"What's safer?" Vivian pushed.

"You, to be honest. I already have a huge target painted on my back, and I don't want you getting hurt. After that jerk slapped you, I felt helpless, but after, getting kidnapped and overpowered... Well, I realized this isn't the best job for you. I'm wondering if they should send you somewhere safer."

Vivian's heart faltered before beating wildly. "You don't want to be partnered with me?" Her voice cracked on the last word.

"It's not about that. Of course, I like working with you, but your safety is important. We already know they're getting close to the Society, and that might be linked to our communication. What if we've put the whole thing in jeopardy? It's nothing personal." Shen's eyes never left the road and his fingers gripped the steering wheel like vices.

Vivian swallowed hard. He said it was nothing personal, but it should be personal. "Are you going back on what you said in Hawaii? On what you've been saying all along? If you're changing your mind, you should tell me."

"No. I just need to know you're safe. I am so distracted thinking about your safety that I'm compromising the mission."

"So, I'm a distraction." The realization hit Vivian like a sledgehammer. Her throat tightened up and she had to turn away to keep from bawling.

"You are not a distraction, but it is distracting to worry constantly. Let's just get this job done, and then we'll figure things out." Shen awkwardly patted Vivian's hand but made no effort to take it in his own. He seemed to be distancing himself from her, first emotionally and now physically. Maybe it was for the best to figure this out now, before they got in any deeper.

The long drive was unbearably quiet. Vivian caught herself wanting to tell him insignificant things going on in her life – everything from Livi's surprising interest in the tech nerd, to the ribbon Evan won for his science fair project. Instead, she bit her lip and held it all in. Maybe he was right. They'd been lying to everyone for months. It was bound to catch up with them.

Shen had grabbed her bag and was standing at the door to a small, ramshackle house. Inside the small abode a group of people pushed their way toward her. Curious faces were inches from hers. Their hands touched her cheeks, still a little wet from those pesky tears.

Shen laid one of the Bibles down on the table, the adults turned away from Vivian and took turns holding it up in awe. The curious children continued to huddle close her. A middle-aged man opened it and began reading in a dialect of Chinese she did not understand. Within minutes the entire group was crying. They lifted their hands into the air and began to sing an eerie, haunting melody. Vivian stared at the group in awe. When the man stopped reading and gently set the Bible back on the table, the room grew quiet.

"Thank you for bringing this. We are overcome with gratefulness. We have never had a Bible in our own language before and we are overwhelmed by God's love. Why do you risk everything to bring this to us? I cannot believe you spend all this money to print this and bring it here, halfway around the world," the man spoke to Vivian and Shen.

"We do it because Jesus loves you," Shen said, then excused himself outside. Their hostess directed Vivian deeper into the small home, taking her bag and exchanging it for a cup of tea.

The growing distance between them over their two weeks together was painful, not just to her throbbing heart, but to her racing mind as well. Holding her breath, reached out and laid her hand carefully on Shen's arm as he drove. She felt him stiffen and suck in his breath. "Is this okay?" she asked, risking leaving her hand there.

He groaned and laid his head back against the head rest, but he didn't ask her to move her hand. "This so hard," he finally said.

Her heart plunged into her stomach, and she removed her hand, dropping it heavily into her lap. "Sorry, I just miss you. I miss us. I'm so confused. You keep saying we're alright but you're distancing yourself from me. It hurts."

Shen sighed heavily and glanced over at her. "I'm confused right now, okay? Can you please give me time to figure out what's going on in my heart? I don't want to end things. I care about you, but I wonder if we should take a break. At least until I can make sense of the storm inside of me. Can you please be patient?

I don't want you to give up on me."

"Yes, I can do that. Wake me when we get there." She turned away and closed her eyes, her heart breaking a little more.

With only a few bags left, Shen navigated the car behind a building on the outskirts of a larger village. A red cross was painted on the rear door of the otherwise plain building. Shen looked around uneasily. This was the delivery place, but usually underground churches, even ones using warehouses, didn't advertise their location with adornments like crosses. He parked the car but left it running.

"Stay here," he ordered with a sigh. He was an absolute mess inside. He steeled himself and pushed the door to the warehouse open. He paused in the doorway, waiting for his eyes to adjust, the only light inside of the building peeked in through the open door. The echo of a car door closing snapped him to attention. Shen cast Vivian an exasperated look. "I told you to stay in the car," he said in English. She ignored him and stepped inside.

"Welcome, welcome, welcome. I am pleased, pleased, pleased, to meet you," a spindly little man said, taking Vivian by the hand and pulling her deeper into the building. Shen followed them at a distance, looking around, nervous they were going to get jumped. He noticed the deep shadows and noted that their only exit was the door they'd come in.

"Follow me, follow me, follow me." Shen shook his head at the crazy old man. "You may place the items there. What are they exactly?" the man asked. That was odd, given that the man was supposed to be a pastor.

"Didn't you specifically request these items?"

"Oh yes, silly me. My memory is not what it used to be. Forgive an old man and remind me." His evasiveness gave Shen pause, but the small man he stepped up and unzipped the two bags before Shen could answer.

"Oh, what have we here?" the man repeated. What was he

fishing for?

Vivian stood off to the side, looking into the distant gloom. She slowly backed up towards Shen and bumped into him. "Um, we have a problem," she remarked in English. His head snapped up to see the shadows moving slowly toward them.

The old man cackled maniacally and laid the contents on the table. Bibles in one pile, flannel graphs in another, tracts in a third.

"Do you admit to smuggling illegal items into our good country?" a lean, uniformed woman asked. "We admit nothing. This man is crazy." Shen said, pulling Vivian behind him.

The woman snapped her fingers and two men grabbed Vivian from her hiding place. "You are a foreigner. Why should I not send both of you to a distant prison to live out your lives smashing rocks and learning to praise our great government?"

Shen prayed silently, *Lord soften her heart. I seek your intervention. Protect Vivian at all costs.*

"She's just a tourist and was along for the ride. I think we must have made a wrong turn. I don't think this is the right place. We'll just take our stuff and go. Better yet, maybe you should take it. Come on, let's go," Shen stumbled over his words, reaching for Vivian.

"Not so fast, young man. Don't you find it odd that we knew you'd be here? We've been monitoring your communications for months. Lover's lose perspective. Let's see what we have here." She smiled coyly and picked up a Bible, flipped through it and tossed it back onto the table. She moved onto the flannel boards, running her fingers over the soft surface. Lastly, she picked up a Bible tract and deliberately tore it apart in front of them. She threw the shreds of paper into the air. Shen's heart broke at the hopelessness he could see lurking behind the woman's empty eyes.

"I am stuck out here in the middle of nowhere. I don't even get paid much to babysit these crazies. Let's say, I let you go for twelve thousand yuan, each."

Shen laughed out loud. "You can't be serious. You know that

no one around here carries that kind of money."

"I am very serious. Aren't I?" The woman looked from one man to the other. They nodded their heads in agreement.

"I have three thousand yuan to pay your fine, but I take these with me." Shen lifted a flannel board. "No one will know how to use them unless they've been taught the lessons that go with them. They are useless without that."

"Well then if they are useless..." The woman casually picked up another board and snapped it in two, "Then I guess I will just get rid of them."

"Three thousand and you can go." She turned away, dropping the broken boards on the ground with a clatter. Shen dug into his pocket and pulled out the money, and the men eagerly snatched the bribe. Shen yanked Vivian toward the door and nearly dragged her to the car.

"Why couldn't you just listen and stay in the car?" Shen chastised her, closing her door against the argument he knew was coming. When he opened the driver's side to get him the look of hurt on her face gave him pause.

"I came with you because we're still a team. You don't have to treat me like a child." She looked away as the crazy old man came running out of the building, waving something in the air.

"Here, here, here, this was my take." Shen grabbed the flannel boards. "You might want to find out who has the loose, loose, loose lips."

"I hope you're happy. Those Bibles will be burned. They could have changed someone's life." Shen leveled a dark look at the man.

"No, no, no. She'll sell them on the black market because the Word of God is too valuable. Must make money, money, money!" He cackled as he walked away.

Shen blinked, then jumped into the car when an officer appeared out the back door. He tossed the boards into the back and tore out of town. When they passed the last house along the dusty lane, he started laughing.

"Have you gone crazy?" Vivian's eyebrows creased in concern.

"The Bibles will get where they need to go. God will see to that. The people might have to pay a lot for them, but at least they will be used. Only God can do that!" Shen focused on driving, despite his moment of laughter his face was back to stoic and brooding.

CHAPTER 26

"Vivian, are you listening?" Livi snapped her fingers in front of Vivian's face, waiting until her sister looked up. "Like I was saying. There I was in customs, setting my carry-on on the table. It was filled with Bible tracts. The checked bags were on the floor next to me. The customs lady kept pulling out Bible tracts and putting them on the table. When she dug for more, I would knock them onto the floor and stuff them into the larger pieces of luggage. My contact later told me that there was a customs agent behind me the whole time, watching and laughing. But he never told the woman! Isn't that funny?"

"Yeah, that's just like God," Vivian said passively. She felt empty, like she was floating through space with nothing to anchor her down. Maybe The Society was right in saying that she and Shen were too attached. Because being detached hurt a lot.

"You okay? You've been awfully quiet since you got back from your last trip. Trouble in paradise? Normally when you get back from seeing lover boy, you're all smiles." Livi put the car in park outside the mansion where their father preached.

"Don't call him lover boy. He is not my lover, my boyfriend, nothing," Vivian said bitterly.

"Whoa! I was only playing around. Do you want to talk about it?" Livi sounded far more serious than normal. Vivian looked at her in confusion.

"Wait, what?"

"Stop it! I'm serious. You listen to me all the time. I don't mind doing that for you. Actually, I'd really like to." Livi looked hurt.

"Ah, Livs, I'm sorry, I'm just tense. I appreciate that you've been a bit more serious and less dramatic lately. Why the change?" The girls unbuckled and made their way into the spacious home.

"Well, Jack and I have been seeing a lot of each other and I suppose he's rubbing off on me. He's trying to teach me the cyber security stuff, but it's way over my head," Livi admitted as they passed by a grand staircase.

"Nothing new there, technology has never been your forte. But I'm glad it's going well between you two, Livi. He's awfully adorable when he gazes at you with puppy dog eyes!" Vivian laughed.

"Stop it! Seriously!" Livi waved at Vivian and left to go up front to sing with the worship team. Vivian had no desire to be up front, nor did she really have the talent. Livi was always the attention getter and the talented one. Although Evan was coming up quickly in his own right, Vivian mused. While he wanted to be a preacher like their father, he also had a love for science, and sports, and, how could she forget, video games. She smiled to herself and slumped into a seat near the back.

Samuel broke away from a few parishioners and made his way to Vivian's side. After a quick side squeeze, he knelt next to her. "Everything alright? You've been extra quiet, almost moody, even. It's odd having Livi being the even keeled one this week. Usually, she's in charge of all of the drama."

"I'm alright, I just have a lot on my mind. Mrs. Hayes told me she wants to see me in the morning, and I have a feeling it's not good news." Vivian looked into the depths of her father's coal-black eyes, oh, how she loved this man. He rubbed her back gently.

"Would you like me to drive you there? If not, my shoulder is always available." He offered what he could.

"No, it's alright, I'll go by myself, but I might take you up on that shoulder offer after!" Vivian cracked a strained smile and gave her dad another side squeeze before he moved up front to join the worship team. Even her father was a great singer. Vivian only halfheartedly sang, her heart ready to crumble to pieces, knowing what tomorrow would likely bring.

Livi plopped down next to her and elbowed her, nodding toward their father on the pulpit, "Pay attention.".

"God desires to have a rock-solid relationship with us but, we get in our own way by letting sin into our lives. Take lying, for example. Dishonesty has been called half-truths or little white lies by the world. But there is nothing little about deceit. Lying can be addictive and will, perhaps, birth further sin. Lying kills your dignity. You chip away at your morals and the very essence of who you are as a person becoming a shadow of your true self. When your reality is so distorted do you even know who you are anymore? Lying kills our relationships with others. It creates disunity. How can the family of God be unified if lies are causing division? Proverbs12:22 tells us that "The Lord detests lying lips, but he delights in those who tell the truth." Is He delighting in you today?"

Vivian felt like she'd been slapped. She stood and squeezed by a confused Livi and left the theater-turned-church to pull out her cell phone. Swiftly coursing through her contacts, she found Mrs. Hayes's number and waited for her to pick up.

"Hi, it's Vivian. Can I see you now? I don't want to wait. I think I know what it is anyway and don't want to put this off." Arrangements made, she slipped back in to sing the final song and see that Livi had a ride home. She was going to face the music.

"Why so sad, son?" Qing Qing was doing his Tai Chi in the tiny space in front of the sofa. "Did she break up with you?" Shen merely lifted his head a bit before dropping it back down.

"No, I broke up with her," he mumbled.

"Doesn't look like that was wise. You're one sick pup." Qing Qing bent over and slid off his slipper, and thwacked Shen hard on the rear with a loud slap. Shen bolted off the sofa and hit the bathroom. He emerged a few minutes later, his face still an interesting shade of green.

"Why are you doing this?" Qing Qing asked, puttering about in the kitchen, making a pot of tea for the two of them. "Obviously, you are lovesick. Why ignore that?"

"You wouldn't understand," Shen muttered glumly, taking the proffered cup.

"Try me," Qing Qing, crossing his arms over his chest.

"She's a major target because of me. She might've been followed back to America. The CCP has her name, travel patterns, facial features downloaded into the surveillance system. It's too dangerous for her. It's like that whole butterfly analogy."

"Pretend I'm dumb and don't know what analogy that is."

"The one where if you love something, you let it go. If it comes back to you, it's yours forever. If it doesn't, then it was never meant to be."

"That's stupid," Qing Qing grunted, blowing on his tea. "A tree whose branches break grows new branches. It does not look for the branch that fell away."

"See, I told you that you'd never understand."

"You think I don't understand what it's like to love someone so much that you don't want to see them get hurt, so you refuse to do anything? Were you not paying attention at all in Beijing?" Qing Qing asked, lifting an eyebrow at Shen.

"Okay, so you understand, but there's a difference between our situations." He muttered resentfully.

"Really, son, what's that?"

"Well, you shut down out of fear. I'm ending things out of concern for her personal safety," he said defensively.

"Concern and fear are just two different words for the same thing." Qing Qing reflected, leaning back against the wall. "Seems to me that you're just as afraid, but you are hiding behind the word love. If you really love her, you'll stop acting like her big brother, and start acting like her partner."

Qing Qing shuffled off into the back room, leaving Shen to his thoughts. Shen moaned and curled up again. What had he done?"

Gloria Hayes sat on a soft chair in her spacious office. Vivian sat across from her, silent tears coursing down her tanned cheeks.

"Darling, I know you are angry right now, but his heart is in the right place. I still wonder if you two got too close. Are you in love with him?" Mrs. Hayes asked, her eyes narrowed at Vivian.

"Yeah, I think I am." Vivian hesitated, eyes downcast. "I've been lying to you for a long time."

"Well, that certainly changes things. I will have to bring this to the board. Since your partnership has ended, I don't think it would be wise to send you back into the field. The deceit must be reckoned with. Until then you will help the team in charge of disguises and smuggling equipment. Your field experience will be helpful; Mrs. Kaminski will help you schedule that. There is also the matter of that woman, Ting. We need to know how much she knows about The Society. You will be helping us with that. Since she's already contacted you, it makes sense to have you and Livi to investigate."

Despite her heavy heart, Vivian was interested. "What would we have to do? Just get her to talk?"

"Exactly. We need to find out what she knows. American contacts, Chinese contacts, they are sniffing right in our backyard. You would be wired and have a team on the ground. Are you feeling up for that?"

"Yes, I would like to help, and stay busy." Vivian stood to leave.

"Vivian," Gloria called after her, "While I care for you, I am very disappointed in your actions. I do forgive you, though. I will call you back in when the council and I have had a chance to discuss things."

Vivian's eyes were still downcast when she nodded, whispering a quiet "thank you" as she closed the door behind her.

CHAPTER 27

Cool, crisp air hit Shen's face as he pulled a donkey along behind him. The obstinate beast was loaded with bags and boxes of Bibles he'd picked up from the mine along the Mongolian border. The donkey pulled back on its lead and brayed loudly, forcing Shen to pause again. He loved nature, but not this mode of transportation. They argued back. Cars didn't.

Fields that lay silent for the winter spread before him, with, dark, heavy mountains looming in the distance. This new position suited him well. He could stay out of the cities, still move Bibles, and be by himself. Seeing God in nature never failed to heal. Shen tugged harder on the lead and forced the donkey forward. He still had hours before he'd reach his destination. The only negative with all this solitude were the thoughts of Vivian that plagued his mind."

He turned his thoughts to the sound of the dry, brittle grass crunching underneath his boots, instead of the aching hole in his heart. Crunch, crunch, crunch. The donkey's hooves stomped in irritation. A grating sound, mostly hidden in the wind, caught his attention.

Behind him, a dust cloud moved toward him. He squinted and tilted his head. A car was coming up fast. He continued to pull on the donkey and turned toward the mountains. He would deal with it if they stopped. Of course, they did.

A man, who appeared to be in his fifties, rolled down the crank style window of an ancient work truck. He spoke briskly, seeming to switch dialects and languages every few words, trying to figure out what Shen would understand. Shen shook his head apologetically, and the man rubbed a hand over his balding head and said, "How about this one?" in the Beijing dialect.

"Ah, that I understand." Shen said. The man's face lit up with a broad, toothy smile.

"Ah, good! Would you like a ride, friend? Where are you going?"

"Oh, thank you, but I'll be fine. The mountains are my aim." Shen turned away and started walking again, dragging the donkey behind him. The truck inched forward, keeping pace with him.

"The donkey can go in the back. It's mostly empty, just a few crates. The mountains are a big target!" Shen thought about it a moment and decided the company would keep his mind from turning to her better than listening to his crunching steps on the dry prairie grass.

"Alright. But I don't want to be a burden."

"No, not a burden. I am sure this trip will bless both of us!" His eyes twinkled brightly with amusement. They worked together to put the bags and boxes in the truck, then rigged up a board to the tailgate as a makeshift ramp. By the time they hefted the stubborn donkey into the truck, they were both sweating, despite the brisk air.

In the cab the man had a thermos of hot tea, steamed buns, and dried meat. Shen donated a roll of cold steamed rice and seaweed cakes, and they had a small feast as they drove carefully toward the distant mountains. They ate in companionable silence for a while before the driver piped up curiously.

"So, what is your name?" Shen asked, as they bumped across the prairie together in the rickety Russian truck.

"Call me Brother Jon. I have all but forgotten my birth name. I suppose the same might be the same for you." Brother Jon glanced at Shen and smiled his toothy grin.

"Yes, but it is what the Americans call a 'necessary evil'. A detail we cannot escape."

"So, what is someone from Beijing doing out here?" He motioned to the vast wilderness surrounding them.

"I wonder the same thing about you," Shen replied, munching on a bit of food.

"I am glad you wondered that." He laughed and patted Shen on the shoulder. "I deliver good news to these rural communities. It is the best part of my life." He focused on picking his path through the grassy fields, to not dislodge the donkey in the back.

"What good news are you bringing today?" Shen eyed him, looking for any hint that maybe this was a brother in arms.

"Oh, the absolute best news in the world. Unless you have any better news." The man was as evasive as Shen had just tried to be moments earlier.

"The only good news I know involves deep love and a tree," Shen said, being as clear as dared.

"Oh, yes, the world's greatest love, and that love that hung on a tree, and now lives in those that believe. I see now, friend, why you are here. I wonder if we have the same destination?" He grinned another toothy grin and bobbed his head. "It is so nice to meet another Christian on the road. Surely the Lord blessed us when he put us on this path together. Come you must tell me of what God has done in your life!"

Several hours later they dragged the donkey down the makeshift ramp and handed it off to a young lad covered in ragged clothes and dirt. They were hurried into a mud hut with a thatched roof, one of several homes clumped together. The donkey was led to a lean-to off the side.

They were welcomed in with warm embraces and directed to sit around a wood burning stove on small stools. The dirt floor was covered with grass mats, likely woven from the long grasses of the prairie they'd driven through. Shen accepted a cup of tea and unzipped his coat a bit. His new friend spoke animatedly to their hosts in a dialect with which Shen was unfamiliar.

The chance-met driver turned to Shen. "They ask if your

contact is someone whose name means the color blue?"

"Yes, it is," Shen replied. "Do they know him?" The driver relayed the question and their heads bobbed vigorously.

"Well, then, this is fortuitous, isn't it?"

"Yes, it is. They say they can keep the items here and will assist him in dispersing them." The man clapped his hands together, smiling widely. "Now that business is cared for, let us turn to other things. Brother, tell me how you came to deliver this good news and how you, from Beijing, come to be so far out here?" More cups of tea were shoved into their hands.

Shen shifted nervously. He shared an abbreviated version of his childhood in Beijing and how he had partnered with foreigners to share the Gospel. The man listened intently and nodded before speaking in turn.

"My family is from Beijing. My Nai Nai and brother still live there. My parents are gone now, and they are the only family I have left. I tried to find them, but the building was torn down last time I visited. I have no idea where they are." He smiled sadly at his reflection in his cup. Shen shifted nervously, again.

"What is your brother's name? Where was this building?"

"An Chen is my brother's name, he takes care of Nai Nai. I think she's alright, she's too stubborn to die. I have prayed for her salvation for years. An Chen's as well. She says her dead relatives have never let her down."

Shen tried to swallow the lump in his throat, but it was unyielding. "I think I know your Nai Nai and brother. And I know where they are living."

The man's face lit up. "How do you know them? The city is so large."

"You said this meeting would result in many blessings," Shen reminded him. "I moved An Chen and Nai Nai myself. The building was scheduled to be torn down, so I found them a street level place with a garden. Nai Nai sits in the sun, blind eyes to the sky, soaking it all in. I left her with an audio Bible in her own dialect. I recorded the entire thing myself."

"Oh! That is wonderful news! We will pray, then, for her

salvation. Will you take me to her? I love serving the rural communities, but I do miss them desperately."

"I can't, but I can give you the address," Shen replied. "I change numbers often, though, so maybe you should give me your contact information." The man grabbed Shen's hands and thanked him profusely, before pulling him into a tight hug. Shen's heavy heart felt a little lighter that night.

Vivian smoothed her black slacks one more time, despite not one wrinkle marring the smooth fabric. She absently tapped a red high-heeled foot on the tile floor. Soft jazz floated through the air, mixing with the subtle hum of voices.

"Stop fidgeting!" Livi smacked her gently on the arm and tilted her head toward the thin Asian woman coming toward them. Ting wore an impeccable suit with a traditional Chinese jade necklace.

"Ting, we're so glad you could meet with us. Thank you for coming." Livi extended her hand to grasp the woman's hand tightly.

"Yes, you are welcome," she said, awkwardly extracting her hand from Livi's exuberant grip. "Who is this?" She motioned to the man sitting with them.

"This is Mat. He's a pastor here in the 'Ville and is all up on the know-how, of both missions work in other countries, and the many churches here that might want you to come speak." Livi introduced Ting to the tall, broad shouldered man that Mrs. Hayes had insisted join them for this meeting. He had a distinct South American look to him, but Vivian hadn't asked him where he was from. Everything about him said deadly, from his fierce eyes to the ropes of muscle that ran down his arms and legs. He was massive.

Ting silently appraised him as he pulled a chair out for her to sit in. He took his place next to Ting with Livi and Vivian across from them. Vivian quietly flagged down a waitress, placed an order for snacks and a water for Ting and turned back to their guest.

"Well, so, you had said before you were here to give updates to the American churches. Is that right?" Livi asked, feigning interest.

"Yes, the Three Self Church is flourishing in China, with the blessing of our government and their open-armed policies for such religion," Ting explained, turning to Mat. "You want me to come speak to your church? There is more to update, of course, I really want to get to know all these organizations that send these religious materials."

Mat hiked an eyebrow up. He seemed unconvinced but snapped into his role. "Yes, we actually are a whole network of churches. We broadcast across the country, so your message would reach well past Nashville." Ting perked up at this news. She angled herself toward Mat, nodding for him to continue. "We know you must have been here for a long while, and it takes so much time to speak to each church one at a time. Would this be beneficial for you?"

"Oh yes, most definitely," Ting enthused.

"How much longer do you have here before you go back home?" Mat asked, taking a sip of his black coffee.

"I should be leaving soon."

"You must miss it. How many churches have you visited so far?" Mat probed.

"Many." She wasn't letting anything out easily.

"What was your favorite place?" Mat asked, popping a chip into his mouth and sitting back to relax a bit.

"California, I liked the best. Many people and good weather." Mat nodded, encouraging her to keep going. "The churches there were receptive to my information and have agreed to stop sending Bibles."

"You know, Ting, it would be very helpful to me to have a list of the churches you've visited," Mat suggested. Ting scrunched her eyebrows, worry lines creasing her forehead. "That way I know who to send the broadcast too. We can make sure to hit all the churches you haven't been to yet."

"Yes, what you say has merit. Can you excuse me a moment?" Ting stood, grabbed her purse and headed off to the back of the building.

Vivian followed behind her; trying to remain stealthy, she moved into the shadow of a pillar between her and Ting. Ting was already putting a phone to her ear and quickly spoke.

"Silent crane," she said in Mandarin. Was that a code word? "I have infiltrated a group of them. The two women match the database, I believe them to be the sisters. They also brought along a bodyguard posing as a pastor, though I did not recognize him. They are asking for a list of churches I have visited, would you put together something for me?" There was a pause before she continued. "Alright, I will send him the list. The database appears to be accurate from our research here. I'll be returning in one week to implement it into the face recognition software."

Vivian slid further behind the pillar, deeper into the shadows, as Ting swept by her. Vivian peeked around the pillar to see that back at the table she had become engrossed in Mat, again. Vivian made her way back to the table the long way.

"Did you find the restroom?" Livi asked, as Vivian rejoined the small group.

"Yes, thanks." She slid into her chair. "Are there any other Chinese contacts here in the US that would be beneficial for us to connect with, Ting?" Vivian asked, tilting her head waiting for an answer.

"Vivian has a good idea, Ting," Mat said, nodding toward Vivian. Ting finally looked over at her and gave her a cursory glance.

"And what is that?"

"Are there any other Chinese contacts here in the US that would be beneficial for us to connect with?" Vivian repeated.

"Oh, that would be very helpful, indeed. We could cover twice as much ground with that information." Mat was pleased with the suggestion. He smiled encouragingly at Ting.

"If it will help then, yes, I will send you that with the list of churches." Ting tapped away on her phone, adding that to the information to send to Mat.

"Well, thank you for the help. Ladies, why don't we be going? I have a sermon to finish for Sunday." Mat stood and shook Ting's hand, then held his arm out to Vivian and Livi to invite them to walk ahead of him.

CHAPTER 28

"So, brother-in-arms, what pulls your heart so?" Shen's friend said no more but seemed to wait patiently for him to answer. His friend knew him too well and it was difficult to hide anything from him.

"I don't know what you mean," Shen replied uneasily to Brother Jon.

"I know the life we have chosen is one of regrets, but your heart is weighed down more than it should be. Your very soul is screaming out to me."

Shen sighed heavily, his throat tightening uncomfortably. "Yes, regrets. They do us no good, though, to relive, so why bother? We cannot change our course. This is the life we have chosen." Shen looked out the window at the wind-whipped plains.

"God is not out to punish us for this life we live. There is much healing in speaking your regrets," Brother Jon said gently.

"My regret is kind, compassionate, loving, and very serious. She grew into a woman at a young age, and it haunts her. I can see the ghost of her regrets in her eyes, and I am nearly held under a spell when I look into those deep, dark eyes. They remind me that I am not a dead man. I want to be alive again. I don't want to resurrect the wreckage of my past, but I dream of a future life with her," Shen spilled, clearing his throat as emotion made it thicker.

"Well, that was very eloquent. The influence she has over

you is very powerful. Is God leading you to her?"

"I thought so, but then I feared for her safety and thought it best to end it. I will never see her again."

"Was she as concerned about her safety as you were?" Brother Jon probed gently.

Shen laughed bitterly. "No, never. She was never worried about that."

"So, she knew what she signed up for and was willing to accept whatever hand God allowed to come against her?"

"Yes," Shen whispered, his heart a complete mess.

"And you pushed her away to keep her safe?"

"Something like that."

"Well, my friend, was that God telling you to, or did the fear get too great for you? God can make every giant we come up against fall. He can set our feet on solid ground and break through every wall the evil one erects. Yet, you pushed her away out of fear?" Shen didn't bother answering. Brother Jon gripped his shoulder. "I don't have the answers, and that's alright, but we can search together and get her back. I will not run away and abandon you. I can feel your heartache. We will find my Nai Nai and Uncle, and this woman who touches you so deeply."

"We found the leak. Well, not so much a leak as a laser beam pointing right back toward you, Vivian." Mrs. Hayes said pointedly, a fierce look on her face.

Vivian sat up straighter and took a deep breath, ready to take responsibility for her actions.

"It was the communications between you and Shen that tipped off the Chinese government. They noticed it centralized around Nashville and that made them suspicious enough to dig further. They got real close to our organization because of dishonesty. They have had an agent tracking Shen for months. The board has voted to put you and Shen both on leave. However, because time is of the essence we will require your help one more time. Is there anything you would like to add?" Mrs. Hayes tapped her fingers on the conference table.

"I am so very sorry for the deceit. I didn't realize how much it was compromising my integrity. I accept full responsibility for my choices."

"Were there any outside factors that contributed to this lack of judgment?"

"No, there wasn't. I simply cared too deeply for my partner but that is over now." She swallowed hard against the lump forming in her throat.

"After your leave is complete you will be allowed back to work on a probationary period. You could have a solid future in our organization, Vivian, if you agree to follow the rules. We recognize your hard work up until this point and do not disregard that. In fact, that is the reason you are being allowed to stay on for now. We will take it one step at a time. Now, please head to my office. I will be there soon." Mrs. Hayes dismissed her and turned to the other board members.

In Mrs. Hayes's office Vivian found Jack going over a variety of equipment.

"What's this?" Vivian asked, pointing to a small, yet simple, USB drive. It lay among dozens of items that were reminiscent of a James Bond movie.

"It will inject a virus that will corrupt this database. The only downside is that it will need to be connected manually. No internet viruses for this, someone must physically attach it to a computer on the Chinese end to deploy the virus," Jack said, sweeping his longish hair back off his forehead and nudging his stubborn glasses back up on the bridge of his nose.

"Who's going?" Vivian asked, trying to not think about how dangerous this was.

"You're going Vivian." Gloria walked up behind them, firm and demanding.

"But you said I was banned from missions in the field."

"Unfortunately, we don't have time to be picky and unlike your sister, you speak more Mandarin."

"I can do that. Who is on the team?"

"Jack, Mateo, Tucker, you. We're still working on what Chinese contacts you will be meeting." Mrs. Hayes snapped her fingers, bringing all attention to her end of the room.

"Alright, Jack, what is this crackpot plan of yours?" Mrs. Hayes crossed her arms over her chest and leaned back against wall. "Let's hear it, honey."

"As I just told Vivian, we will need to inject a virus from this USB into the system. The main challenge will be getting in there without raising suspicion. I must get my hands directly on their computer system."

"That's my job," Mateo said.

"I thought Jack was doing the computer stuff." Vivian looked around confused.

"No, my job is to covertly get Jack in there so he can do his thing, with Tucker backing us up. It'll be Vivian's job to talk us out of any sticky situations should they arise."

"I want you to have more than one of those USBs. Should something happen to one of them, you will need another one," Mrs. Hayes said, pointing a thick finger at Jack.

"Yes, Ma'am. I can disguise one as a necklace that Vivian can wear. Is she, you know, going like that?" Jack waved his hands up and down vaguely in front of her. She was still in her finery from the meeting with Ting.

"And what is wrong with me looking like this?" Defensiveness crept into her tone.

"Oh, no, honey, he doesn't mean any harm. He knows you are in that database and not allowed in China, he wants to know what your disguise and identity will be," Mrs. Hayes explained. "Tucker, will you take her to see Max?"

Tucker, a tall, muscular, sandy-haired young man a few years older than her, led her through the maze of hallways. "So, ya been to China before? Mrs. Hayes said you were decent with the language," he asked, his voice carrying the familiar local twang.

"I've been there a time or two. Who is Max?" Vivian asked,

ignoring Tucker's probing but innocent question.

"Oh, he's the new costumer. He worked in Hollywood on those fancy spy movie sets. He can make you look like an ol' grandpa or a British aristocrat. What's your preference?" Tucker eyed her and turned away.

"I guess I'll have to speak with this Max about that. I'm not really sure."

"Max, meet Miss Vivian. Vivian, this is the famous, Max of California." Tucker gave a gallant bow and excused himself, and Vivian turned to take in Max. He was a diminutive black man with lime green sneakers, lemon yellow slacks, and a hot pink button-down shirt. His head was as smooth as a bowling ball and enormous diamond earrings adorned his ears. He thrust his hand out to Vivian.

"Oh, so nice to meet you. I have heard so very much about you! You're pretty much famous around here, you know?" Max pumped her hand with little effort as he continued gushing. "I can't wait to get started. Do you know who you want to channel?"

"Wait a minute, back up. Famous?" Vivian echoed.

"Oh yes, you were the first to use the pregnancy suit. Now, what is your inspiration for this trip?"

"Well, I hadn't thought about it," Vivian admitted. "I've never been given a choice. Being biracial, the possibilities are limited."

"Oh, pshaw, not true! We could make up all sorts of stories for you. Hmm… what do I have? Come, come, come." Max waved her after him as he scuttled through the large room filled with garment bags hanging from rolling carts.

"Have you ever been to Hawaii? You are exotic and I think we could borrow the credentials of the Hawaiian royal family this one time." Max tore through the garment bags before grabbing several. "Well, have you been, or haven't you?"

Vivian snapped out of her stupor, memories of Shen sucking the air out of her lungs. "Y... yes," she whispered, following behind him to the changing room. She firmly put thoughts of

Shen out of her head as she changed.

"Okay, give us a spin." Max clapped as she stepped from the dressing room. "That red is stunning!"

Vivian did a slow spin in a gown she would have chosen for a wedding or gala. "I'm supposed to fly in this? It seems a little too much, don't you think?"

"Oh, no, this isn't for travel. You'll have a suit for that. This is your in-country ensemble. Red and yellow are considered lucky in China, but with your skin tone I think gold will be better. So, red, gold, and black will be your colors."

"How will this help me blend in?" Vivian was thoroughly confused.

"Oh, you are the main distraction. We are going to play that up, girl. Go back in and try that black super suit on." The lights reflected off the gold rings lining his fingers as he waved toward the changing area.

"Max, can I ask you something?" Vivian stood in the small changing room and slid the elegant strappy dress off her shoulders, carefully hanging it back up.

"Of course. But I can tell you right now that I already know the question. What is a guy like me doing in a place like this? Amiright?"

"Well, that's not quite how I was going to put it." Vivian slid her long legs into the slim black slacks.

"Well, honey, it's called grace. When we reach the end of ourselves and stop looking at the world for fulfillment, we come back to the beginning. It was exactly that one line, too, that sparked a curiousness in me about God. I was browsing a book rack and picked up a very old Bible and flipped to Genesis one. In the beginning God created. I was struck with awe. I'd only ever heard of evolution, so this was like reading some deep, dark secret. It was that deep, dark secret at the end of the tunnel that made me want to dig further."

She stepped out from behind the door and handed Max the suit jacket to hold while she tucked in the deep red shirt. She shrugged the coat on and did another spin. “In the beginning God created. Such an enormous truth, and yet a nearly infantile thought, at the same time.”

Max nodded. “So, here I am. God’s servant. Now, let’s get your wardrobe packed up. Everyone else is already waiting for you.”

CHAPTER 29

"You are sure that your people will work with me? I have always been solitary." Brother Jon scratched the top of his balding head and chewed on his tongue.

"Yes, they want to help you to bring more good news to the hills. I will take you to Nai Nai, and then I have a mission to go on. It's an urgent matter and I must meet with my team soon," Shen explained, checking that the shirt he'd hung in the hotel bathroom was dry enough, so he hastily folded it and shoved it in his bag.

"So, why do you look left and right, like you are being chased? You are easy to read, like a book, you know that?"

Shen laughed and shook his head. "Truth is, I am nervous about being in the city. The surveillance system won't take long to pick me out of the crowd."

"No, you are just not using your imagination. Will you trust me?"

"Of course, I trust you."

"How do these cameras work?" Brother Jon asked, folding his own clothing to pack up.

"They detect your facial features."

"Then let's change your face. I'm not in their system because I have been in the rural areas for so many years. What is that toy that children like? It is flesh colored and comes in a bright egg. It can be pulled and squished." Brother Jon tapped a finger on his chin, deep in thought.

"Putty. What would we do with that?" Shen asked.

"Use it to reshape your nose bridge. Wear your hair forward so it covers one eye. Put a ball cap on. Wear glasses. And we can get you some colored contacts."

"Are you sure you aren't actually a spy?" Shen laughed and tossed a pillow across the room at the missionary. Brother Jon caught it, laughing.

"I will go get your disguise. You stay here and work on your hair. Do you need to contact your team?"

"That's done. I have my orders and just need the disguise. I'll take you to see Nai Nai first, then be on my way."

"Well, then, let's get started."

Several hours later Shen tilted his head back and forth and was surprised he could barely recognize himself. A pair of glasses sat on his face, secured to his nose by the sticky putty that Brother Jon had shaped in such a way as to hide his natural nose bridge. His hair was brushed over his left eye. A hat with reflective silver images topped his head.

"You don't have to be up on all the technology to know how to outsmart it." Brother Jon patted Shen's cap and nodded his approval. "Let's go, brother."

Vivian adjusted the cute little glasses she had been assigned by Max. It included a prosthetic nose dyed the same color as her own skin. Her hair, hastily permed, hung in gentle ringlets framing her face, with sunny highlights reflecting the harsh overhead lighting. Her chic outfit stood out against the everyday fashions of the crowd around her. She was purporting to be a royal delegation from Hawaii with Mateo, Tucker and Jack as her entourage. Her hands shook as they filed through customs. She expected the State Security forces to come running any second, but they breezed through without any issues, despite the vast number of dubious gadgets Jack had managed to sneak into every possible case and crevice of their baggage.

"Our contact will meet us and take us to the nearest hotel. He will disable any security devices, from what I understand," Mateo whispered.

"Oh no, we don't need him to do that. I'll find even more devices than he would," Jack jumped in, his chin tilted up proudly.

"Well, y'all can take your gizmos. I don't need 'em. Everything can be fixed with a Sig-Sauer or a Baretta, right boss?" Tucker drawled, patting his hip as if he were packing heat.

"You wouldn't have made it past security, T. So, let's just focus and get somewhere secure. Our contact will, well, contact us." Mateo said, hefting his military style rucksack.

Vivian, feeling uncomfortable out in the open, snapped her finger at the group of men and headed to the side of the terminal. She found a quiet spot, cautiously located the nearest cameras and turned her back to them, then withdrew behind a large kiosk. Mateo followed her.

"It'll take him longer to contact us if we're out in the open. Have you learned nothing, boys?" Vivian chastised the group.

"Well actually no… It's my first time out of the US." Jack quipped, readjusting the large backpack weighing him down.

"Haven't you been undercover before?" Vivian remonstrated. "I realize some things are a bit new, but basic protocol doesn't change much from one branch to the next, even if it's a civilian one."

"Touché! We're very new to this civvy org. We're still putting together our team. So far, it's the three of us and we're working on adding several more faces. Interested in joining?" offered Tucker.

"What exactly is your job?" Vivian asked, curious.

"Well, when the governments can't come to an agreement and civvy's are involved we step in, covertly. Everything from rescuing trafficking victims to hostage situations. Since we don't have our full team yet, we're picking up smaller assignments like this one. Escorting a royal pain in the-"

"Why, you brat!" Vivian squeaked, smacking Tucker on the arm as he laughed.

"Am I interrupting anything?" a familiar voice penetrated the shadows. Vivian's head snapped up, looking around. The voice was Shen's, but the man standing in front of her was not. Instead, she saw a nerdy Asian man with an outdated longish hairstyle and retro 80's gear. She had the strangest urge to either run the other way or pull him into a hug, but she fought it and got down to business.

"It's about time. Let's go," she barked at him. Head held high, she stepped into the flow of traffic heading outside. He ran to catch up, followed by Jack, Mateo, and Tucker.

They walked silently next to each other. Vivian was a mess inside fighting regrets, needing and wanting to say what was on her heart. The airport wasn't the place, nor was this mission the right time.

Shen led the group to one of the Society's cabs, which dropped them off at a pre-selected hotel. Vivian checked into a room by herself, grateful for the privacy. Shen had gone through and removed the listening devices, so she took off her glasses and nose prosthetic.

Lord, why is he on the team? Out of an entire country, why was he the one picked to be the contact? She wasn't sure her heart could take it. *Get it together, girl. He's going to be here with the team and you're going to have to be able to handle it.*

A knock echoed through her hotel room, announcing the arrival of the team for a meeting. *Take a deep breath, show time.*

Soon the guys were lounging on the sofa and chairs, with all eyes on Shen and Mateo.

"If we fail this assignment, we will all end up in prison. For life," Shen was saying.

"Way to be a negative Nancy," Tucker muttered.

"You cannot fake it 'til you make it here. There are no gray areas here. If any of us are caught, no amount of government intervention will get you out of the consequences." Shen's shoulders sagged as he continued. "What is she doing here?"

Shen thumbed over his shoulder at Vivian. Her jaw dropped. Mateo opened his mouth to answer.

"Oh no you don't. *She* can answer for herself," Vivian began. "*I,* sir, am here to pull my full weight on this team. I am the translator and diversion. I am here under the pretense of-"

Shen cut her off. "I know the story, but anyone could've filled that role. Why you, specifically?" Shen turned back to Mateo, clearly waiting for an answer. Mateo was smart and snapped his mouth shut..

"Well, Mama Bear picked the team, including her. You'll have to take it up with her," Jack jumped in. He shot Vivian a pained smile, and she nodded her gratitude.

"This isn't like your other assignments. You must stay focused the entire time," Shen said quietly to her. She sensed the stress and fear in his voice.

"I'm aware this isn't a pleasure trip. Now, boss, please go over the plan," she said coolly.

"Alright. Our target is several miles away. We will take the taxi over, carrying only what we need. You will be presenting a made-up award for International Relations in Hawaii to the head of the Caishen Conglomerate. The media you will see are actually paid actors who know nothing about The Society. They are being told it's a movie scene. While you are busy giving interviews and presenting the fake award, we will sneak away so we can get Jack to the computer system." Mateo had rolled out a map and building schematics as he spoke.

"What is this Caishen Conglomerate?" Vivian asked.

"They collect data on foreigners who frequent China. They are also the security firm who runs the facial recognition software. As we learned from Vivian spying on Ting, they will be implementing a new database containing most, if not all, of our operating agents tomorrow. Now, this," Mateo tapped a section of the schematics, "is the location of their central computer system. It will be heavily guarded. We cannot leave bodies lying around, T. You got it?"

Tucker threw his hands in the air defensively. "I don't know what you mean, boss!" A smirk crossed his handsome face.

"Sure, you don't. We're using the tranqs. These guys will enjoy a nice little nap while Jack injects the virus. Then we get back to the princess here and get the heck out of Dodge."

"Why do you need to get out of a car?" Shen shook his head, his forehead scrunched up.

"It's just a saying now, but refers to an old West town," Vivian explained, a genuine smile playing on her lips.

"Okay, guys. Let's go do some surveillance, then regroup back here," Mateo ordered them to move out.

An hour later, the group looked like tourists taking in the city sights. Mateo had slid a pair of large, funky glasses on that had screens built in. He tapped the side of the glasses and scanned the building. Vivian had listened to Jack proudly explaining to Livi that they were plugged into the facial recognition software in the building they were infiltrating, so Mateo could look through any camera he wanted. He slid the device off and handed it over to Tucker.

"What do we know about their schedule, shift changes, and security protocols?" Shen asked, waiting for his turn with the space age toy Jack was smugly nodding at.

"Once they are on shift, they do not leave their posts until they are relieved. There are no breaks for those near the computer system and servers. So, we will not need to worry about any other personnel while we are there," Mateo informed him.

"Do they all have to be tranquilized? Too bad we cannot give them stomach issues, so they simply have no choice but to leave their posts," Shen said, slipping the glasses on. He sucked in his breath. The amount of information on the screen blew him away.

"Ipecac induces vomiting, but we wouldn't be able to control how long they would be gone, and we have to get them to eat it somehow. Tranqing them allows us total control on that front, and I like full control. Anything less and we are in danger," Mateo said firmly.

Shen nodded "Do we have enough intel for now? How much longer will we be here?"

"I'd like to stay for a bit longer. Why don't you take the princess back to the hotel? We'll meet you there," Mateo suggested. Shen handed off the device and turned to Vivian.

"Shall we, princess?" He held his hand out in front of him, giving her the lead.

"Don't you start calling me that, too." She shook her head at him, but that small smile still played on her lips. He set his jaw stiffly and followed behind her.

"I'll take you back, but I am not staying. I have other business to attend to. Do not leave your room while I'm gone," he instructed her sternly as they wove their way through the large crowds.

"Are you going to see Nai Nai?" Vivian asked knowingly offhandedly. Shen let out a breath and shook his head.

"Yes." He sighed. "I met her long-lost son, so I left him for a long visit."

"Can I go with you?" Vivian asked, her eyes sparkling with hope.

"I'm afraid Nai Nai won't take that news that we aren't together anymore very well. Especially if you are with me." He shifted his weight nervously and watched her, as if hoping she would protest.

"I just want to say goodbye. This will be my last trip to China." Shen stopped walking. Vivian took several steps before she realized it and turned back to him. He looked like he'd been slapped.

"Yes, you can come, but please keep it to a simple goodbye. I don't want to deal with the fall out of Nai Nai's pestering questions for every visit until she passes on. Let's walk." They changed direction and headed toward the district in which the Nai Nai lived. The silence was heavy between them. Unspoken thoughts swirled about them.

"How have you been?" Shen asked, nearly whispering the question.

"Have you ever been blindsided with something? It feels like it did when my mother was suddenly gone. It hurts. I hurt." She glanced over at Shen to see pain wash over his face.

"I'm sorry. I was a coward. I was completely terrified of losing you. I thought letting you go on my own terms would be easier," he admitted.

"Has it been?" she asked, trying not to sound accusing.

"No! I've been miserable. I can't stop thinking about you. I can't stop wondering what you are doing, how your family is, what silliness your brother has gotten into." Vivian smirked at that last one. "I... I'm sorry. I can be the bravest man in the world delivering good news, but I fell apart at the thought of losing you." His voice cracked with emotion. "I have never connected with another person like I did with you. I can never have you in my life," he finished lamely.

"You won't know that until you ask." Vivian slowed.

"Ask what?"

"For me to be in your life." She shyly looked up into his eyes.

"You would consider having me back? After all I put you through?" All the background noise of the city and streets faded away. Vivian backed into an alley between buildings. Shen followed her, his hands visibly shaking.

She held her arms open. Shen stepped into the embrace and pulled her close. Tears fell unabated, and his voice caught in his throat. "I've missed this so much. I've missed you so much." He pulled back for a moment and laughed gently. "These glasses really make you look different." He kissed her forehead, as if testing the water. She canted her head, inviting him in closer. He ran his thumb along her jawline, placing his fingers underneath her chin and bringing her face closer to his. "I've missed you," he whispered, pressing his lips gently against hers. Vivian's head swam and she had to grip his coat to stay steady. His touch was gentle yet firm, hesitating, giving her equal power to pause or go deeper. She pulled him tighter and moved a hand up to right his hat, which was now askew.

They pulled apart, lips swollen, and fixed their attire before silently moving back into the flow of pedestrians, together this time. They walked hand in hand all the way to Nai Nai's condominium.

Before they went in, Shen pulled Vivian to the side. He traced her new nose bridge, a trace of humor on his lips. "I have no idea how we'll be together, but I'd like to try. I have decided not to let worry get between our love. If anything happens and we're separated, we will meet up on the Mongolian side of the mine. Even if one of us isn't there, keep coming back. Will you promise to meet me there?"

"This sounds like a goodbye." Fear rolled through Vivian. "I won't say goodbye. Never again."

"Not forever, but we will need to be temporarily separated, even if the mission goes well. Correct?"

"Yes, I realize that, but that didn't feel like a quick little I'll-see-you-tomorrow-for-dinner goodbye."

Shen leaned in for one more soft kiss.

As Chen answered and led them through the small unit to the enclosed garden where Nai Nai sat in her chair, bundled against the winter chill. A man Vivian didn't recognize sat next to her.

The conversation between the two paused and Nai Nai's face lit up as she animatedly spoke to Shen. Vivian couldn't understand the old Beijing dialect, but the woman clearly was delighted that Shen was back. The man next to her looked Vivian up and down before nodding knowingly. She and Shen were still holding hands.

"Is this the joy of your life, brother?" the stranger asked. He was a little round, with a balding head, and a vibrant smile. Shen dropped her hand as he and the stranger hugged, clapping each other loudly on the back.

"Yes. Brother Jon, this is Vivian, but please, for her safety, refer to her Princess Vaiana." Brother Jon held his hand out to Vivian, and she gladly shook it. Nai Nai squealed and waved her arms, chattering away. Vivian needed no translation. She stepped into the Grandmotherly embrace. Nai Nai patted her back and waved Shen over. He knelt so Nai Nai could pull him into a hug, as well. She flapped a hand one last time. Brother Jon joined the group hug, and they laughed at the awkwardness of it.

"Well, my brother, she has something important to tell you." Brother Jon prompted Nai Nai.

"Yesu! Yesu! Wo ai Yesu!" She thrust her hands into the air and lifted her eyes to sky. She looked like she had just climbed the highest mountain and stood at the top, triumphant.

"Oh, praise God!" Vivian breathed aloud.

"She listened to the audio Bible you recorded for her. She got confused at some point when she fumbled a button, and An Chen messed it up even more. She must have skipped to the New Testament, because suddenly she kept hearing about this new man, Yesu, who went around performing miracles. She was angry when he was so harshly opposed for his kindness to the poor and hurting. When she understood this Yesu was the one you have spoken about with her so many times, her heart began to melt. She realized what a miracle it was that we met in the mountains."

"You recorded the Bible for her? That's so sweet," Vivian said, nudging Shen playfully.

The grandmother chattered away. Brother Jon shook his head. "Bu."

"What's she asking?" Vivian knelt and took the woman's hand.

"She wants to be baptized," Shen answered.

"Great! Let's do it!" Vivian stepped next to the woman again and rubbed her arm.

"Well, we use bathtubs, and I am nervous we won't be able to get her out! I did not come all this way to be charged with murdering my mother," Brother Jon explained. Vivian laughed, picturing the wet, sloppy scene.

"Once at my father's church we used a piece of fabric underneath the person and used it to pull him back above the water. You could wrap it around her several times, so it doesn't come loose. It would be gentler than using ropes," Vivian suggested.

Shen and Brother Jon considered the plan for a moment before asking Nai Nai, who, of course, immediately agreed. Brother Jon went in to start the bath water. Shen followed him to look for a sheet, leaving Nai Nai and Vivian alone. She moved to the empty chair, but Nai Nai grabbed her hand and spoke rapidly.

"Whoa, slow down, Nai Nai. Man dian. Slower," Vivian cautioned. She only caught a few of Nai Nai's words, including Shen's name. "Nai Nai, wo ai Shen." Nai Nai nodded quietly, seeming happy with that pronouncement.

When the bathtub baptismal was set, they put a low stool in the water and wrapped the sheet around Nai Nai. Shen lifted her into the warm water, settling her gently onto the stool. Brother Jon announced her as part of the family of God, and the two tipped her over backward, immersing her in the water, while An Chen flitted around behind them like a worried mother hen. Tugging on the sheet, Shen and Brother Jon easily pulled her back up and settled her, sopping wet, back onto the stool. If her cloudy eyes could sparkle, they would have. She was absolutely radiant.

CHAPTER 30

Shen looked around uncomfortably at the small group dressed in suits. He looked down at his own and fought with the tie, trying to make it match everyone else's. He had never worn such elegant clothing. Vivian, however, was stunning in a classy black pantsuit with deep red button-down shirt, as if she were born to wear it.

"Here, put this on. It's the backup Mrs. Hayes asked us to bring." Jack handed a necklace to Vivian, then retreated to his case of gadgets and gizmos. She fingered the lotus flower on a long chain. Shen eyed the necklace; he wondered if she still wore the koi necklace he'd given her.

"May I?" Shen whispered behind her.

She extended the ends of the necklace toward him so he could secure it around her neck. "Careful, it's heavier than it looks."

"Remember, meet me at the border if anything should separate us today." Shen leaned in close to her. Mateo looked up at them and raised an eyebrow but said nothing. They stepped apart, aware that there would be no time for a private moment.

"I promise to meet you there. Will you promise me?" Vivian shot back at him.

"Of course. I just got you back. I don't want to live without you ever again," he mumbled under his breath, just loud enough for her to hear.

"All right team, gear up. We roll in five," Mateo said. Vivian headed to the bathroom to put on her glasses with the prosthetic nose and double check her makeup. Mateo waited for her to walk away to confront Shen. "You feel like telling me the history there?"

"No," Shen said defensively.

"It better not affect the team's safety. I will hold you personally responsible if it does," Mateo warned.

The group left in a hurry, and Brother Jon drove them personally in a sleek, black limo. Vivian carried a briefcase which held the "award" she would be presenting to the Caishen CEO. Vivian's cell phone rang. Everyone looked at her, but she was as shocked as they were.

"Hello?" she asked.

"Put me on speaker phone. The whole team needs to hear this," Mrs. Hayes said urgently. Vivian fumbled with the buttons but got it on speaker for the entire team to hear.

"Ting, our Chinese spy, cut her stay short this morning. She is boarding her plane now. You'll have one shot at this, team. We still don't know who leaked the database to the CCP, so there is a possibility they already know you are coming. Stay on your toes, get this done, and get home."

Agreements echoed throughout the car. "Yes, Mama Bear," Tucker practically yelled.

Brother Jon let them out at the entrance. The men took up positions surrounding Vivian, with Jack and Mateo in the front, Tucker and Shen behind her. Shen took stock of his new colleagues. Tucker and Mateo were clearly military men, with their strong bearing and confidence. Jack stood out with his lanky bone structure and scrawny frame. Though Mateo had made clear he wasn't there for the muscle. Jack nervously playing with something in his pocket and Shen shook his head. Clearly this was his first assignment, and not something he was comfortable with.

The entrance was alive with would-be reporters. Shen took in the crowd as Vivian paused, unable to pass through. He narrowed his eyes. Interspersed in the crowd were several muscled, intimidating men, not who The Society would've hired to play a part. He scanned the assembly, growing more nervous as the number of stout men increased with each sweep.

Right there, ducking behind a brawny body, was Dandan. His heart constricted. How had she known he was going to be here? Who had access to The Society and the ability to track his movements, predict his plans? He grabbed Vivian's hand and tugged her backward. She spun, confused, as the crowd pressed in on them. Jack stumbled and nearly fell, something flying out of his hand and disappearing onto the sidewalk. A soft crunch was eaten by the street noises.

Mateo pulled Jack back up and righted him. "That better not have been the primary apparatus," he whispered harshly at Jack, who was nearly cowering. The tech expert gave a nearly imperceptible nod. "Great." Mateo cut himself off and turned to Vivian with his hand extended expectantly.

"No, she can't take it off here, too many witnesses. We must get her inside," Shen said, taking control. He didn't want to let on about Dandan's presence if he didn't need to. He wasn't sure what her game was, but until he knew, he would keep the info to himself.

"Alright, let's get her in there, then," Tucker said, grabbing Jack by the scruff of his wool business coat and shoving him in front to create a path. Vivian followed, with Shen and Mateo closing in behind her. Building security guards opened the door to her and the team, but the crowd shoved their way in behind her before they could close them again.

"Who is in charge here?" Tucker bellowed out. His arms stretched out wide, creating a buffer between Vivian and the pressing crowd. The sight of an enormous American man, dressed to kill, muscles bulging against the seams of his suit, took the wind out of everyone. An eerie silence settled on the crowd.

With Tucker captivating the guards and the rest of the press of people, Shen discreetly unhooked the necklace from Vivian's neck. He passed it to her and nodded toward Mateo. "Be careful, my friend from Chengdu is here," he said, not taking his eyes off the congestion behind them.

"What? Here? You're sure?" she sputtered, passing the necklace to Mateo, who pocketed it.

"Yes, be careful. You ready?" She sucked in a deep breath, squared her shoulders, and nodded. He pushed her into Mateo and joined Tucker. He stood nearly as tall as the white country boy and was easily as muscled. Shen yelled out in Mandarin and their voices mingled, ringing out over the bobbing heads.

Mateo led Vivian and Jack toward a podium set up in the building's lobby. She looked back and breathed a sigh of relief. This job was the end of her time in China, and there was no one else she would rather have by her side than Shen. Her whole world felt right when he was near her.

A gangly Chinese man trotted across the lobby toward her as she neared the podium. "I am so sorry, Princess. I am not sure where all these people came from. Please, allow my security to deal with the stragglers." The man had heavy makeup on, his nails were painted black, matching his pure black outfit of a long, tunic and wide-legged pants. He climbed up on the low stage and tapped on the microphone. "If you will please allow our esteemed guest to reach the stage. If you have not been invited to this event, you must leave."

"We just want to see the visiting royalty," a female voice bounced back. Vivian scanned the crowd and then saw Dandan stepping out from behind a broad wide Chinese man.

"Well, you should greet a person of royalty with much more respect," Vivian shot back. She took the stage and stepped around the greeter at the microphone. "Be orderly or leave," she said firmly in Mandarin. The crowd gasped.

"You may call me, Pat. You sit here," their chaperone pointed Vivian to a chair just left of center stage. "Come, come! You, here!" He ordered the company's security to stand around her as Mateo and his team pulled away to mix into the crowd.

"When will we get the blessing of hearing from Her Royal Highness?" Dandan asked, walking closer to the short stage, her own hired muscle taking up positions near her. The crowd gave them a wide berth.

"Her Royal Highness will begin once the CEO has arrived. Now, stand down, please." Pat glared at Dandan, and Vivian hid the smirk creeping onto her face. She had a role to play and time to buy.

Mateo and gang moved silently down the stairs. According to the building schematics, they would find the main servers and computer system in level B7.

"You're sure their system will recognize us as employees? If it doesn't, we'll be leaving in the back of a police car," Mateo whispered to Jack, glancing toward the next hall where they knew a camera to be.

"Yes, I programmed us into their system myself. As far as the computers are concerned, we work here. I don't feel like learning what a Chinese jail is like." Jack seemed exasperated that they didn't trust him.

"You go first, then," Mateo offered. Jack hesitated for a second, but then took the steps two at a time. Shen followed him, not trusting the boy to handle any guards that pop up. At the bottom of the stairs, Jack looked at a black screen to the right of the door. It scanned his face, flipping through dozens of possibilities before giving a green light to open the door. He pulled it open and held it for the rest of them to enter. Shen took point as they crept down the hallway. They turned with the corridors until basement became warmer and they could hear the whirring of machinery – thousands of computers and servers working together to crunch numbers and track millions of people. While they had several warehouses that housed even more computers and servers, this was the main hub, where everything was remotely controlled.

Shen paused and held up his hand, then pointed silently forward. Mateo pulled out a skinny tranq gun from his jacket and screwed it together. Tucker handed him the cartridges of tranquilizers. Once Mateo had his weapon assembled and loaded, Tucker took point and led the way to the door. He allowed the camera to scan his face; the terminal blinked green, and he whipped the door open. Several faces looked up in surprise, and they stood in a rush, a chair falling over backward. Mateo aimed and fired. He shot rapidly but consistently, hitting each man in the face. Clear pellets burst on contact, releasing narcotic fumes. The targets dropped instantly. The last man ducked and crawled across the floor toward an alarm system. Shen and Tucker moved together in perfect unison, reaching the man at the same time. They pulled him toward them and threw him down on his back. Tucker putting his foot on the guy's chest kept him immobile until Mateo could pop him in the face.

"Get to work!" the team's leader snapped at Jack. "Don't drop it this time." A lotus necklace flew through the air, and Jack fumbled a bit but caught it. He righted the downed chair and began typing rapidly.

Shen walked over to a bank of monitors filled with security cameras. He spotted the lobby where Vivian stood regally on a small stage. All eyes were on her. His most immediate worry relieved, Shen's thoughts turned elsewhere. How did Dandan know they would be here? He narrowed his eyes and scanned the faces in the crowd.

"Can I search the building using their software?" Shen threw over his shoulder at Jack.

"Yeah, why? You expecting to find someone?"

"Yes. Trouble, that's who I'm expecting," Shen said grimly.

"Let me get this going and I'll do that for you in a moment." Jack disconnected a miniature memory stick from the necklace and inserted it into the computer he was working at.

CHAPTER 31

"Excellent international relations are vital to the growth of not only this beautiful country, but the entire world. Working together as one company and one royal family promotes unity, and many others will look to us as we continue this partnership. Modern relationships rely on cultural understanding and generosity. We come from different backgrounds with different values, traditions, and beliefs. By learning to work together, we make exchanges between our countries more beneficial and productive. This will have a profound impact on our world," Vivian recited, smiling blandly down at the crowd and thankful she'd been able to memorize her speech. Below her, the crowd cheered. Sweeping the audience, she saw Dandan standing in the front row to the left. Even with the crowd getting loud, she was determined to keep the woman in her sights.

"It is with immense gratitude that I present the East Asian Award for International Relations to Caishen Conglomerate for their efforts in Foreign Affairs." She handed the fake award to the CEO of the company, a shy smile played at the corners of his mouth as he accepted it. She felt kind of bad for fooling the man, but firmly squashed her sympathy with a reminder of what they would do with the information they possessed.

Vivian stepped back and allowed the man access to the microphone. She tuned out his eloquent acceptance speech, reflecting that it was too bad it wouldn't ever been seen. The cameras were fake. She wondered how the team was doing before refocusing on the CEO while keeping an eye on Dandan. When the CEO was finished, she stood up to reclaim the microphone. "Let's take a few questions," she suggested with a glittering smile, and hands shot into the air. The actors knew their lines well and shouted out their questions.

"Yes, you." She pointed to a young University student in the front row.

"What has the international community gained by this partnership?" the young man asked, his voice the first of many. Vivian and the CEO worked together to answer the prearranged questions. While she knew the correct answers, and most of them were easy questions, the CEO did not know that. At one point he nodded to Vivian in thanks as she redirected a tough question. Just as the Q&A session was winding down, Dandan stepped up, her hired hands parting the crowd before her. She stood with a hand on her hip and her head cocked to the side.

"So, what does the *royal* family gain from this?" She sneered on the word royal. She obviously knew Vivian's identity. "Shouldn't China treat all the people like this *royal* person? Since equality is one of the 12 values, I want the royal treatment."

Vivian looked to the CEO; his shy smile was gone. He clearly was not the spitfire personality that ran this company. He was a 'yes-man,' a friendly face put out in front of the world to make nice with the public.

"No, China shouldn't treat everyone like royalty. The party comes first. If everyone were treated with such methods, the country itself would suffer. Am I correct, sir?" Vivian took the lead, knowing that the phrase "The party comes first," was sure to get a positive reaction.

"Yes, the party comes first. We owe all we have to our wonderful government and the memory of Chairman Mao," he played the party card just as she expected. Vivian discreetly glanced at the clock on the far wall, noting the time. Clearly, she needed to buy the team more time. Pat took the microphone, dismissing the crowd and false media.

"I would love to have a tour. Do you think you could arrange it? I would also like to enjoy a meal with you. Is that reasonable?" Vivian batted her eyelashes at the company official.

"I want a tour, as well." Dandan stood out from the crowd in a thin jacket that would do nothing against the harsh Beijing winter winds, but the showstopper was underneath – a traditional red silk dress that barely covered her upper thighs. Her thin legs were covered with black hose, and she strutted on five-inch red heels. "Oh Mr. Cai Shen, it's so good to see you again. I'm Fu Ming Jie's daughter. You wouldn't mind if I tagged along for the tour, would you?" She slid in beside the CEO and linked arms with him. She flirted shamelessly, puckering her lips. The man chuckled nervously and nodded. If the guys didn't hurry up, Dandan was going to make her move, and Vivian would be on her own.

◆ ◆ ◆

"So, who's this guy we're looking for?" Mateo asked, drumming his fingers on the table next to Jack's keyboard. Jack ignored the incessant tapping and continued uploading the virus.

"He used to be a friend of our organization. He mostly donated assets, but he has sway on the Council. Friends in high places, as they say," Shen said, walking back over the bank of monitors. "What's taking so long? I thought you said this would be quick?"

"It's supposed to be fast, but there's a slight problem." Jack didn't even bother glancing up at them.

"What do you mean a problem?" Mateo whipped his head in Jack's direction.

"Let's just say they added a layer of protection since the last time I traipsed through their system. They might've detected me last time and added this protocol to prevent it. But from here I have root access, so I should be able to dismantle it. Okay! I've got that running. Let's get looking for your friend

Or is it foe?" Jack left the computer and headed to the camera monitors.

"How can you be so casual right now?" Tucker drawled in his soft Tennessee accent. Jack just shrugged and pulled a small keyboard out from where it was wedged between screens.

"Why are you sure he is our leak?" Mateo asked, following Jack over.

"Because that's his daughter." Shen pointed to the screen of the lobby, where it looked like Vivian and Dandan were facing off. "She recently had me kidnapped. I was giving him the benefit of the doubt, but now I am sure he must've known all the details."

Jack's jaw dropped. "You were kidnapped? Boy, I don't want to run into the guys who can hold you down."

"Well, I have some bad news for you. Do you see all the muscle in the crowd?" Shen pointed them out on the screen as Jack paled slightly. "She's up to something, and I have a feeling her father is nearby. He's a well-known and powerful businessman. Ming Jie." Jack's finger flew over the keyboard as faces flashed across one of the screens, when suddenly it stopped on a plump face.

"That's him. Where is he?" Shen tapped the screen. Jack tapped a bit more and the face shrank to a small corner of the screen, and a map popped up with a blinking red dot.

"Right there, in a room off of the main lobby." Something beeped behind them, and Jack ran back over to the mainframe.

"What's the history here? People don't just suddenly turn against us," Mateo asked, glancing at Tucker. Tucker took the hint and moved to the door to stand ready.

"His daughter has been after me for years," Shen began.

"But you have eyes only for those of royal blood lines?" Mateo asked. Tucker tried to cover a laugh with a cough, but it was obviously a snicker.

Shen barreled on, not addressing Mateo's jab, "Dandan gets what she wants, and she desperately wants to control me. I doubt she is here for a social call. We need to finish up so we can get Vivian and get out of here. Are you almost done?" Shen demanded; he was growing impatient. This was taking too long.

Jack looked sheepish. "Well, that little problem? It's a little bigger than I thought. It'll take me a little while longer."

Mateo placed a reassuring hand on Shen's arm. "Well, our girl is well trained, she's got them giving her a tour. But your other little girlfriend is going along and seems to have the CEO eating out of the palm of her hand."

The screen showed Dandan with her arm linked through the CEO's, Pat walking next to him with Vivian on the other side. A group of sturdy men trailed behind them.

"How much longer? I don't like this at all." Shen's stomach lurched with anxiety.

Pat took the lead on the tour, hitting all the spots he must've thought the two modern women would find interesting. They visited a cafe, several offices packed full of cubicles filled with typing minions, and even a massage room.

"Nothing less than the best for our employees," Pat informed the two women. The CEO merely nodded in agreement. He had been silent most of the time, practically drooling over Dandan.

"You have so many security guards!" Vivian steered away from Dandan, hoping she was distracted enough by sinking her claws into the enamored executive.

"Yes, we take security very seriously around here."

If only Pat knew what was happening in the very bowels of this building, Vivian thought.

"We try to balance the strict rules around who comes and goes by providing housing and financial support for nursery school, so our employees can continue to grow their families while working."

"Oh, how thoughtful of you; it must be wonderful to work here. Where shall we go next? Would you show me your office? I'd love to see where the man in charge resides," Dandan cooed.

Vivian felt nausea roll through her stomach.

"Oh, I'm nobody really. Pat, see about arranging a special dinner for these ladies." He paused, finally pulling his lustful gaze away from Dandan to take in the room. "Where did your men go?" It was only then that Pat and the CEO realized that Mateo and the others were missing.

"Oh, who knows. It's hard to find good help these days. Isn't it?" Vivian gave Dandan a cutting look.

"They should not be wandering around without an escort. Find them!" The CEO snapped at Pat, and they moved to the side to speak with an administrative assistant, leaving Vivian and Dandan alone with the Chinese girl's goons.

"It's been too long since I saw you last. How have you been? I do hope you haven't started making wedding plans. I hear it's hard to set that up from prison. Right, boys?" Dandan said slyly. Vivian felt more than saw several of the men close the distance to stand directly behind her. A hot, heavy breath soaked her neck, even through her thick hair. Dandan continued her little game.

"I didn't know you wore glasses. Those are very cute. Can I try them on?" Vivian's eyes grew wide as a hand gripped her side, fingers digging into her skin. Dandan swiped the glasses off her face, knocking them to the ground. The prosthetic nose broke off and went rolling across the floor. A burly man with a mohawk stepped on it with a quiet "oops."

The fingers gripping her side dug deeper. She closed her eyes, breathed a prayer and twisted out of his hold. She dropped and rolled to the side and backed toward the elevators. Dandan and her men stood still for a moment, shocked, before turning toward her.

Vivian continued to back toward the elevators. There was a ding and the doors opened. The man with the milky eye stepped out with Ming Jie, Dandan's father, and stood next to her. She felt the cold barrel of a gun into her back, and she froze. Dandan snapped her fingers and her men surrounded Vivian and the man, who moved them back into the elevator. "We'll meet you downstairs, gentlemen!" Dandan called to Pat as the elevator doors clanged shut.

"What do you want from me?" Vivian asked, working hard to keep her voice steady, and frankly failing.

"Oh, it's not what I want from you, it's what I am going to take from you. You have his heart, and that cannot stand. He will see you die with his own eyes, and he will have nothing in this world." Dandan swung her hair around, hitting one of the men in the face. "Nothing but sweet Dandan to comfort him."

Vivian scoffed. "You're a fool if you think killing me will bring him to you. He has something greater he serves, a purpose beyond his needs. Haven't you figured that out, yet? If you break him, it won't drive him to your arms. When will you learn he just doesn't love you?"

Dandan's eyes grew large with fury. She slapped Vivian across the face so hard her head snapped back and hit the back the wall of the elevator. Pain exploded across her face. "Shut up! You are nothing but a vile American!" Dandan shrieked, her scream ringing in everyone's ears.

"Daughter, maybe a little more subtlety?" Ming Jie suggested. Vivian felt a trickle of blood running off her nose. The man with the milky eye waved his gun at Vivian as Ming Jie shoved a white handkerchief into Vivian's hands. "Press the hold button," he ordered, and turned back to their captive.

"Get that nosebleed under control. When we step out these doors, you will not try to run, or show any sign of distress. We could kill you here and now, but the cleanup would be quite messy and expensive," The gunman growled. Vivian's cheek was red and puffy.

"So, you support your daughter's criminal activities. I was told that you were a righteous man. I suppose the enemy of our souls will go after the weakest link, won't he?" Vivian said, handing the bloodied cloth to one of the guards who pocketed it.

"What is she talking about, Baba?" Dandan looked from her father to Vivian and back again.

He grabbed Vivian by the hair and wrenched her head back.

He buried his face into her neck, his hot, stinky breath near her face. "I'll get my payment in the afterlife then, won't I?" he snarled. He released her hair and she stumbled. Someone pushed the door open button, and they were in the lobby again.

Dandan opened her mouth to speak, but oncoming footsteps broke her concentration. She looked around, to see four men in black suits coming up on her fast. Vivian let out a sigh of relief and swung her elbow back hard into Dandan's father's gut, sending him stumbling back into the elevator. She dropped and rolled to the side and tried to kick the knee out from under the gun toting goon. He grunted but didn't go down, instead leveling the gun at her head. Something flew by her head and exploded on the man's face. Whatever hit him was clear, and he crumpled in a heap outside the elevator. Chaos exploded as the building security joined the fray.

Shen grabbed Vivian around the waist and hauled her toward the door, but the way was blocked by guards. He looked around the lobby for another escape route, and moved toward Jack waiting in elevator, holding the door open. Dandan's father was slumped against the wall of the lift, holding his midsection, still gasping for air. Shen led Vivian through the chaos to within a few feet of the elevator door. Tucker and Mateo converged on Shen and the group backed into the elevator together.

Mateo punched an ugly face that slammed into the small space as the doors tried to close. The man snarled but didn't move. Mateo pulled back and punched one more time. A satisfying crunch of the man's nose was the last sound of the lobby as the doors closed and the lift shuddered and began going down. He pulled out a phone and furiously typed before pocketing it.

Shen let go of Vivian, turned around and grabbed Dandan's father by the front of the shirt. He lifted the older man up so his stubby legs dangled in the air. "You coward! Why?"

"What Dandan wants, she gets. It's that simple. She's only ever wanted you; why shouldn't she have what she wants? Nothing I've ever done has gotten me rewards here on earth.

Why not make my daughter happy?!"

"You are a fool." Shen dropped him on the ground snagged the tranquilizer gun Mateo was still holding, shooting several rounds into his pudgy face. Jack's mouth dropped open, but Shen ignored him.

"Here." He slammed the tranq gun back into Mateo's hands and pulled Vivian close. He held her face and searched for any injury.

"Are you alright?"

She merely nodded, too numb to say anything.

The lift lurched to a stop, but the doors didn't open. "What's going on?" Tucker asked, ready to run for it.

"I took us down to the maintenance level," Shen replied. "We should be able to go through the delivery entrance. Where is the driver supposed to meet us?"

"I already have the driver circling the block, with a little blessing we won't have to run far to find him." Mateo nodded. "On the count of three, you'll open this door and we're going to break left and right. J, to the left with me. T, to the right with you two." Mateo took a deep breath, looking around. "Everybody ready?" Upon receiving assents, he nodded. "One. Two. Three." The door dinged open, and they broke out of the elevator.

Vivian, Shen, and Tucker dashed down the hall, and threw open a door marked deliveries. Mateo and Jack weren't far behind them. The group ran down the steps, dodging deliverymen, and burst onto the street. A passenger van striped yellow and black slowed down, and through the window, a familiar face grinned toothily at them.

"Let's go!" Shen yelled, yanking open the sliding door of the van. Mateo jumped in the front seat, and the rest of them piled in the back. The door slammed shut as Brother Jon sped away. Several of Dandan's men ran to catch up, but Jon was driving too quickly for them to keep up.

Inside the van, they all seemed to be collectively holding their breath. Moments later, sirens rang through the streets, and flashing lights loomed near them. Jon sped up, running red lights, swerving to miss pedestrians, and circling blocks multiple times, trying to shake the cop cars.

"Brother Jon, plan two," Shen announced, breaking the tense silence.

"What do you mean by 'plan two'?" Mateo asked, turning to look at Shen. "Tell me!" Mateo bristled.

"We're taking you to the American Embassy. That is the safest place for everyone," Brother Jon offered.

"But not for you, unless you request protection," Vivian said, trying to work through all the possible angles Shen was considering. She turned on him. "But you're not coming, are you? You promised!" Her stomach dropped out of her body and sobs shook her shoulders. "You promised."

"Meet me at the border, I will be there. I don't make empty promises." Shen wiped the tears that poured from her face. "How much farther, Jon?"

"Only a few blocks," Jon answered. "You might have to make a run for it, I think they know. Yes, see that roadblock? Shoot!" He jerked the wheel to the side as a police car swiped the side of their van. Another rammed into the rear hard enough that the hatch popped open. The van spun around several times, but not before one more car slammed into the driver's side.

Jon screamed as the door bent into his legs, pinning him to the seat. "Go! Run! Don't worry about me!" he yelled. Mateo had already jumped out and was throwing open the sliding door. They all piled out, jittery but unharmed, and sprinted toward the American Embassy. Vivian cast one last glance back at Brother Jon, where he still sat pinned in the van. He was surrounded by officers.

Tucker took off ahead of the group, with Mateo and Shen close behind. Vivian ran as fast as she could, but it was hard in high heels. She kicked them off and ran barefoot on the frozen cement. Tucker made it to the gate first and was yelling for them to move aside when a shot rang out. Vivian turned and saw Shen go down. Her scream faded into the nothingness as Mateo tried to drag Shen toward the safety of the Embassy grounds, but Shen shoved him away.

"Get her to safety!" was the last thing she heard Shen say. Mateo dropped Shen's arm and ran over to her. She thought she was still screaming but heard nothing. *Was she floating?* Somehow, she made it to the boundary without using her legs, and with her heart in pieces. She watched as Shen was hit and kicked by officers. She couldn't hear his screams, but she knew he must be screaming. A blanket of silence had fell over her.

CHAPTER 32

"And now we turn to the recent scuffle outside the American Embassy. The Chinese government is stating that the man who was brought down by a PLA bullet was a deranged tour guide who had been attacking American guests as they fled to the Embassy. The identities of these victims have not been released." The television clicked off, and the sofa dipped as someone took a seat next to Vivian. She didn't bother looking up; she knew who it was without needing to look. The Society had flown Livi in the moment they heard about Vivian's breakdown. Vivian had absolutely refused to go anywhere but to Mongolia, to the mine.

"Mrs. Hayes told me they are working on getting updates on him, but the CCP isn't cooperating. He's been on their list for a long time," Livi said, trying to sound encouraging.

"That's why he avoided the cities, but The Society asked for his help, and he would never tell them no," Vivian said, opening her eyes and looking vacantly off into the distance.

"Vivian, I know you want to stay here because you both agreed that this was the meeting place, but what are you going to do? You can't hide in a cave for the rest of your life," Livi gently probed.

Vivian narrowed her eyes to dangerous slits and turned to her sister, ready to explode, but the look of peace on Livi's face calmed the churning rage in her heart.

"Who are you?" Vivian asked. Livi's eyes grew wide with

concern. "No, I don't mean it like that. I just mean. Well, you've grown and changed. A lot. You are settled, and so much more mature. How many times have I been the comforter when some boy broke your heart or you missed a sale at your favorite department store?"

Livi laughed. "Yeah, I do love me a good sale. Or what about the time I cried in the store at the register because the coupon I had was expired! Wow, that seems like a million years ago."

The girls shared a long, slow hug. "I know I must face reality, but I can't walk away from him. If he said he would meet me here, I believe him. I know he will make it here. I don't know how I know it, but I feel it in my core," Vivian said with a heavy sigh.

"When is the virtual meeting with the council?" Livi asked, extracting herself from Vivian and her nest on the sofa.

"8:30 PM local time. So, in about an hour." Vivian glanced at the time on her watch. "I'll either be resigning or, well, I'm not sure really. I am not going anywhere, that's for sure."

"I'll stay as long as I can, but I have a new role with The Society to train for. I'll be going back to school, too," Livi said, grabbing a bottled water out of a mini fridge. "Want one?" Vivian nodded and caught the bottle Livi tossed her.

"What's the new role?"

"Well, they're starting two new teams. One is to rescue trafficking victims. Mateo, Tucker, and Jack will be on that one. The other will be investigating demon worship and paranormal activity. That group will intercede on behalf of victims, as well." Livi sipped her water, looking far more grounded than usual.

"So, which group will you be part of?" Vivian asked, pride in sister surging into the shattered portions of her heart.

"Well, first I need to complete my degree. Until then, I will be training to help on two fronts. On the interceding teams that talk with the victims after the locations are secured, and on the team helping the victims adjust, get job training, go through therapy. That sort of thing."

"What degree did you decide on?" Vivian asked.

"Well, I thought I could help a lot of people as a therapist,

I'm thinking of being a child therapist. Give others the help I should've asked for when we lost Mom. I want to help those lost little girls." Livi wiped a stray tear.

"Oh, Livi! I'm so proud of you!" Vivian threw her arms around her sister and the two shared a good cry.

"Sorry to interrupt, but the meeting is about to start." A head poked into the small room. "I'll see you in the conference room." Vivian drew in a long, steadying breath. She hurried to join the rest of the team at the conference table in a room down the long corridor, part of the faux mine hundreds of feet underneath the surface.

A computer projected an image of the Nashville conference room on a large screen. Mrs. Hayes and the entire council were convened, along with Mateo, Tucker and Jack.

"Thank you all for joining us," Mrs. Hayes began. "We are grateful that you are safe. The mission was successful; what Jack did was nothing short of a miracle. The virus corrupted the database, swapping out our agents' profiles with fake pictures. For now, we are restricting all activity to emergencies only. We need to lay low for a while. I have read the report, but we would like to hear from Mateo. What went wrong?" Mrs. Hayes was larger than life on the screen. While her face was kind and gentle, her fierce demeanor made her nickname "Mama Bear" seem accurate.

"An extra layer of cyber security had been added to their network. It took longer than expected to deploy our ailment into their system. That wasn't the true challenge, though. Our Chinese counterpart figured out who leaked the database – someone named Ming Jie. We were told he mostly donated assets and funds, but he seemed to have deeper connections in our organization." Mateo explained. A low murmur took over the Nashville conference room. Heads turned back and forth as each council member looked at each other.

"Thank you for that assessment. What happened next?" Mrs. Hayes's eyes were fierce.

"This Ming Jie's daughter showed up. There appears to be a

bit of a history there between our Chinese agent and this young woman. She was also familiar with Vivian."

"Is that true, my dear?" Mrs. Hayes asked Vivian.

"Yes, Ma'am. I have met her one time in the presence of my contact. She was a bit hostile, though she did allow us to hide at her apartment. Do you have any update on my contact or his friend?" Vivian asked, cringing inside a bit at the pleading in her voice, but she was beyond trying to hide this from the world.

"We will cover that in a moment," Mrs. Hayes replied then turned back to Mateo. "Your exit made a bigger bang than we had anticipated."

"Yes, it couldn't be helped. There was a kidnapping attempt on Vivian, and we had no choice," Mateo gave her a reassuring smile through the screen.

"Are you alright, dear?" Dayita, the council representative from India, asked.

"Yes, thank you for asking." Vivian looked at her feet.

"That wasn't in the initial report," Mrs. Hayes said pointedly. "You certainly have had an exciting mission. Well, we narrowly avoided an international incident. We are in the clear there, and will be laying low for the time being. Now, as for our contact. He was shot in the leg during the escape attempt, but we do not know the extent of his injuries. From what we know, he was immediately taken into custody. He is being charged with numerous crimes, including assault and attempted kidnapping. Our hands are tied on this. We cannot try an extraction. We are using diplomatic channels to gain access to him, but it seems they want him to be an example."

Vivian struggled to breathe but kept her panic in check. She looked to the screen for any sign of hope from the council. Mrs. Hayes was speaking again.

"Vivian your sister, will have to return soon but you are to stay in Mongolia. We have use for your language and smuggling skills on the ground there. This mine will be your new base of operations. Will six months be sufficient time before returning" Vivian's tongue stuck to the roof of her mouth. She couldn't answer so she simply bobbed her head in agreement.

"Alright, ladies and gentlemen. Safe travels to you Livi, and may the Lord hear the desire of your heart for those staying." Mrs. Hayes nodded to each person on the Mongolian end, and the screen went black.

An incessant dripping slowly penetrated the veil of misery that had settled over Shen. Pain beyond pain. The physical pain he could sink into. No, it was the emotional agony of knowing he would not be able to keep his promise that plagued him. He was so close to having her in his life forever, but that dream was smashed.

"They are coming," a hoarse voiced whispered harshly in Shen's ear. He groaned and rolled over to his side. Several young boys helped him sit up and lean against the wall. One eye was swollen shut and he could barely see out of the other. He had just enough vision to take in the gloomy world he would now call home.

"20934. Get up." Shen shrugged off the help of the other prisoners and stood stiffly. Chinese prisons weren't known for their medical facilities, though they were well known for inflicting grotesque injuries. What help he had received had been from the prisoners and the little bit of traditional remedies they had stashed in their small, shared cell. His clothing was nothing more than shredded rags, covered in dried blood and filth. The one bright side, if one could call it that, was that the authorities had not figured out his identity, nor his connections to Vivian or any of The Society. She had left the country safely. At least he could die in peace, knowing she was safe.

He hobbled down the hallway to the interrogation room and sat on a short stool before a table. A group of six officials sat across from him.

"You are 20934. The one with no name. You will be sent to Qincheng Prison. It would help you if you shared the names of the Americans you were assaulting," a middle-aged warden said, his uniform crisply pressed and adorned with the insignia of his position.

"I volunteer for Inner Mongolia," Shen croaked, his mouth dry.

"Why would you request such a location? You know there is no chance of escaping there, just the same as anywhere else?" A deputy pointed out.

"I like it cold," Shen sneered coldly. In truth, it would give his soul a little rest, knowing he had gotten as close as he could to fulfilling his promise to Vivian.

"Done. Next!" the warden yelled as Shen was shoved off the stool and into the hallway. He was taken immediately to a different cell, one filled with dozens of prisoners sitting snugly together on the floor. Shen's grotesque appearance gained him a few precious extra inches from the crush of bodies. Pain radiated up and down the length of his leg as it still bled. He figured infection would take him long before the CCP finished him off.

The night was long, and he almost couldn't get up the next morning from being frozen in one tight position. The small cell emptied as he joined a group loading into a large military transport truck. The drive took all day with no stops, not even for restroom breaks or for food or water. They were still several hours away when a young man started vomiting and convulsing. The truck never stopped. Shen shuffled with the other prisoners around the now-unconscious man when they reached the frontier.

The new facility was guarded heavily, but the prisoners often worked in nearby factories and on maintaining the railway that stretched across the horizon. The group was stripped of their clothing and any personal articles that had somehow managed to make it this far. Shen nearly cried when they yanked the koi necklace. He knew it would likely be sold. Then the prisoners were hosed off so they could be scrubbed down. Shen could barely stay upright, let alone wash his body. He managed to get his head and upper body cleaned up, but his leg was now gushing blood again thanks to being ripped back open by the hose.

"20934 to the medical facility," a guard barked, and Shen stepped to the side and slid a clean shirt on

"Carry your pants but wrap this around you." He threw the pants over his shoulder and wrapped an old pair of pants around his waist. He hobbled as quickly as he could after the guard, another one following behind him.

Shen was surprised to see the medical facility nearly empty. He sat on a bed while his leg was irrigated, stitched, and an antibiotic cream was slathered on his blazing hot skin. The medical attendant gave him a shot in the thigh that he assumed was an antibiotic. He shimmied into his pants and rolled up the leg, so the fabric didn't stick to the ointment. By the time he reached his new cell he had missed the evening meal, and his stomach clenched angrily.

He sat on his bed in the corner fighting against his anxieties. He closed his eyes against the hunger, pain, and regrets. He'd been here before. This place of pain, misery, and emptiness. It was this very thing that had finally brought him to the Lord.

I laid it all down for you, Lord, to serve you. I have endured pain, hunger, loneliness, closed doors, sharp thorns of cruelty, and unanswered questions. All those trials pointed me back to you. I will trust you one last time to not leave me here to rot. It is all in your hands. The flight of the sparrow, the prisoner in the deep, dark prison and the life of a lonely girl back in America. Help me to endure this one final trial, Shen drifted off into a fitful sleep.

CHAPTER 33

Two Years Later

Vivian gripped the steering wheel tightly, not even noticing the brown parched grasses surrounding her. She'd made this drive along the border so many times she could do it in her sleep.

"You'll be back for the wedding, right? I can't get married without my sister standing up for me." Livi practically bounced up and down in the seat of the Land Rover, a few miles from the Chinese-Mongolian border.

"Of course, I'll be there! I already have the time off. I'll be back for a whole month. Evan's been bugging me to go fishing with him" Jack had proposed a few months ago, and the wedding was being held at The Society's vast property.

"I hope it doesn't rain. I guess that'll be the least of my worries, but I really would like to have an outdoor wedding and reception." Livi prattled on about wedding colors and other minute details. "*Ahhhh!* Watch out!" she screamed.

Vivian looked over at her sister, who was pointing out the windshield. Vivian looked up and out the front windshield and gasped in horror. She tried to swerve but couldn't without losing control , so she slammed on the brakes. The car hit the body that lay in the dirt like a speed bump with a thump. She stopped the car, breathing heavily, trying to quiet the panic that constricted her chest.

"Did I just run over someone?" Vivian asked, gripping the steering wheel tightly.

"Yeah, I think you just did. Why would someone be out here? There is literally nothing." Livi pointed to the vast brown landscape by which they were surrounded.

Vivian put the car into park and reached for the door handle. "You're coming with me; I hope you know." Livi opened her mouth as if to argue, but she clamped her mouth shut and swung her door open.

The girls slowly approached the prone body.

"Did you kill him?" Livi whisper yelled. Vivian ignored her sister and stepped closer to nudge the person's leg. A groan floated up to them. "Oh good, at least he's still breathing," Livi said loudly.

Vivian knelt to the body. It was a man; his face was scruffy with an overgrown beard and body and clothing nearly blended in with the surrounding dirt, sand, and filth. She swiped a finger along the back of his shirt and looked closely at it, rubbing her forefinger and thumb together.

"What are you doing?" Livi asked, nudging the man's leg again.

"I think he rubbed the dirt all over himself as camouflage. Yup, he's got a heartbeat," Vivian confirmed, having found the pulse point on his neck. "I wonder if he's a Chinese refugee. We have to get him into the truck. Back up the car, but don't run him over again."

Livi ran off to move the vehicle, leaving Vivian with the stranger. She pushed the thin, dark hair away from his face and squinted her eyes, trying to guess the man's story. She shook her head and refocused on directing Livi where to park, eventually standing to pop the hatch of the Land Rover. With Vivian taking the man's legs and Livi hefting his arms, they managed to wrangle him into the back of the car

He remained unconscious and outside of a few moans.

Vivian tried to drive carefully, but the Gobi Desert wasn't known for its smooth terrain. The roads were less roadways, and more like lightly traversed twin tracks. They finally made it through the mine complex and screeched to a stop, where workers poured out of buildings and came running as Livi swung open the hatch.

Several workers hauled the man inside. The mine had its own small medical facility, but it wasn't a hospital. If he needed serious treatment, it would take days to get him there.

"What happened?" Chingis, one of Vivian's coworkers, asked in heavily accented English.

"He was laying on the ground and blended in. I didn't see him in time to stop and... well. I, um..." Vivian stammered.

"She ran the guy over like he was a speed bump," Livi piped up.

"What is speed bomp?" Chingis asked, shaking his head.

"Bump, brother, bump. They are used to slow down speed demons," Livi said, crossing her arms impatiently.

"Demons?" His eyes grew wide.

"No, not real demons, just people that like to drive fast. Back on subject, here. She ran him over, but he was still alive. Did he die?" Livi asked, no shame in her investigative game.

"No, not die. Will live. Come. Come." Chingis hurried them into the small exam room. The man had been stripped of his shirt. Tape was wrapped around his ribs and an IV was hooked up to his arm, dripping fluids into his parched body.

"Who is he?" Vivian asked Chinua, the medical student who was serving the mine as an intern. She only spoke Mongolian, which Vivian was slowly learning.

"No," the young woman answered, using the only English word she seemed to know, clearly not understanding Vivian's question. She adjusted the IV flow rate, gave him a shot, and left.

"He's got a cute koi tattoo on his chest right over his heart," Livi said, pointing to his chest. "It's really pretty." Vivian looked around Livi to see the tattoo. The detailed black and gold fish stretched across his left pec, surrounded by blue water. Several pink lotus flowers drifted around the water. It was truly beautiful. Vivian looked at his face, but it was turned away toward the wall. She couldn't see any particulars with his head turned and his face covered in a rough beard.

"Well, I guess our job here is done. Why don't we go eat?" Vivian said, turning to go. Her foot caught on the gurney's tire, and her arms flailed in the air as she tried to catch her balance. She knocked the IV pole over.

"Vivian!" Livi screamed, she grappled with the IV pole to keep it upright but as Vivian went down the tubing popped out of the machine. The machine began to beep wildly. Chingis came rushing in, yelling something in Mongolian that Vivian could only guess were chastisements. She pushed up from the floor and brushed off her pants, her pride the only thing wounded.

Chingis chattered away over at the table. Vivian assumed it was more criticism directed at her, however, a male voice whispered something. Vivian and Livi looked at each other and then at the man.

"Sorry, Chingis. Bu hao yi si. I mean namaig uuchlaarai." Vivian stumbled over the many translations rolling through her brain.

"Huo? Nà shì nǐ ma?" The man said, his voice gravely. "Wǒ dāyìngguò wǒ huì lái de." He looked at Vivian and gave a weak smile.

"What did he just say, Vivian?" Livi asked, gripping Vivian's arm.

"Alive, is that you? My name means alive." Vivian's heart pounded in her chest. She searched the face for any resemblance to the man she loved, but either her memory failed her or his time in China had changed him. "He kept his promise." She stumbled forward, her knees nearly giving out on the way. He pushed up from the table on his elbow and reached out to caress her face.

"Yes, I kept my promise. I only wish I could give you a whole man, but you can have what China didn't manage to kill. If you'll have me." He broke into a ragged cough that shook the entire table.

Vivian couldn't reply, her throat was clogged with emotion.

She couldn't even see through her torrent of tears. "Well, if that isn't the most romantic thing ever!" Livi shot at them, and Vivian and Shen laughed together. He brought his forehead to hers and she stared into his eyes, eyes she had been sure she would never see again.

"Of course, I'll have you. Why do you think I've stayed here?" Vivian answered tearfully. He pushed up fully and crushed her to his chest in a tight hug. Neither of them noticed as Livi and Chingis slipped out to give them privacy. Vivian tipped her head back and smiled, her shattered heart suddenly mended. Shen cupped her head and brought her mouth to his. He pressed gently at first then more fiercely before pulling back and beginning to chuckle.

"What is so funny?" Vivian asked, happy but confused.

"I thought I was a dead man, but here I am alive. Vivian. Alive."

EPILOGUE

Squeals of laughter echoed across the open field. A light breeze pushed away the bugs and the early summer heat.

"Mama! Baba! He won't stop chasing me with that snake! Make him quit!" Seven years old, black ringlet curls falling out of a ponytail, and running as fast her little feet could carry her, Mei grabbed Vivian's legs and hid behind her. Four-year-old Jack Jr. was soaked up to his knees, mud smeared across his ruddy cheeks as a green garden snake dangled from his pudgy hands. Vivian wasn't so sure the snake was even still alive. Not her problem.

"Mei, go clean up. We need to go see Nai Nai and Uncle An Chen." Mei's eyes lit up and she squealed, dashing off into the house to clean up.

"I'm so glad she adores Nai Nai so much. I'll get Oliver from your father; can you find Genevieve? I think your brother was toting her around." Vivian smiled as Shen threw his arm around her father's shoulder. Samuel was in his glory as a grandfather. Between their four and Livi's two children, life was anything but boring.

In Livi's house, shrieks of laughter bombarded Vivian. She dodged Jack Jr. as he chased her middle child, Charlie. She plucked him up out of the way and threw him over her shoulder.

"Mama, put me down!" Charlie wailed halfheartedly.

"No, Nai Nai is waiting for us. You don't want to make her wait, do you?" she asked. Charlie pushed up on her shoulder and looked at her with a wide smile.

"No way. And Uncle An Chen?"

"He'll be there, too. Go wash up with Mei while I find Genevieve." Vivian plopped him down near the powder room, where she could hear the water running on full blast.

"Uncle Evan had her. I think she's his favorite," Charlie said, disappearing into the bathroom. Vivian peeked into the empty living room before turning to the basement door that stood open. She tilted her head to listen to the flow of male voices coming from the depths of the basement. She crept down the stairs and focused on listening.

"Jack! You can't use a computer to win in this house. It's talent only, buddy, and you do not have any of that," Evan was saying. She peeked around the corner. Evan held a pool cue as 5-month-old Genevieve sat on the pool table and patted the green felt. She swiped a pool ball and tossed it, clapping for herself. Evan took his shot, which missed, but Genevieve clapped for him anyway.

"Thank you, Gigi!" Evan swooped her up into his arms and nuzzled her neck, sending her into a squealing laugh. She grabbed his Afro and dug her hands deep into the poof. Vivian's heart swelled. She was so grateful this was her life, filled with friends and family.

"Alright, Evan, I've come to collect your pool buddy. You're welcome to come babysit anytime you're on break from Seminary." Evan passed the baby off to Vivian, gave them both a squeeze and went back to his heated pool game with Jack and eight-year-old Trey, Jack and Livi's oldest son.

"Come on, baby, we need to find Qing Qing and go see Nai Nai." The baby sputtered a bit of nonsense and drooled down the front of her sundress. Vivian held the baby close to her heart and soaked in the joy that filled the house.

Later, after all the children were tucked into beds, Vivian and Shen went from room to room praying over each child. They even prayed over Qing Qing's first floor bedroom but didn't go in and bother the elderly man.

Shen pulled Vivian into a tight embrace and kissed her cheek.

"I have never felt so alive as I do right now."

"I know exactly what you mean. God pushed us together, pulled us apart, and then made it work. What a ride." Vivian tilted her head up toward Shen. "There is no one else I'd rather walk through this life with."

ABOUT THE AUTHOR

Christian Romance Author

Jolene O'Dell is a writer, wife and mother of seven from Southwest Michigan. She is prolific reader who started writing short stories at a young age but wasn't able to dedicate herself to the craft until her many children grew a bit older. She is the winner of the 2021 The Well Oasis Award for Christian Fiction. When not surrounded by her many children, she can be found with a book in her hands or out on a long walk in the woods.

Made in United States
Orlando, FL
12 July 2022

19657497R00135